STAR
RIGGER'S
WAY

STAR RIGGER'S WAY

JEFFREY A. CARVER

Nelson Doubleday, Inc.   Garden City, New York

Published by arrangement with
Dell Publishing Co., Inc.
One Dag Hammarskjold Plaza
New York, New York 10017

For Cindi

STAR
RIGGER'S
WAY

1

STAR-FREIGHTER *SEDORA*

Gev Carlyle struggled to put the frustration out of his mind. It was essential to maintain control of himself; he knew that. But the alien kept staring at him from across the ship's gloomy bridge, like some frightful catlike apparition.

Who could stay calm looking at something like that?

"Cephean," he said, his voice trembling. (A rush of *impatience* interrupted him—the alien's.) "Cephean!" he demanded furiously. His eyes went out of focus as he tensed, struggling to frame his words. He refocused and gazed at the creature again. The cynthian was as large as a tiger and black as coal dust, and he was plump and furry like an enormous Persian cat. Cephean's eyes blinked slowly, indignantly. They were gold-flecked obsidian, with irises of molten copper.

"You told me that your ship operated the same way as mine. And you know how to fly your own ship. Correct?"

"Hyiss-yiss," insisted Cephean. "Hoff khorss."

"Of course," Carlyle muttered. He reminded himself: there must be confidence before it can work. The cynthian said that he was capable; but who could be sure? The telepathic link with the alien was incomplete; the cynthian, alone, perceived the thoughts behind the human's words. And somewhere in Carlyle's instruction, the cynthian was misunderstanding. There was only so much he could explain about flying the starship, anyway. How could he "explain" intuition?

Cephean stared at him with his coppery eyes. Waiting behind his front paws were his two small companions, the riffmar, which followed him everywhere. The riffmar were thin-trunked, walking ferns with root-toed feet; from their midsections they waved muscular, slim-fingered branches. They pranced about and squeaked and twitched their fingers disconcertingly.

"All right," Carlyle said. "You have to feel what I am doing when I fly. And you have to help me. When I guide the ship, when I turn it, you back me up as steadily as you can. Don't struggle, and don't work against me. Do you understand? Just follow."

Cephean looped his tail behind his triangular ears. His eyes flickered. "Hi khann ff-hollow, Caharleel," he hissed.

Carlyle nodded, thinking that they *should* be able to work together—they *had* to, if they didn't want to die together, adrift between the stars. Whatever their differences, they were both riggers in their own fashions. "Let's go, then." He pointed the way. (He felt a twinge of *preoccupation*—Cephean's.)

"Are you paying attention?" he asked quietly, angrily.

Cephean sputtered—then dipped his head and padded over to the stern-rigger's alcove, with the riffmar dancing behind. He stopped and sat in front of the rigger-seat which Carlyle had dismantled and adapted for his use.

Carlyle shook his head. He swung the seat pad forward to rest against the cynthian's furry spine. The cynthian tensed, fur rippling and his eyes flashing—and then slowly relaxed. Beside him, the riffmar settled down to wait out the session. Carlyle crossed the bridge to his own place in the pilot-rigger station. He averted his eyes from the sight of the empty alcoves which his crewmates had once manned; and, resisting a compulsion to relive *that* horror, he lowered himself into the seat and rested his neck against the neural-foam pad. Engage, he thought.

Numbness spread through his body, stealing his hearing and touch. His eyesight darkened and collapsed. Then his senses sprang from his body like electrical fire and blossomed out of the starship and into space, into the rigger-net. Into the Flux. He stretched and looked around.

The view was an atmospheric panorama: the starship floated in a vast, luminous space. Sculptured lemon clouds drifted in the distance, and russet layers of smoke twisted outwards to form a sea as broad and as deep as the entire arm of the galaxy. This was the "subjective sea," interstellar space rendered as an airy red and orange-yellow watercolor, with sloping and intersecting layers, and rivers which ran and twisted at all angles. Some stars were visible, mostly as flecks of carbon dust adrift in the luminous space; however, a few stars and their associated nebulae stood out more clearly, as whorls or as discontinuities in the flow of the sea.

The image—which was partly real and partly a creation of Carlyle's imagination—was a good one. It was vivid and bright, and it was a good analogue of normal-space. He hoped that Cephean could interpret the landscape, and more importantly, that the cynthian could follow his lead.

Sedora's rigger-net sparkled around him and pulsed with energy as he flexed his limbs. Below the net he sighted his immediate objective—a dark, channeled intersection of two planes. That was the Reld Current, a smooth-running river deeply submerged in the multi-layered sea of the Flux. It was a major current in the Flux moving toward *Sedora*'s destination; and it was as safe a place as any for practicing teamwork with Cephean.

The Reld Current would be easy.

But after the Reld, they had to sail into the Hurricane Flume, and that was a different sort of current altogether. The Flume was a "channel" where dozens of streams came thundering together, meeting and tangling with terrible energy. They would reach it in six or seven shipdays. The Flume was a perilous place to take a ship, but they had to go through; from within its chaos streamed the upwelling currents to Cunnilus Banks, and that was where *Sedora* was bound. In Cunnilus Banks lay the star-havens and safety. If they could fly on through to Cunnilus Banks, they would be virtually home free.

But to reach the Banks, they had to go through the Flume; there was no other way. Carlyle was almost too frightened to think about it. *Sedora* was not a one-man or even a two-man ship. She was a four-rigger freighter, a massive hulk riding on a lone rigger's back. *Sedora* had carried a crew of five; and Carlyle had been the fifth, the extra. But that was before the accident. Now only he, of the original crew, remained—with this alien, Cephean. Singlehandedly, he could manage the ship in the easy current of the Reld. But the Flume would hit them like a cyclone—and if he and the shipwrecked cynthian did not function as a team, the Flume was going to be the end of *Sedora*, and of them.

He glanced around to the stern. *You there?* he asked.

Hyiss.

He released the stabilizers and reached his steely, spidery, sensory arms outward and down into the Flux. Slowly he coaxed the ship downward toward the Reld; and he hoped that Cephean would assist him.

As *Sedora* reached the streamers at the edge of the Reld, Carlyle cursed the cynthian's clumsiness. His anger rang in echoes round the net and vanished to the winds of space. Somewhere astern, the cynthian hom-humm'd to himself and responded late to Carlyle's guiding actions. The ship bucked and plunged like an angry whale.

Gently, Cephean! Do you see the river?

Whass? Whass?

A "river," yes—that would be a good functional image, and it was consistent with the actual flux-currents they were riding. Carlyle settled the image in his mind. The misty lanes of the Reld congealed beneath *Sedora* and darkened to the color of molasses, then flattened to water swirling downstream between low-profile riverbanks. The sky overhead turned to night, glittering with fairyland stars. *Sedora's* net shimmered and passed into the dark surface of the river, and Carlyle eased the ship down until her hull settled in its waters.

Carried by the flow, *Sedora* moved downstream in the night.

Somewhere, lost in the distance ahead, was the Flume. It did not yet betray itself, but Carlyle knew it was there. And now, as he studied the horizon where the meandering Reld vanished into darkness, he detected a dim streamer rising, almost imperceptible against the stars. Above the river's end, in the night sky, the streamer met Cunnilus Banks, a faintly gleaming cloud of particles above the horizon. The sight gave him the first surge of hope he'd felt in many days. Regardless of how distant his goal lay, it was reassuring to glimpse it.

He plunged his "hands" deep into the river, just to feel the cool slipstream.

The ship lurched, and yawed to one side. Cephean had bumped the stern.

Cephean! Follow!

Ff-hollow-hing, Caharleel!

No rapport, he thought despairingly. He strained against the current to bring the ship into line. What was it his old friend and crewmate Janofer had once told him? That a crew needn't necessarily understand one another . . . that the crux of teamwork was congruence, simple congruence of vision. And Skan—that without unity none of the rest was worth a mote in the Kryst Nebula. Indeed, that was why they had asked him to go and to train for a time on *Sedora*. It had been their hope, and his, that on *Sedora* he could learn something which they had been unable to teach; and perhaps later, with more experience behind him, he might return to rig again with his friends.

It seemed as though he would learn now, or he would never learn at all.

This Cephean was an enigma—a bit like Legroeder, so alone with his thoughts, even in the net where personal barriers tended to relax. But Legroeder, despite his aloneness, always worked in harmony whether as leader or follower. Carlyle suspected that Legroeder was fearless, but Janofer and Skan said that he simply gave what was needed, and no more.

But this was Cephean here with him, not Legroeder, and Cephean wasn't giving what was needed at all. Carlyle guided the ship into a gentle turn; the cynthian responded late, and incorrectly, and the ship swung toward the riverbank. Carlyle was forced to reach deep into the waters, using his hands as rudders to bring the ship back into line with the current. He tried again, coaching: *Gently, Cephean! Steer very gently!* But again the ship went off course, and again Carlyle had to jockey and trim and correct for Cephean's mistakes. The Reld Current was running smoothly, but, despite that fact, the ship drew closer and closer to the shallows.

Finally he cried: *Cephean, pull out the net!* The cynthian obeyed, humming and grumbling; and when Cephean was gone, Carlyle strengthened the entire net himself, and he turned the ship and held it against the drift, held it until it was safely back in the mainstream. The effort was exhausting, and as soon as he could manage, he set the stabilizers and withdrew from the net.

He blinked and gazed about the gloomy, reddishly lighted bridge. Cephean and the riffmar were gone. The rigger-stations were empty. Most of the instruments, burned out from the accident, were lifeless. The bridge looked as though it were dying with its former crew.

Carlyle went straight from the bridge to the commons. He

drank an ale so quickly he scarcely noticed its taste, and then he went at once to his cabin. He needed to sleep, to regain the feel of his own body. Soon enough he would find the cynthian and face the melancholy bridge, and try once more.

2

THE RIGGERS

Starship-rigging had been regarded, since its inception in the Twelfth Century of Space, as clearly one of the most peculiarly demanding of professions. Piloting a starship involved a mastery of technology, of course; but more than that, it required curious aptitudes of personality, of emotional set. Star-rigging involved not only spaceflight but also the mastering of the Flux—that subjective realm underlying the normal-space of Prime Reality, a realm akin to but distinct from freewheeling fantasy, and as intricate as the mistily mapped waking dream.

Successful navigation of the Flux demanded the exceptional dreamer, the rigger, trained to construct a vision and then to reach *into* it and to gain a literal fingerhold in a reality where the spaces flowed as oceans and the currents were unconstrained by the laws and distances of normal-space. The rigger's net was a harness, trussing the ship to him like a backpack as he rode the ebb and flow of the space itself. Rigging was an exquisite mating of imagination with the reality of the Flux—a strange way to live, in many eyes, but a fine way to travel among the stars.

The net itself was a glittery spangle of ghost neurons flung into the Flux like the exploded tentacles of a man-of-war. Interfaced through organic neural foam and amplified by the flux-pile, it was the rigger's skin against the elements, his

wings and fins in the turbulent air/sea among the stars. A
rigger steered by intuition and by experience, by his own individual imaging powers, and by the currents of the space
itself.

The dreaming could be difficult; but far trickier was the
intuition, especially among members of a crew. Because no
two riggers viewed the Flux identically, teamwork in the net
demanded a gestalt, a near-perfect intermixing of visions,
perceptions, and intuitive judgments. Several riggers func-
tioning as a gestalt could sail a ship smoothly and speedily
between stars. But working at odds in the net, they could
tear a ship apart and leave the pieces bobbing lifeless in the
Flux.

To Gev Carlyle the most intimidating aspect of rigging,
by far, was the teamwork. He had never ceased fearing the
nakedness, the emotional turmoil—the laying forth of embar-
rassments, of fears, of weaknesses both real and imagined.
But one rigger had to know another's fantasies, both to find
the common lines of strength and to know what images
should not be tread upon; indeed, sailing a ship in a space
built of fear was surely courting disaster.

But sharing was so difficult with fellow humans, with his
friends. How could he possibly hope to succeed with this
alien stranger?

Would he have to resort to the dreampool?

He hoped not. Lord, he hoped not!

Gev Carlyle's sleeping dreams were filled with visions of
old friends.

There was Legroeder: dark little man, pilot-rigger of
Lady Brillig and a lover of dream-gestalt plays; friendly, but
often shut away in his cabin, a place secluded and strange,
and madly adorned with mystical-sequenced pearlgazers
which no one but he understood. And Janofer: gentle, beautiful keel-lifter, fond of stories and music even in the net,
briefly a lover and always a friend. And Skan: com-rigger

and hard-balanced thinker, the one to believe in when decisions fell due, but fearsome when his balance failed and he plummeted into one of his black depressions.

They were the three who had sent him here to *Sedora*. Why couldn't they be here now—or he back with them on the deck of *Lady Brillig*?

Ah, *Lady Brillig*—glittering domed beauty of a ship, light and comfortable and responsive as a kite! Who was the fourth in her rigger-net now? Who, *Lady Brillig*?

Such dream remembrances gave way to others, though. Darker memories. Memories of danger and fear here aboard *Sedora*, of burned flesh and dead men. What were their names?

Thoughts better left unremembered.

Carlyle awoke troubled. After eating, he went to seek out Cephean in his makeshift quarters, halfway around the circle of crew-deck from his own. Cephean made the human cabin look small, both by his own physical size and by the astonishing litter created by his new personal belongings. The cynthian seemed unaware of Carlyle's entrance. He sat with his back turned three-quarters to the door; he was idly batting the two riffmar into floating somersaults. Carlyle cleared his throat. The ferns squealed and scuttled away behind Cephean, their oversized hands flailing excitedly. How strange, Carlyle thought, to be so utterly dependent—both Cephean and the riffmar. Cephean was clearly the master, but the riffmar possessed the prehensile branches, the hands. Would Cephean be helpless without them?

He shook his head. "Cephean, let's talk."

The cynthian gazed at him, ears raked forward. (He sensed *mild interest*.) "Hyiss?"

"Cephean," he said, and hesitated. Where to start? "All right. You need my help and I need yours, and we're both incredibly lucky even to be together here to try. But why isn't it working? We both know how to fly, but the last time in the net was worse than ever." He gestured pleadingly. "Don't you want to reach port, Cephean? Don't you want to go home again?"

"Hyiss-yiss," Cephean said, his whiskers curling and springing straight again.

"Did you have trouble understanding the image?" That was the kindest assumption he could make.

"Hh-no." (Carlyle sensed . . . something . . . and was disturbed that he could not identify the feeling.) "Hi heff ffly wiss hyou," Cephean hissed, his black velvet face split in what seemed to be a grin.

"What went wrong, then? Why didn't you coordinate with me?"

Cephean's breath whistled slowly in and out as he apparently considered the question. Behind him, the riffmar rustled and *sssk*'d quietly as they buried the roots of their feet in the nutrient tray. Cephean touched a forepaw to his nose and rubbed slowly. "Hi ss-ry." (An impression of *shame* flickered across Carlyle's mind.) "Hyou ffly ha-lone, Caharleel." (He sensed a strange, dark longing, unidentifiable and then gone altogether.)

Why did he have to play these guessing games? What was Cephean really thinking and feeling?

The cynthian stirred, watching him carefully.

"No," he said. "We'll try again, in a while. But if things don't work better this time, we'll just have to try another method." He did not name the dreampool, but it loomed in his thoughts. The cynthian started, and suddenly looked away.

Odomilk. An image of the strange pods drifted eerily through Carlyle's mind. Responding to the commands, the riffmar leaped out of the nutrient tray and danced across the floor to a wooden cache. They lifted out two odomilk pods and carried them back and placed them on the floor in front of Cephean. The cynthian carefully cracked a pod with his teeth and sucked at the yellowish liquid which oozed out.

He looked at Carlyle with upturned eyes, making plain his wish to be alone.

Sighing, Carlyle went back out into the corridor. He paced and then went to the commons, in the center of the crew-deck circle. It was a silent place, a human lounge empty of human voices, human presence. He shivered; the lounge was haunted by memories. His thoughts drifted to the men who had relaxed here with him, and tears began to blur his vision. He blinked angrily. He strode to the counter which curved along one side of the lounge and drew himself a beermalt. Then he sat on the opposite divan and tried to steady himself, to clear his mind. He toyed with a flo-globe, watching the colors flash mistily, randomly. They reminded him of the unharnessed Flux after the accident, after the deaths. Dropping the globe, he switched on the wall-generator and watched sparkle-patterns flash in ringlets around the room, the patterns, changing slowly: stoic . . . erotic . . . pastoral. . . .

Slowly his thoughts dissipated, and he stared darkly at the wall, the beermalt growing warm in his hands.

The next session in the net began not much differently from the last. Cephean hummed away at the stern with his own thoughts, while Carlyle pleaded, pressured, cajoled—and *Sedora* sideslipped and trembled in the smooth-flowing Reld. They were sailing an image of streaming clouds.

Cephean, open up—listen—turn your thoughts out into the net.

The cynthian whistled an unintelligible reply; and the ship swayed in the clouds, thumping.

Follow! Damn it, Cephean!

F-hollow-hing.

Carlyle flew a practice turn. Then, as before, he had to strain, working against Cephean's mistakes to bring the ship back onto course. He flew straight, resting. Janofer came to him in his thoughts, quietly, unbidden. Her presence surprised him, but he said nothing and waited until she spoke.

Can you go it alone, Gev? You may have to try.

Don't ask me that, Janofer. Dear Janofer, sweet keel-girl, you know I can't go it alone. But you always ask.

A wrong fit in the net warps it like a gravity-abscess in a calm stream . . . dangerous. You are sometimes like that, Gev, for all that we love you . . . dangerous.

Do you think I don't know? All right, I'm a lousy rigger.

Janofer, face darkening: *That's not what I mean, Gev. You're a fine rigger. But—*

Skan, appearing suddenly: *You're a lousy matcher, Gev, that's all. You'd be fine in a one-rigger . . . except you'd be lonely. Too bad you don't have a bit of Legroeder in you.*

Skan. *Always right but never tactful, damn you. Stay with me awhile, Jan will you?* Sad, already distant gaze: *Can't, Gev—I can't. I'm gone, now. Later, perhaps, if you really need me. Perhaps then, for a while.* And then she was gone, and so was Skan.

Perhaps then, but not now? Janofer: so kind, so courteous —you hurt me even when you're here.

But the ship was drifting from its course now, and he reluctantly refocused his thoughts on flying. *Sedora* challenged his efforts to steer her true—and there was no assistance from Cephean. More strength was needed; he was taxing himself heavily as he flexed his ghost-neuron arms in the current. He cried out, demanding new strength from himself; *Sedora* answered slowly, but when he eased off for rest she immediately began to slip. He was losing control.

Then a curious thing happened. Legroeder appeared in his thoughts, wordlessly, and entered the net at the keel-station. Smiling enigmatically at Carlyle, the former crewmate lifted *Sedora* from the keel, helped steady her axis along the blue haze of the mainflow, and pointed her bow just tangent to the distant glitter of Cunnilus Banks. The maneuver went as smoothly, as easily as though *Sedora* were *Lady Brillig.*

All right, Carlyle thought. *Why not?* The strength of Legroeder, he knew perfectly well, was his own inner reserve focused through a wistful memory. But if he could fly through a memory, what harm?

Sedora sailed sturdily under their coordinated control, and Carlyle almost forgot about Cephean, silent at the stern-station. Then a turbulent stretch loomed ahead, an orange tributary streaming in from the left, setting the blue haze of the mainflow swirling with dangerous eddies. *Legroeder?* Yes, still there. *Sedora* shivered into the turbulence, and with Legroeder's help he stretched out steely arms and labored like an oarsman to maintain control. But they needed more strength; they had to aim directly into the heart of the turbulence to complete the passage.

As quickly as the thought, Janofer and Skan reappeared—and all three backed him in the net as he hooked his nails into the fabric of space and wheeled *Sedora* to a new heading. Without fanfare Carlyle found himself a part of a perfect gestalt, and as one, the four riggers brought *Sedora* into a downwelling and leveled her off again in a smoother layer of current.

The fantasy was a white lie. Never in the past had he achieved gestalt with his three crewmate-friends. If he had, he would still be on *Lady Brillig*. But the image was perfect in his mind—it was the gestalt for which he had yearned—and *Sedora* flew now like an eagle. That image multiplied in scope, and they winged silently over sprawling tufted clouds which glittered whitely and handsomely beneath him. He forgot his terrible loneliness. Janofer's music breathed soothingly through the net, and Skan's com lay steady and sure over the gestalt. Even Legroeder, pretending to ignore them all, smiled with secret affection.

Time, in the gestalt, passed unnoticed.

But the image was as taxing as it was exhilarating. Carlyle, bearing the load of four riggers in one, became aware finally of the strain he was enduring—and by then it was too late. His strength turned to souring wine, his senses dimmed and flattened, and *Sedora* suddenly balked in his failing rein.

His friends' voices were faint, now, their faces escaping his memory. The ship tumbled. He wanted to sleep—no, to collapse. *How long have I been flying?*

Caharleel! A whisper out of nowhere.

Cephean! My god! Can you help? Can you hold the keel steady? The fine spiderweb of the net was fraying, its grip in the clouds lost.

Hyiss.

Cephean's leverage from the stern increased dramatically. Carlyle felt relief. Then alarm. Could the cynthian handle the ship—now, of all times? (He sensed a blur of *annoyance*, and *bewilderment* at . . . what? . . . at the humans who had materialized to help run the ship, and then had vanished. And . . . *eagerness?*) Before he could understand, the sensations disappeared. The cynthian had sealed the lid on his feelings, and now he hissed as he wielded the ship over Carlyle's failing control.

Cephean took the ship deeper—diving steeply *down* into the Reld. The cloud-image vanished, and the ship was suddenly underwater, and sinking with terrifying speed.

This was all wrong. . . .

Cephean! What are you doing? Carlyle's heart leaped with fear. He tried desperately to oppose the cynthian; but Cephean refused to yield, and in the struggle for control the net strained and sparkled brightly, heatedly, and began to tear, to shred. The ship tumbled deeper, deeper—and suddenly broke down through the Reld and was beneath it, and the Current was only a shimmering ocean surface above them as they fell toward the abyss. Here in the depths, space was dark; it was the midnight of cruel dreams. *Sedora* was off her course and out of control, and what nightmare it was bound for Carlyle did not want to guess. If the cynthian aimed to destroy them, there was no surer way.

Fear turned into panic. Carlyle, like a stricken diver

screaming for air, acted badly, instinctively. He triggered the maneuvering fusors to turn the ship upward. The fusors burst into life, and the ship began to groan—until finally it rose, roaring and shaking, on the torches, its wake casting a light into the darkness. Carlyle had forgotten to numb the sensory field astern, and the fire of the jets crawled upward along his spine, setting shots of agony alight in his soul. Cephean screamed soundlessly; in the stern-rig he was near the heart of the sun-fury, and beyond any help Carlyle could offer now. The cynthian's outcry flew in whispers: *Ru-hinned . . . ss-/-how . . . de-h-mise!* The rest was lost—too fleeting—but Carlyle heard a distant cry as the cynthian sprang free of the net.

The fusors were dreadfully inefficient in the Flux; but they generated an image of directed movement, and that gave Carlyle the confidence he needed to reassert his control over the ship. Like a crazily inverted river, the Reld came back down toward him as the ship rose; then the river fogged, and sputtered in the jet flare. When he finally shut down the fusors, *Sedora*'s keel was again drifting in the hazy stream of the Reld. She was held cockeyed but steady by the tangled remnant of the net.

Carlyle set the stabilizers and withdrew, shaking and twitching, from the net. He sensed the cynthian nearby, jittery and numb and bewildered, but he was far too exhausted to look. His veins flowed with lead, and before his eyelids could open he foundered into unconsciousness.

Images of the quarm fluttered naggingly, incessantly. A strange communion: cynthian heads bowed in a circle, clusters of riffmar shivering, forgotten. Ears, whiskers twitching. Thoughts fleeing from one's body to join, to intermix like buffeting winds—to share dreams and strange worlds, to animate imaginary bodies. Time slipped quickly, spanning eons, or stretched and staggered, and flowed like clotted milk. There was distaste here, disdain. Sour anger toward

. . . toward others in the quarm, personalities which slipped into and out of the self without invitation. Resentment?—that intimacy should come so easily, so unavoidably.

(But wasn't the quarm a relief, a boon to the lonely mind? Wasn't it a natural end to solitude, an inborn gift of being cynthian?

Why did Cephean so want to be alone?)

Carlyle felt dizzy and confused, uncertain of his own identity. The cabin walls blurred, resisting focus, as he struggled to recapture consciousness. Recollections filtered into place. He had awakened on the bridge, exhausted— years ago, it seemed—had stumbled to his cabin and bunk. He had slept—how long?—a full shipday. Jesus. There had been memories, dreams—the *quarm*, whatever that was—he had picked up more from Cephean than he had realized.

And the flying, earlier—lord, flying as four people, he must have been trying to kill himself. Small wonder he had slept solidly for a day.

Rousing himself, he went to the commons. Hunger soon made him feel awake, and he ate ravenously, a meal of sea- tarns and warmloaf. Scarcely another thought went through his mind until he had finished; then, afterwards, he fixed a mug of hermit brew and sat and collected himself—knowing that he ought to be looking for Cephean.

But he was rather comfortable, basking in the ochre morning glow of the commons, and instead of getting up right away, he put his feet up and thought. As he sipped the brew, memory-faces rejoined him. Skan led the conference, shaking his head: *"No flow, Gev. You've got to bring that cat right into the rigging—wring him out, make him work."*

"Thanks, Skan. Care to help?"

Skan, smiling broadly: "I have, Gev."

Janofer, flowing and concerned: "Perhaps you should think of using the dreampool, Gev. Or, if you must, go the whole way alone."

The dreampool—assisted intimacy. Not for nothing had he kept it out of his mind. It terrified him, even with another human. "Just like the old days? That's not much help, Jan. That's how you've always spoken to me."

"I've tried, Gev—you know that. But always there was something that wouldn't connect between us."

"How many times did you try? Twice? Three times?"

"Which nearly broke me. It wouldn't work, Gev—it just wouldn't."

"Hm."

"You're coming up on the Flume, Gev. Don't be thinking about us. We'll help when we can, but if you depend on us you'll burn yourself out."

Skan: "The cat—you have to get the cat working with you or you'll never make it."

"He seemed to be trying, last time. But god knows what he was doing. He acts suicidal."

Legroeder, from somewhere, looked up and nodded, but distractedly, as if his real thoughts were elsewhere. Janofer, whispering, drew close and brushed him with a kiss, a breath of moist wind from afar, and then withdrew, her voice a fading note on the air. He was alone again.

He drained his mug and left the commons, thinking to find Cephean and—what? Okay, it was time to act like a commander and start kicking ass.

Right.

But Cephean was not in his quarters. Carlyle stood in the corridor under one of the humming, brushed-bronze stabilizer arches and, feeling fretful and a little silly, considered where to look next. Well, what might Cephean have been doing while he slept away the last day? Unsupervised, probably almost anything.

The bridge was deserted. Likewise the communications coop. He went back down the ramp, worried now, and began a systematic search: dreampool theater and exercise room, then the lower deck and utility storage, lifecontrol, airlock, and conversion room. In the central part of that deck was the prep room leading to the fluxfield chamber. Lots of bad memories there. He checked without entering the chamber; the suits were all in place, and the monitors were steady, indicating that the pile shields had not been breached.

No Cephean.

That left only the cargo holds, accessible from the next lower deck; the primary holds were grouped in a broad oval around the bulk of the flux-chamber. Carlyle was actually not even certain just what *Sedora* carried, but it was likely to be costly merchandise. Not that it mattered much, at this point; nevertheless, he hurried below.

The corridor was eerily silent, and he found himself moving stealthily, peering through each sealed cargo port like a thief. He came to number three port and cursed, whispering, "Damn you, Cephean!" The port was retracted, and a tattered bit of something lay on the deck: a broken riffmar leaf. Carlyle stepped quietly inside. The hold was gloomy, and crisscrossed with anchoring webs from which were suspended individual pieces of cargo. He recognized the articles almost immediately—Lifecybe organic computer cores, each in a fried-egg shaped cradle with umbilical to a central life-maintenance unit. He was surprised; he had not guessed that the cargo was *that* valuable.

Cephean was on the far side of the hold, hunched over one of the cradles. Carlyle started that way, ducking and threading his way among the anchoring strands. Suddenly he was stopped in midstride by a snap of light, a flash from nowhere which danced in a quick series of circles about the room, then vanished—and for a moment he totally forgot his purpose, his destination—but when he shook his head and completed the stride with his left leg, the spell evaporated and he was aware again. But what? Oh—the light was external stimulation for the computer cores. Mesmerizing but, one hoped, not dangerous.

He crossed over to the cynthian. Cephean looked up at him, eyes dark, glinting.

A welter of emotion crawled through his mind: loathing, curiosity, scorn, anger. A mixture of his own feelings and Cephean's. He struggled to sound diplomatic, thinking of the precarious position they were in. "Cephean, what in hell are you doing?" He heard a whisper, and looked down at the two riffmar, who rustled quickly around behind Cephean. (He sensed *disconcertment, frustration*.)

The cynthian's whiskers curled, and he hissed, dipping his head, the words coming out in a sigh. "Caharleel—hyor comffusor noss hwork."

Carlyle scowled. "Of course not . . . *now*. They'll work when they're installed in computer tanks. Right now they're just being kept alive for shipment."

"D-heds now," Cephean insisted.

Carlyle froze, eyeing the cynthian. What was that supposed to mean—*dead?* He shoved past Cephean and looked into the nearest cradle. The neural tissue of the core, visible beneath a clear dome, quivered faintly; it was dark and smoky. A glance at the cradle monitor confirmed that the core was indeed dead. He turned slowly, raising his eyes to the cynthian.

Cephean's ears were flattened to the sides, the fur along their edges trembling. His whiskers twitched. "Hi h-make miss-thake," he hissed. His eyes darted about the room, his foreclaws extended and retracted quickly, clicking softly on the deck.

Carlyle's breath escaped in gasps: "You . . . made . . . a mistake?" He caught the cynthian's eye and held it. "*You what?*" He glared, infuriated by Cephean's sullen gaze. "What did you try to *do?*"

Cephean sputtered and pawed his nose. He half-snarled an answer, incomprehensible. The riffmar lurched forward, rustling, then retreated. Carlyle was startled, but he demanded an answer. Cephean broke from his gaze and cried,

"Hiss whoodens hans-ser h-me!" He hunched mournfully and shook his head. The golden flecks in his eyes gleamed like flames. *Guilt*, Carlyle thought scornfully.

He circled around to check the other Lifecybe units. He found one more ruined, and he returned, confounded, to Cephean. "Why are you wrecking my cargo?" he shouted. Even if the cargo didn't matter in the end, what did this creature think he was doing?

Cephean sputtered and gave in, after a fashion. "Hi hask ssem."

"The computer cores? Asked them what?"

"H-insfor-m-hationss. H-abouss sshiff," he hissed. "H-how iss ffly."

This was incredible. "What did you want to know? Why didn't you ask me? This is just a mass of nerve tissue—only works when it's part of a system. It's delicate! You can't just —it doesn't even *have* information! And what did you want to know, anyway?"

The cynthian made no reply. Carlyle looked around in disgust. The two cores were an expensive loss, but more appalling was Cephean's lack of understanding or of good sense. Which probably went a long way toward explaining his incompetence in the net.

Cephean peered at him. (*Resentment*, he felt.)

"Damn it!" Carlyle said, making his decision. "Time we got some things straight!" Cephean looked startled, the color dimming from his eyes. (*Apprehension* crossed Carlyle's mind. Had the cynthian already guessed?)

"Cephean, I'm not going to like this either—but when it's over, I think we're going to understand each other a little better." He took a deep breath. The riffmar squealed; he glared at them. "Follow me."

Cephean obeyed and followed him out of the hold, ducking his head and hissing.

3

IN THE DREAMPOOL

The dreampool theater was lighted only by a deep-sea gloom. The pool was encircled by a smooth, padded ledge; the water itself radiated the ocean-blue light. The water was still, and its depth visually indeterminable. The water appeared to simply merge with the inner wall, and only the glow could be seen in its depths. Good place to dive and never come up, Carlyle thought, though of course the depth was illusory.

The intensity of the light fluctuated as they moved about, varying inversely with their proximity to the water. "Whass?" Cephean queried, loping around the pool and coming back to eye Carlyle suspiciously. The riffmar fluttered to a halt.

"Dreampool," Carlyle said. "Rigger crews use it to help develop rapport. Intimacy. I didn't want to use it because it was designed, really, for human minds—and frankly it can be pretty damn personal." He swallowed. "Well, we're going to test it between a human and cynthian."

Cephean's flickering eyes seemed to turn inward. The riffmar shuddered sympathetically. "H-no-o, no-o!" he hissed. He glared at Carlyle and drew back defensively, his whiskers pointing forward.

Carlyle exhaled through his teeth. He wasn't asking; he was telling. This was something which had to be done.

"Cephean," he said sternly, "if you don't, we will be adrift in this spaceship for the rest of eternity. Now maybe you wouldn't mind that for yourself, but how do you like the thought of looking at *me* until you die, eh?"

Cephean shivered. Hissed.

"That's what's going to happen, because we're not going to fly this ship again until we've had a session in the dreampool." He held his breath, keeping his anger and his uncertainty in check. How far did he dare assert himself?

The cynthian muttered and, to his surprise, acquiesced. "Hyiss."

Carlyle sighed gratefully, and explained the procedure. Then they sat at the pool's edge, ninety degrees apart from one another—Cephean having to splay his hind legs and sit stiffly upright to fit on the ledge. "Now," Carlyle said, "look straight into the water, and let your mind follow your eyes. Listen to my thoughts and do exactly as I do."

The cynthian hissed an acknowledgement, and Carlyle let his gaze drift down to the center of the pool. He studied the luminous surface. He remained aware of Cephean's attention, and of his own worries; but as he stared into the water his tensions began to subside. His thoughts focused themselves, without guidance, onto the pool with its internal glow. Something began perturbing the water beneath its surface, causing a subtle wavering in the light. Soon it was the variations rather than the light itself which he watched—shimmerings in the cool sapphire-emerald bath. The flickering of an open flame, but without warmth—it was alive, and it reached out and entered his gaze with the energy of an alert, probing mind. . . .

The first thoughts were his own memories, focused both through his own eyes and the eyes of another. Murky. Then deadly clear:

Sedora's fluxfield chamber's secondary shield curved around him like a queer eggshell, sealing him into the serv-

iceway between the outer shield and the main core baf-
fling. The mutter of voices from the wall intercom barely
reached him, and he worked at his chores with some relief
at being alone and having his thoughts to himself. Not that
he minded his four new crewmates, but he had only been
with them for a few weeks, and that was hardly enough
time for real relationships to develop. It was good to be off,
to be out of the rig, to worry about simple machinery for a
while.

That anomalous reading, now, was probably a misalign-
ment in one of the feedback elements, a bit too steep to be
compensated for from the bridge. It was easily corrected,
except for the awkwardness of just moving around in this
damn chamber suit. He stooped and took a flow reading,
turned a handscrew, and then backed it off a hair. There
was a flow surge for some reason, but it only lasted a moment before the readings leveled off again. He played the
screw back and forth very slightly; it wasn't a critical adjustment, but it was always good to have the flux-pile working
as smoothly as possible. Finally (did he hear a ringing, an
echo of some kind?—hard to tell, probably his own heartbeat
pulsing in his ear), he moved over to check the other elements, one by one.

When he finished the final adjustment, he rubbed his forehead against the suit faceplate, trying to scratch an itch over
his eyebrow. It was time to be getting back to the bridge.
And there was that ringing again—was it coming from the
outside?

The exit was on the far side of the pile, and it took him a
few minutes to work his way around the circular catwalk.
He stopped at the intercom. "This is Gev. Adjustments are
all right in here. Has the power smoothed out in the net?"
His voice was dull, a muffled echo inside the chamber suit.

No answer. And there was that noise.

Then the exit port opened, and clanging exploded around
his head: general-alarm klaxon. Stunned, he sealed the

hatch and hurried to the prep-room intercom. "Bridge! Bridge!" Still no answer; either no one was in the net, or communications circuits were out. The alarm meant a vital systems failure.

He quickly checked the pile console; there was no danger here, but there was a massive interruption in the net circuit. He headed for the bridge at a run. The suit still encumbered him; panting, he flipped open his visor for more air. He shouted into a corridor intercom, and this time he was answered by a hiss. The corridor illuminators flickered but remained alight.

He mounted the ramp to the bridge—and gagged as he inhaled a lungful of smoke. Choking, he slapped his visor down and panted rapidly, hoarsely, to draw filtered air through the suit. The bridge was gloomy and filled with acrid haze. He moved cautiously, squinting and blinking tears and thinking: there is burning flesh in this smoke. The instrument panels were blackened but no longer burning. He turned to look at the rigger-stations in the outer circle of the bridge. His stomach dropped. His crewmates were dead in their alcoves; their bodies still smoldered in the rigger-seats. Marc, the com-rigger, his neck and cheeks collapsed, his eyes sunk in their sockets, smoking. Gayl, Abdul, Niesh—all the same. He stared at each one for the same long minute. Numbness blocked every nerve, every emotion, every thought except a detached *awareness* of horror.

For a time he did not move at all. But gradually the haze began to clear from the bridge, and he knew what had to be done. He remained shock-calm, and though the stench continued to burn in his nostrils and his stomach threatened to convulse, he did not become sick. Garbed still in the chamber suit, he wrapped the four bodies and carried them to a small, unused freezer-hold. He ventilated and scrubbed the bridge, and he finally shut off the clamoring alarm. He examined the instruments and recorders, and he reconstructed and logged the accident to the best of his ability. And *then* he went to pieces.

He stayed in the commons; he was afraid to leave. Through tears and shakes and stuttering outcries to an empty ship, he relived and relived the accident. It had been a freak happening: a Flux abscess. Uncontrolled energies from the Flux had flared through the net, cauterizing every delicate nerveway tied into it—including the space communicators, the neural foam of the rigger-stations, and the riggers themselves. What had caused it? There was no way to be sure. Perhaps a subjective firestorm, a nightmare brought to life by the fantasies of one of the riggers. Perhaps a gravity-abscess, an unexpectedly close approach to an analogue of a star or black hole from normal-space. Perhaps something altogether different, some uncharted phenomenon of the Flux. It was always so difficult to know; abscesses existed along that delicate boundary between fantasy and subjective reality, and few witnesses ever survived to tell.

And might his own tinkering with the flux-pile have contributed to the accident? He thought not. He *prayed* not. But how could he be sure? Would he have to chase back the demon of guilt, too, before he found peace?

It had been his luck that he had been out of the net, his luck that he had not died with the others.

Luck? He was in a crippled ship, with long-space communications completely burned out. He was alone, more alone than he had ever been in his life, more alone than he had ever dreamed possible. And *Sedora* was a four-rigger freighter. Was it even conceivable that it might be flown by just one?

Reliving the horror for the hundredth time, he tried to summon the living faces of his dead crewmates. But they were gone now; he could recall neither their faces nor their names. A mercy, perhaps—but lord, the emptiness of having forgotten the last humans he might ever see.

(*Whasss?*)

Eventually, though, other names returned to him: Janofer, Legroeder, and Skan. The names began to click through his head like the chatter of a rad counter, rhythmically: Janofer Legroeder and Skan. Janofer Legroeder and Skan.

The faces came later, as he stalked the commons, battling with his thoughts—or as he moved dazedly about the bridge, watching the healers slowly regenerate the neural foam in the rigger-seats so that he could make the attempt to fly. The faces of friends, and their voices—along with the memories, the dread.

Finally it was time to discover whether or not he could, in fact, fly. When the pilot-rigger station was ready for use, he suppressed his apprehension and entered *Sedora's* net. It glowed fuzzily about him, shimmering, reflecting his nervousness. Hours went by as he struggled just to become settled again in the net, to establish a basic vision. And when at last he did, he was astonished to sink his fingers into the stuff of space and to feel the ship moving at his bidding.

Sedora, as it turned out, could be flown by one; but she was ponderous, and she flew as though laden with water. He could work only short, numbing shifts, and even then his endurance was strained. The ship moved on its course; but his thoughts flew ahead to the Hurricane Flume, the maelstrom to which all currents in this region of space led. There was no escaping the Flume. He could shape it to the image of his choice, but he could not make it less treacherous. He tried to consider alternatives; but there were no alternatives. The Flume danced constantly in his mind, and he was sure that he hadn't a chance in a thousand.

Therefore hope, when it appeared, was exceedingly strange. It was in the fourth day after he began flying that he noticed the signal—a part of the windrush, the starsong of the net. But like a warbling bird it twittered incessantly and would not be ignored. Finally he decided that *perhaps* he was hearing a distress beacon; and, lacking anything to lose, and with a bit of tightly suppressed excitement, he wheeled *Sedora* upward into the clouds to find the source of this distraction. The search very nearly drained him—ten hours, in all, of puffing through crazy blue skies with golden veils and spun hair arching across the stars like a yellow-brick road.

But in the end he found it: a flattened raisin of a spacecraft, drifting abeam of *Sedora* in the queer, atmospheric near-distance of the Flux. He grappled it in his net and took it spiraling up with him through layered images of space, through regressing visions, into spinning darknesses . . . until the stars exploded in bright pricks of light. Withdrawing from the net, he looked out through the clearplex port into normal-space.

The ship drifting alongside *Sedora* was squat, strange. Alien.

Suited, he left through the sidelock and floated across. He rested, enjoying weightlessness and gazing off into the galaxy; it was splendid and brilliant around him, exotically beautiful. From space, *Sedora* was silent, a gun-grey cetacean linked to him by a snaking lifeline. He turned, and his soles touched the alien hull. As he searched for an airlock he wondered who or what he might find—and whether, perhaps, the strangeness was only beginning.

(*Hyiss?*)

Before the disaster, though, was departure—boarding *Sedora* at Deusonport Field, with mixed and hurt feelings. It was *Lady Brillig* he wanted to fly. But if they said that a tour as helper-rigger on a slowship might teach him, then helper-rigger he would be. Deusonport Field: scattered cloudy, blue-tinged sun, green hills and forest about the perimeter. Should be a cheery sight upon return. Relaxed, amidst the frenetic commerce of the Aeregian planets.

But what should be so troubling about the leaving behind of friends? (*Who asked that? Who is wondering?*)

Earlier still, now, *Lady Brillig* out of Jarvis on Chaening's World: Legroeder and Skan as usual; and Janofer, never quite stationary—her moods like air currents, never remaining simply petulant or contemplative or buoyant or depressed, but always a turbulent mixture, and her attention rarely focusing for long upon any one friend, but forever shifting from one to another to somewhere beyond thought. Why could he not have been closer to them? To her?

But why desire closeness? Rejoice in isolation. (*Who?*) (*Whass?*)

Before *Lady Brillig* there was only the training, the school. The buffeting among childhood peers. Homeless, familyless. (*Hyiss!*) (*What?*)

And . . . earlier? . . . later? . . . the flight-shell of another spacecraft altogether: the battery of riffmar in turmoil, working to confused commands while he fought to control his fury and discover what was *wrong*. The riffmar were maddeningly inept, never mind that they responded directly to his control. *Mindless plants!* he shrieked soundlessly, but it was not a curse so much as a statement. Oh, why oh why had he come such a way to this nowhere place in space to be stranded? Why had he let Corneph *get* to him like that?

A riffmar, confused by his unsure control, stumbled near. He swatted it with his left paw and flattened it. *Six more left, by damn, and they'd better start flying!* But they wouldn't, not unless he determined what was stalling the craft, and instructed them. If only he knew more about these things!

(*Strange, to be flying without knowing . . .*)

Bring me syrup, he ordered, and glared at the two riffmar scurrying to comply, wrestling between them a large stalk from the bin. He took it moodily in his jaws and sent the two off to tend the riff-bud cultures, and then to feed themselves. While they were wriggling their tendril toes into the nutrient beds, he crunched the sweet stalk and brooded.

He had left Syncleya in a terrible fury, actually a tantrum. True, it wasn't his time yet to learn to fly (not for another four seasons), and he *had* taken the shell from the space-

docks without knowing if it were properly checked and pre-
pared—all right, that was questionable judgment, admit-
tedly, and perhaps he had compounded the error by heading for deep space rather than one of the worlds—but *who
would have thought that a simple shell could malfunction?*
Everyone knew that flying was bloody simple—use your
riffmar to run the shell, nothing complicated, and let your
mind steer the ship, like the interdreaming of the quarm,
but with no other broil-damn minds cluttering up your
thoughts.

(*You had never flown before? But . . .*)

(*Hone-ly held-hers f-hly!*)

(*Elders? Then you . . . aren't that old. Oh.*)

Lord-o, it wasn't the same for the others. He just *had* to
get away from the quarm and from Corneph's incessant *nag-
ging,* never letting him rest for a moment without conform-
ing to the quarm. Share, merge, unite, never leave a thought
untouched. Here: become a plant, become an alien (he had
never even *seen* an alien!). Broil-dammit! Was he strange,
just because he alone could not stand it?

Ooh, to be free of them! That's why he had fled! But he'd
never meant to make it permanent.

(*Did the others offend? Is that why you do not wish company?*)

(*Whass?*)

Now he was stalled, stalled! Why would the damn thing
not fly? Seated in his sunken dais, he grilled the riffmar on
their findings (though he had not been tending them, so
how could they have found anything?). He hurled abuse at
the quivering creatures, and finally he leaped screaming,
scattering them in fright. *Odomilk!* he shrieked, and when it
was brought he sucked on the pods with a vengeance, while
the riffmar huddled in their nutrient beds. Nothing like pun-
gent odomilk—but still, there were the riffmar to be attended to. Certain chores they could perform by rote, but
hardly what he was demanding now. And he had best be

careful; there were only six of the sluggards left. Here, an idea: perhaps there was a maintenance recorder.

Humming, he set the riffmar to locating the memory cube and then, once they found it, to obeying the cube's silent recitation. Hey-now, the thought-flow amp seemed to be working, so maybe it was just the controls out of kilter. That was more like it—a pity he hadn't thought of the recorder sooner, but after all he was a forest-singer and not a flight-crafter. Corneph—that sot-rotted nuisance would be unbearable if he knew of this. His bloody arrogance could drive anyone from home. Corneph, with his stinking empathic whistle, diving like a fool into the quarm and dragging you off on a mindlark whether invited or not. Lord-o-lord, to be rid of him was worth even this!

A riffmar peeked shyly at him, awaiting recognition.

Useless plants! He recognized it with a powerful swat. Hah! Two with one blow!

Oh damn, now he needed those two to fly!

Alarmed, he prodded the limp ferns—but it was no use; they were dead. He sprang to all fours, whiskers curling and twisting. What had they been meaning to tell him?

The four living riffmar huddled at the control tree, so obviously paralyzed with fear that he approached with unusual caution. What had they learned?

Ssss. They quivered, struggling to coordinate a reply. *Hssshell ffly . . . h-need more uss.* One of them collapsed, strained beyond its limit, and the others lifted it gingerly and carried it to the nutrient bed. *Sssss.*

That was it, then; he was finished. He had caught the image before it faded. The controls had been upset by a passing storm; now, with the help of the maintenance memory-cube the problem had been corrected, and all he needed to fly again were six riffmar to operate the controls. And all he had left were four.

Rage boiled in his stomach. He could not fly with only four, and there was no way to speed the growth of the young buds. He could switch on the distress beacon, but there would be no one to hear it; he was far beyond cynthian space. So that was it; he was finished.

He was also embarrassed beyond description.

A groan erupted from his throat, and through a deepening haze he saw the riffmar shrinking from him. *Damn them!* Wailing, spitting, he leaped at the control tree—rebounded with a crash of breaking elements—and launched himself at the riffmar. Two of them fell to his claws, but in his madness he lost his thought-control, and the other two fled shrieking to safety behind the nutrient bed. He forgot them and bounded back over his dais; he skidded, and slammed broadside into the wall. He staggered away, stunned, and hurled himself yowling into the control tree again, where with a smashing of splinters he tumbled, battered, to the deck.

Later, on awakening, he tore savagely into his stock of bramleaf, and he gorged himself on odomilk. He ignored the riffmar, ignored the broken tree, ignored the shell's warbling distress beacon—and concentrated solely on glutting himself to the limit on bramleaf and odomilk. When he finished he sank groaning into the dais, laid his head upon his tail, and slept.

(*My god, such violence! You've no discipline! No wonder you can't coordinate worth a damn in the net.*)

(*Ffsssss—hyou who kannoss kheef hyor mines hwhere iss be-hlongss, Caharleel!*)

On awakening this time, he hissed in pain. His stomach was a hard knot of complaint; his fur was matted and disheveled; he wanted badly, oh so badly, to regurgitate, or, failing that, to die. He fumed in silent agony, his eyes watering, his thoughts orbiting one another in meaningless jokes. Could he maybe work the little knobs himself, with his big, clumsy paws? Yeh. Ooh, to throw the fiercest tantrum in history! But he could hardly move, for the abdominal cramps.

Eventually his head cleared somewhat, and he turned

grimly to the final challenge: arranging for himself a good, classical demise. He looked balefully at the two riffmar *sssk*ing in the nutrient bed, and his blood heated once more.

But no; he must spare them, at least for the moment.

Had he grounds for demise? Dereliction in space was embarrassing, to be sure. Depressing, infuriating, humiliating. But was it humiliation enough? It was hard to be certain, and he had little experience in such matters. What he really needed, now, for a demise that would put even Corneph to shame, was to be perceived as being a victim rather than an idiot.

(*Demise? What do you mean, "demise"?*)

Later, mulling, and gnawing at his tail, he was startled by a CLUNGGG reverberating through the shell. And a buzzing outside—was there something out there? Some*one?* Fascinated, nervous, he moved over to the wall and listened. What, what? There were *thumps,* small thumps moving in a progression around the outside of the shell. Lord-o, now what? Was space itself going crazy?

He listened more carefully, and extended the range of his thoughts beyond the inner shell. Why, there were the stars and space—too broil-damn *much* space!—and . . . an *alien!* He pulled back, sputtering, and then reached out again. A creature from another shell, a biped, enclosed in a form-fitting suit of some kind. Walking about on the outside of his, Cephean's, shell. Searching . . . for him?

Blood rushed to his head, then ebbed. And suddenly the meaning came clear. The creature had heard the distress beacon—and who had activated *that,* anyway?—and he was here for a rescue!

Now what better humiliation could be asked?

Feeling suddenly much brighter, he sent the two riffmar to ready the airlock to receive the alien—and to prepare the space-balloon, since clearly they would be transferring to the alien's ship. While *he,* with assurance at last, began plotting a truly graceful demise.

Cephean, you mean you came aboard with me . . . (vision of the cynthian and the two ferns, plus baggage, drifting across space in the flimsy clear bubble, squeezing with considerable prodding into *Sedora's* airlock; Cephean clawing the bubble open like a plastic bag) . . . *meaning from the start to . . . kill yourself?*

Fffssilly ssfhool! Hnow hyou haff h-made me ffssay iss!

But can't you see I'm trying to help you get home again?

Ffssthufid! H-noss h-my home-ss.

Carlyle, facing the cynthian through a gauzy veil: *Cephean, if we get out of this, you can find a way home. I'll help you. Is humiliation the only reason you're not cooperating? You want to scuttle my ship, destroy it, take me down with you? Wouldn't you rather go back—laugh at Corneph, make* him *look like the fool instead? Put him in his place?*

Cephean lurched about in great agitation, almost crashing through to Carlyle's side of the veil: *H-no, no! Noss Corneph hin mi-mind-ss! H-noss hafter thiss!*

Cephean, I didn't take you off your ship to embarrass you, or even just to save you. I needed help as badly as you did. There's no humiliation in offering *help, and that's what I want you to do—offer me help.*

The boundary layer shimmered like a curtain, threatening to part, and Cephean pushed his face close to it to peer at Carlyle. *Ssso? Whass-about hyor frenss hyou halways heff?*

You mean Janofer, Skan, and Legroeder? They're not here in person—they're different. I thought you knew. They're out of my memory and imagination—sort of like your quarm, I guess.

Hyou heff no quarm! Scornfully. (Or perhaps enviously?)

No. But we wish we had something like it, or something like what you saw between the others and me in the net. But wishful thinking is as close as we come. We're alone. The way you seem to wish you could be.

Hyiss.

We're condemned to it. Except for short times, when

*we're in the dreampool—and then it's scary, but we do it be-
cause it helps us work together in the rig. The way I want
you and me to work.*

H-why hyor frenss noss helff?

*They were never there. That's my whole point. I was
flying alone in the net—just me, with my memories. Perhaps
I could do it again for a while, but never long enough to get
us through the Flume.*

Whass iss Flume?

Again? Here:

The Flume. Breakup of the Reld Current, and the vicious
spawning ground of new currents. The Flume varied in detail with each vision of the Flux, but in its most basic char-
acter remained the same. It was a place riggers passed at
peril and with utmost attention to control. They were like
ancient sonarmen—sounding their ocean depths carefully,
guessing shrewdly at reflection layers, scattering layers,
deep transmission layers. The only certainty was change, the
intrinsic frailty of any given condition. Things happened
fast: a vortex luring a ship into subtle pathways to unknown
space; a waterspout lifting a ship whole and pinwheeling it
lifeless back into the sea; white-water rapids smashing a
ship and flinging the pieces to the heavens. Or: the ship
dancing across the flux-eddies like a skipping-stone over
water, the reins of the net allowing the rigger to guide it
through the danger zones, to master the flow and bank into
the chosen exiting current, and to send the ship high and
fast toward its destination.

H-we kann noss!

*Yes we can, Cephean. That's why we're here—to learn
how. Are you ready for an experiment in cooperation?*

The cynthian drew back, sputtering. *Whass?*

The setting changed abruptly. They stood together on a
hillside meadow under a beaming sun. The meadow lay
upland in a range of rugged hills; all around and downland
from it sprawled pockets and cushions of forest. *Whass!*

Cephean was astonished and indignant, and his eyes flashed like copper buttons in his black velvet face. This, Carlyle perceived, was a bit like the tricks old Corneph used to pull. Well, too bad. *This is your world, isn't it, Cephean? Syncleya?*

Hyiss. Suspiciously? Or angrily? Either way, Carlyle could sympathize. The dreampool drew from both of their minds; and probably Cephean did not realize that neither of them was wholly in control of the process.

There was a sound of giggles, badly suppressed. The two riffmar poked their heads out of the grass, and sat up hiccuping.

Another sound—a hissing chortle, from the top of the hill. It was Corneph, gazing down with delight; he was a somewhat smaller version of Cephean, with a brown and white streak down his black breast. (Carlyle sensed sudden *malevolence*—from Cephean.)

Not far downslope from Corneph, Janofer sat serenely watching; and presumably Skan and Legroeder were somewhere about.

That's the whole cast, Cephean. Carlyle turned, scuffling his feet in the turf; he breathed great lungfuls of the open air, and gazed about at the almost torturously green countryside. *Will you show me around?*

Cephean spat and sputtered in perplexity, and finally pawed his nose, his tail lashing about behind his head, and allowed: *Hyiss, ss-all righ-ss.* He sprang downhill on all fours, the riffmar hurrying at his heels, and vanished into the woods. Carlyle followed, surprised by the sudden display of speed. He found Cephean in the woods, unconcernedly waiting beneath a stand of slender, smooth-trunked trees.

Ssthoff.

He stopped. Clearly Cephean had something to show him. The cynthian sat and simply looked off into space, his molten eyes wide. The riffmar stood perfectly still.

A sound passed through the air like a shadow, a musical tone. Or had something touched just his thoughts, and not the air at all? He couldn't tell what it was that he was hearing—even when the note repeated itself, and other notes followed, notes of different pitch and different timbre. Clear, piping notes—but were they in the air or in his mind?

Notes fell like rain. Reedy mournful sounds, and crystalline belltones, and a shower of melohorns, and a whole skyful of tones for which he had no name. There seemed to be no melody. But other patterns emerged, as though from the depths of his mind, blossoming into his thought. Visuals: of colors and of blending, sagging clays, of red sands tumbling, sliding from cliffs. And smells: of fresh-cut greens and broken cedar. His vision blurred, and instead of seeing Cephean he saw a whole community of cynthians, crafters at work—directing riffmar and the larger, brawnier roffmar at construction tasks. In the background, low-slung pack delmar grumbled and sighed. The controlling thought-commands rushed cacophonously through his skull.

The vision shifted with merciful speed, and he glimpsed a quarm, a circle of female cynthians, the everyday telepathic clamor subdued to an intense mumble; a circle of minds traipsing together in other worlds. The vision shifted again, and here were cynthians at study (investigating what?), their sparkling eyes gazing into oddly shaped crystals. Hum of probing thoughts; and instructions for younger cynthians (such as Cephean?). The vision shifted again, and broke altogether.

The music-rain trickled wetly, and stopped. He looked at Cephean in amazement. The cynthian was now resting, utterly relaxed, beneath a cleverly woven bower of trees. Carlyle blinked. Had the trees bent themselves to Cephean's designs? The music had so engaged him, he had seen nothing of what had happened. *You did that?* he whispered.

Hyiss.

The visions—had they been a deliberate presentation, or a distraction, or merely background noise?

The question died unasked. A boisterous scream shattered the stillness—and Carlyle whirled about in consternation and looked back through the woods, squinting. What the hell? he wondered. The scream sounded again, louder. Finally he looked up. An enormous flying beast soared low over the woods, then descended, crashing through the trees, and landed on the forest floor with a CRUMP and a horrible strangling noise.

Carlyle's throat constricted at the sight. It was a *koryf,* a dragon-creature from the wilds of Garsoom's Haven. He had seen a real koryf once, on that world. The beast had so terrified him that he had humiliated himself by hiding and abandoning his guide to face the creature alone. The guide had escaped unscathed, fortunately, but Carlyle's pride had not. The humiliation and the fear rushed back now, and before he even realized what he was doing, he was looking frantically—and futilely—for a place to hide.

The koryf was hideously crumpled and gray, like a deflated elephant skin hung on a misshapen skeleton. Even from a distance its stench was gagging, and its teeth were highly visible, long and yellow. The beast screamed again, and spat acid saliva that fell smoking among the trees.

Whassss! Cephean hissed shrilly.

Carlyle glanced at him blankly, then came to his senses. Quickly he explained to Cephean what the creature was—and that it was going to try to kill them. *This one's from my memory,* he said woefully. He wheeled around, looking desperately for a place of safety.

The koryf furiously beat its wings, smashing tree branches recklessly; and it lurched toward them with a cry of death. Carlyle backpedaled, urging Cephean to flee. But the cynthian was paralyzed by indecision—until the laughter of another cynthian (that toad, Cornephl) hissed through the woods. In sudden fury, Cephean raked his ears forward and flashed his teeth. *SSTHOFF!* he shrieked at the monster.

The koryf lunged, spitting and wailing, and tore a tree apart with its jagged incisors. Sputtering, astonished, Cephean fled after Carlyle.

You can't stand against it, Carlyle insisted, huddling behind a tree. Cephean glared at him. The riffmar scuttled on past and didn't stop.

Carlyle tried frantically to remember just what it was one *did* do against a koryf. *We can't outrun it, not far, and we can't fight it unarmed. We'll have to outwit it.*

Sss-how?

Suddenly he remembered. *It's stupid. It's telepathic but it's stupid.*

The koryf was crashing very close, now. His words spilled out in a jumble. *We have to distract it—it can only concentrate on one thing at a time. If we can each get its attention, we'll confuse it. Then—jesus I don't know, but if we don't do at least that much it will kill us for sure.*

Corneph, somewhere, hooted.

Hyou bross heem, Caharleel! Cephean said accusingly, not specifying whether he meant Corneph or the koryf.

Carlyle scrambled and shoved Cephean ahead of him. The koryf lumbered through the last shielding trees. The stench was terrific. Carlyle ran with Cephean until he had gained some distance from the beast and then sagged, gasping, with his back to a tree. Cephean snarled in the direction of the koryf, and turned to resume his complaint. His whiskers quivered with anger as he stared at Carlyle.

Carlyle was saved from an inquisition by the sound of Janofer's voice. *He had no choice, Cephean.* Carlyle looked around in amazement; but Janofer was nowhere to be seen. *He can only get so much help from us, Cephean—we are not so real as we might seem. But Cephean, you can help if you will only try. Do what he says now—you must, for all of us!* Her voice was soft, as always, and urgent—and it stirred warmth in Carlyle, along with a trace of bitterness and humiliation. Could a cynthian sympathize with such weaknesses in a human?

Cephean snorted and looked off into the woods—thinking, rubbing his tail against his ears, pawing at his whiskers. Finally he dipped his head around to face Carlyle. *Whass h-we d-hoo?*

The koryf screamed as it deciphered their location and began smashing its way toward them. Entire trees toppled before the creature, and the air was fouled with sulfurous gusts.

Carlyle shouted instructions: *You run to the right and I'll run to the left! We'll both try to keep its attention. Keep it confused, and keep track of me, too. Now GO!*

The nearest tree suddenly erupted from the ground, its roots dangling. The koryf shook the tree in its jaws, dirt flying in all directions, then dropped it with a crash and set to the attack. Carlyle and Cephean bolted in opposite directions. The koryf hesitated, infuriated—then lunged after Cephean. Carlyle turned, screaming: *STOP! STOP!*—but when the koryf gave no notice he took a deep, full breath and charged hard on the beast's tail.

His first thought was to throw stones to distract the monster; but there were none lying in reach, so instead he scooped up a clod of earth in each hand and when he was near enough threw them both, with all his strength, at the koryf's head. He missed. But he found a broken branch on the ground, and—as the koryf snapped close to where Cephean crouched, hissing—hurled it straight on target. The branch glanced from the koryf's head—and that got its attention. The beast swung about in rage and, screaming, set upon Carlyle.

He ran in terror. He ran until his lungs ached for wind, and then he stopped and looked back. The koryf was following him; but stalking the koryf, at a safe distance, was Cephean. Good, so far. But moments later the koryf was dangerously near, crashing recklessly, its acrid breath warm in Carlyle's face. Carlyle waited, ready to dash, and projected his thoughts in an effort to bait the koryf: *Come to me, come to me!*

The beast spat hideously. Suddenly into Carlyle's mind came an image of red, dripping flesh. He stiffened with horror, thinking that it was the koryf's thoughts he had intercepted—but the koryf suddenly lumbered to a halt and looked back at Cephean, slavering. Carlyle realized then what the cynthian was doing, and he projected his own image of bloody meat, gruesome and (he hoped) appetizing. The koryf's eyes flashed back around, half a second faster than its head motion, and it fixed Carlyle with a raspy-breathed gaze. Before it could decide to attack, though, an image of a wounded, struggling animal appeared, and again the koryf turned with a thrashing of its wings toward Cephean. Carlyle backed off by a few steps, and projected the same image, larger.

The koryf's confusion lasted about a minute; then it made its decision and charged full-bore after Cephean. Carlyle whooped after it, screaming and hurling branches and clods of soil. The creature ignored him for a time, intent on its prey; but after Carlyle had struck its head with several chunks of wood, it finally turned, shrieking loathsomely, its eyes sparkling with hatred, and advanced toward Carlyle. Backing away, Carlyle stared fearfully at the creature, thinking that Cephean would be too slow to save him; but the baiting images reappeared in his mind, and the koryf paused in its attack, turning again to look behind him.

This time they were able to hold the creature longer. Carlyle was so delighted by the sight of the koryf glowering with indecision that he shouted: *We're doing it, Cephean!*— and at once the spell was broken, and the koryf turned on him, its teeth snapping in his ear. Carlyle ran, and he did not stop running until he was out of the trees and realized that he was dashing headlong across open meadow.

Stupid! he thought. The koryf broke out of the woods directly behind him and began to close the distance between them. Carlyle cut to his left, reeling from the hot breath, and in a glance over his shoulder saw the koryf beating its wings for flight, for a swooping kill. *Cephean!* he cried—and at that moment the cynthian appeared at the edge of the forest and literally screamed an image of a gutted, bleeding animal. The image was so powerful it assaulted the mind, and Carlyle staggered—but so did the koryf. The creature hesitated. Carlyle echoed the cynthian's image; the koryf vacillated.

Carlyle thought quickly and framed in his mind an image of a snoring mouse. He concentrated all his thought on that image: a tiny, weary, sleepy animal. Cephean reinforced the image at once. The koryf grew even more confused, and suddenly seemed less vicious. Outside the forest cover, it appeared even uglier and more gangling—still terrifying, but less mythical. Carlyle thought of *sleep . . . peace . . . satiation.* He envisioned himself after gluttonous eating: loggy, muddleheaded, too sluggish to even think of moving. That image, too, was reinforced—a cynthian gorged on odomilk.

The koryf refolded its wings and settled down to observe from a more comfortable position. It seemed an oversized, large-jawed bag of bones. Its inclination to attack was failing. Lowering its weighty head to the ground, it seemed to decide that there was no point in making hasty judgments.

Two minutes later, it was snoring loudly and vulgarly—and Cephean was studying Carlyle with flickering, astonished eyes.

Carlyle caught his breath. Finally he grinned. There was Janofer at the edge of the forest, now, smiling. And there Corneph appeared and hissed grudgingly, his smirk gone. That seemed to please Cephean.

Carlyle wondered what the cynthian was thinking. But if Cephean had believed Janofer earlier, did any of the rest matter?

* * *

Carlyle lifted his eyes and looked across the dreampool with unutterable fatigue. His neck ached, and it cracked painfully when he stretched. His arms and legs were sodden; he was drenched with sweat. The theater seemed incredibly hot. He gazed at Cephean. The cat was grumbling and sliding down from the ledge with something less than his usual poise.

Carlyle stepped down, also. He nodded to the cynthian, but that was all; and clearly Cephean felt like talking no more than did he.

About an hour had passed in the dreampool theater.

4

HURRICANE FLUME

The day before their arrival at the Flume, Carlyle found himself taken by a liking for the riffmar. He whiled away an hour playfully boxing with them; and later, as they sunned themselves under a lamp in the nutrient bed, he came back and squirted them with a water bottle. They giggled hoarsely and seemed to enjoy the attention. Cephean said nothing about all this, and Carlyle wondered whether it was the riffmar with whom he played, or an amused cynthian. He did not ask; but he rather hoped that it was the riffmar themselves. Boldly, he assigned them names: Idi and Odi. Cephean refrained from commenting on that, as well.

They had practiced several times in the net since the dreampool. The cynthian still seemed awkward but was cooperative, and Carlyle felt that he would gain nothing by pushing him harder. They were nearing the end of the Reld, and there was little time left for worrying; they would enter the Flume, and they would succeed or they would fail.

And as for the future—well, if there *was* a future, he would consider it when it arrived.

Carlyle finished a last hot mug of brew and then summoned Cephean from his quarters. The time had come. Even the riffmar moved solemnly as they went to the bridge. Without exchanging a word, they took their stations.

The net was flushed with energy as a result of Carlyle's final retuning of the flux-pile. He flexed his spidery wings, trimming the excess energy. When the net felt right, and when *he* felt right, he looked calmly and alertly about. The Reld Current was a river running fast, and grumbling as it accelerated toward its end.

Ready? he asked. *Hyiss,* answered Cephean.

The images and decisions that followed were mostly those of Carlyle, but not entirely so—and not all that weren't belonged to Cephean. Space itself, in continual flux, bore the pair in its own malleable but headstrong manner toward the approaching nexus.

The Reld became a powdery, tumbled ski slope; and they sped downhill into an obscure evening mist. Carlyle folded the keel net into skis, and they thundered pleasantly, swiftly through the snow. The tremors of the skis moving against snow raced through his thighs and were carried by the rest of the net. *Sedora* bounced heavily through the banks and curves, but was riding well.

There was no telling when the vision might change, or how. Was the cynthian viewing a compatible scene? *Cephean, what do you see? How does it feel?* Cephean homm-humm'd in reply, and Carlyle caught a stunning glimpse—a fleeting landscape, prismatic and crystalline, and dustily wet. And downhill speed, mounting. Carlyle was reassured.

H-you wanss chahange, Caharleel? Cephean queried nervously.

No, this is fine for now. The cynthian was uneasy, then—but he seemed alert and ready to assist. What more could be asked?

Their speed increased, and the snow became hard and patchily icy. The skis rumbled, and began to shimmy and skitter on the run. Daylight over the snowscape was fading into twilight, which impaired visibility and made Carlyle nervous.

Without warning, he slammed into a mogul and was

thrown into the air, quivering. He kicked frantically against nothing, then crouched in mid-air, trembling, trying to guide himself back down to the snow; but the ship's mass took him off balance and twisted him sideways and off keel as he fell—and it was Cephean who brought them down safely, swinging his heavy tail outboard to counterbalance Carlyle's torque. They landed hard, skidding and swaying, and swooped onward down the trail.

Good work! Thanks!

Yiss.

The air began turning to mist, and the snow softened under the runners. The image was disintegrating. The snow wilderness blurred into speeding, hazy clouds; and then the current shifted, dropped—and turbulence grabbed at them like a vacuum.

They had been dumped into the Flume.

Carlyle pulled his arms in close, held his breath, and tried not to become excited. *Sedora* plummeted in free fall, and he had no idea whether he should try to slow it or steer it or leave it alone. *Ride it easy until something develops,* he called finally, finding security in the sound of his command. Where a moment ago had been silence, there was now a rushing of wind.

Whass haffenss? An urgent, frightened whisper.

I'm not sure.

Ahead (below), the turbulence was visible in the form of glowing streamers: chaotic, thundering, furiously inter-clashing. *Sedora* dropped into the whirlwind and was swept up by one of the streamers. It rode the streamer through the maze, buffeted by turbulence until its entire frame shook alarmingly. Carlyle drew the net in harder and tighter. *Sedora* raced ahead along the streamer—and something was changing . . .

Another vision, he called as he tried to decipher what was changing. It was a new noise, a change in tone. It was a deeper rushing sound, a rumble, a subdued but growing roar. At last, he perceived. *Waterfall ahead!* he bellowed. *Ride it hard or it will break us apart!* The streamer had transformed back to an image of water—a hurtling river swollen and fresh with the rush of a thousand mountain streams, melting glaciers and rainfall surging headlong to an approaching gorge.

If the cynthian replied, his answer was lost in the hiss of the current. Carlyle dug his arms deep into the icy waters, and strained to stabilize the vessel against the roll and the pitch. The water was dark and frigid and roiling, and to either side of the channel it smashed foaming against bulging rocks. The sky overhead was an eerie green with fast-moving clouds, and the banks edging the furious rapids were multicolored rock. Etched against the sky were orange- and blue-forested mountains, through which the river raced. Carlyle's thoughts drifted; if he could only stand on one of the banks and *watch*, the scene would surely overpower him with its serenity and its queer beauty. But he could not; the current was heavy and turbulent, and *Sedora* jolted and bobbed like a balsa chip. Carlyle tightened his grip in the water and held his breath against the numbing cold. He turned his arms into tensile-steel rudders, hard and strong against the flow. The vessel steadied—and he knew that Cephean was holding his weight at the stern. He wondered if the cynthian was as scared as he was, with his stomach somewhere in his heart.

The roar crescendoed steadily. Ahead, the channel narrowed and the water whitened. The chasm should be just beyond the neck formed by two huge and sullen bluffs ahead. The far end of the narrows was filled with mist—rapids. *This could be it ahead!* he shouted to the cynthian. It could be the heart of the Flume, the confluence of the hurricane forces of this region.

The net shimmered beneath the water, running just ahead of the speeding ship like a school of hysterical sea sprints, glittering and flashing against the ominous dark of the water. Carlyle prayed that the net could hold together in the Flume's fury, because the net was all that could hold the ship together. *Hold, Cephean, hold tight!* he screamed. His scream was lost in the thunder.

The ship accelerated; the banks edged closer on both sides. Carlyle's arms ached fearsomely from the strain and the chill, and he was sure he couldn't hold on even a moment longer. He looked frantically to the sides for a place, any place that he could moor the ship to rest and recover. But the thought was absurd—the banks were speeding death to the ship, lined with shallows and blurred, treacherous boulders. There was no choice but to keep moving, not that they could have stopped if they'd tried, and he *had* to hold on, to cling desperately to the channel as it swung from side to side. His gaze sped along the water ahead of the ship, seeking the darker ribbon of the channel, and the ship fishtailed as he steered. He cried to Cephean: *Tighter, tighter!*—and the cynthian leaned harder still into the stern.

The banks escalated abruptly to become two close sheer walls; and the water rocketed through the gorge. They could not guide; they could only cling and pray. *Sedora* thundered through black roiling water and silver foam and spray, dashed left and right amidst shining boulders, cleaved miraculously to the center of the current—and shot over the edge of the falls.

The ship sailed, floating—but it was dropping like a cannonball. Mist and spray surrounded them, and the landscape flashed dizzily as they fell (skirting how many light-years, Carlyle wondered ludicrously). The ship was falling outside the main body of the waterfall, and they had a few fragmentary moments of calm, of apparent safety; they seemed to be falling slowly, drifting rather than tumbling, but the cataract basin was incredibly far below them and growing fast. Carlyle's mind raced; the impact would utterly destroy them if they did not hit with their strongest point forward. *Nose first!* he cried. *Be ready to bring the stern about!* They would have to come about instantly under their own power or be churned to destruction by the whirlpool.

The basin mushroomed. Carlyle steeled the net to its limit; he would lift the nose as Cephean kicked the stern . . .

Sedora slammed into the basin like an ungodly pile-driver, an exploding jackhammer, and smashed his thoughts and teeth and steel neural arms, and blasted his soul into pinwheels of fire.

He wrenched before blacking, and Cephean kicked—and the ship screamed through its skeleton and skin, caught by torrential waters, and it foundered and twisted in the whirlpool and refused to yield either to control or to the thundering currents; and then it bent like a maddened porpoise, hung poised for a breathless moment, an enormous and powerfully coiled spring shaking in the vortex—and it rocketed shrieking out of the maelstrom and coasted straight, shivering and, unbelievably, intact.

Against a deadening weight, Carlyle forced his eyes to open and to see again, and he was astonished to discover that the madness had passed. The thunder died away behind them and *Sedora* streaked straight along a sparkling smooth river, and the way ahead was open as far as he could see.

We cleared it! he screamed.

Hyiss yiss yiss yiss yiss! howled the cynthian, who was so joyous at finding himself alive that he cast open all his feelings for Carlyle to see. (*Anxiety! Terror! Wonder! Relief! Intoxication! Anticipation!*) *H-where we gho?*

To the Banks, to Cunnilus Banks, you lunatic cat! shouted Carlyle gleefully. He was astounded at the relief in his own heart.

But the relief lasted just moments, and then *Sedora* lurched and scooted sideways and dashed like a startled barracuda, and the two riggers jerked their attention back to the net. Their pathway led among scattered and shifting currents, where the aftermath of the Flume broke into upwellings and downwellings and dying threads of energy. They still had hours of flying left to locate a current that would take them upward to Cunnilus Banks and safety.

The effort was grueling and tedious, and allowed no time for rest. The way was ambiguous, and shifted constantly. There were no charts for this highway; there was only vision and intuition. Carlyle found a wisp of a streamer and clung to it, an image of jetting atmospherics. The streamer carried them from one track to another, and he prayed that he was choosing the right way. The net strained between them when their visions strayed from one another; and more than once Carlyle shouted in anger, and Cephean slewed the ship threateningly. Carlyle cursed him, and received a bitter, hissing reply. But neither could have managed alone. They pooled their strengths and their guesses; when one's vision blurred with fatigue, they steered by the eyes of the other.

The currents nagged them and often seemed to deceive them, but in the end *Sedora* hurtled coasting out of the winds, and Cunnilus Banks glittered before them like a starry, snowy fairyland in the night sky—warming and welcoming to the weary travelers.

Carlyle settled back in the net and took a long rest to watch the sparkling snowdrift of stars. After a time, he spoke. *Not a bad piece of flying—eh, Cephean?*

H-you kidss h-me, whass, yiss, Caharleel? Hi needs broil-damn odomilk.

Ho, you weasel, I ought to teach you to drink ale. Or maybe a spot of whiskey, no?

H-no, yach! H-you ffoison h-me, yiss?

I'll bet it's something Corneph's never tried.

Ss-rue, fferhaffs, yiss.

It's settled, then.

Yorgh. Hey, whass?

Carlyle was as startled as the cynthian. Janofer, clear and

beautiful in the net, was staring at the two with mock-beady eyes. *What's this, Gev? You two are starting to sound like old friends: vicious.*

Never.

Don't be embarrassed. It's nice.

Yeh. Enough's enough. *Cephean, you ready for that ale?*

H-you kray-ssee, the cynthian muttered, and he vanished from the net.

Carlyle faced Janofer again, more comfortable now that he was alone. *I'm coming back to join you. Think we might make it together in the net, now, ourselves?*

Janofer smiled sadly. *Perhaps, Gev, perhaps.* She blew him a kiss. But then she was gone.

Perhaps? That was no answer. He flexed the net, feeling rather hopeful nonetheless. At least he could dream again of the future. Soon he would be back on Chaening's World, waiting for *Lady Brillig* at the Jarvis Port field. And Cephean—well, he presumed the cynthian would want to go home.

Right now, though, he had to get *Sedora* aimed on her final heading. He set about leisurely sighting the ship's lateral position along Cunnilus Banks, and he took a fix.

He cursed silently——and his hopes darkened. They were much too far abeam to reach *Sedora's* cargo destination, Gammon's Annex. What the hell could he do now? He had scarcely considered the possibility of reaching port, but the wrong port. What would the shipowners say about that? Surely . . .

Hey, Skan?

The com-rigger appeared silently, and listened as he outlined the problem. Skan shook his head. *Gev, you can find more things to worry about. The Guild will handle it. You saved the ship, remember?*

Oh, yes, the accident. He would report to the Guild and they would handle it. He hoped. But would he be able to get home? *All right, Skan.*

Now go get drunk with the cat. Waving jauntily, Skan vanished.

Carlyle considered. He wished he could be as sure of things as Skan. Well, he had to pick a port, and from here Garsoom's Haven was a likely choice (and what the hell, he could show Cephean a real koryf). He extended the net and brought *Sedora's* nose up and to the right, and pointed it carefully toward Garsoom's Haven. Then he set the stabilizers.

He pulled from the net and rubbed his eyes. He was most definitely ready for an ale, whether the cynthian was joining him or not.

And the way ahead was clear. Whether it was the right way or not was another question altogether.

5

GARSOOM'S HAVEN

Not until they had arrived in the system of Garsoom's Haven did Carlyle begin thinking in concrete terms about his future. And even then his thoughts were none too clear.

They had left the shining mists of Cunnilus Banks, had left the Flux, had brought *Sedora* spiraling up out of the subjective sea to normal-space. Garsoom's Haven Spacing Authority masered them immediately. "Welcome to Garsoom's Haven. Your arrival in our space was noted, and we have dispatched a tow ship to solar orbit 61 by 72 standard. Will you need any assistance beyond the ordinary?" The communication was too prompt to have been sent at lightspeed from the planet; the Spacing Authority either had Flux-modulation relay satellites scattered throughout the local solar system, or a network of manned dispatcher posts.

Carlyle looked out the viewport, where Garsoom's Haven's sun was a small, orange-yellow disk darkened by radiation filters. He could not yet see Garsoom's Haven itself. The sun was the nearest in a strand of jewels edged by a dim veil nebula.

"Rigger-ship?"

He jerked his thoughts back to the communicator. "Garsoom," he said. "*Sedora*. We need help. We've had a Flux-abscess accident, with crew casualties, and we seek emergency haven. Please advise the RiggerGuild—" he had almost forgotten to add that, "and stand by while we test our drive to see if we can make rendezvous." He glanced at Cephean. The cynthian watched impassively, eyes unblinking.

"*Sedora!*" The voice was suddenly demanding.

"Yes, Garsoom."

"*Sedora*, this is Garsoom's Haven Spacing Authority. We have apprised the RiggerGuild of your accident situation and have dispatched a tow ship to intercept you in your present orbit. Do not, repeat do *not* engage your ship's engines except in emergency. RiggerGuild Code specifies that in the event of any rigger-ship suffering a Flux Space accident, any port shall provide assistance and safe transit for the rigger-ship and crew and passengers, from the point of first possible contact . . ."

Embarrassment flushed Carlyle. "Quite correct, Garsoom. Thank you. We will not engage engines."

". . . assistance if necessary," continued Garsoom. "Do you require medical assistance, and do you have adequate life support?" The operator was speaking carefully, asking the questions required by the RiggerGuild Code.

Carlyle answered, "We have life support, and there are no injuries among the living. Garsoom." He glanced at Cephean. "Part of our Code. The port has to do everything it can to help us. Otherwise it's in violation of our Rigger-Guild." As if he cares, Carlyle thought. Whatever's on his mind, he's hardly said a word in two days.

"Hh-why?" Cephean said suddenly, lifting his eyes.

Startled, Carlyle shrugged. "Well," he said, "the accident might have damaged our space engines, so we don't risk using them. Especially if there's help."

(He sensed *disapproval.*) "Yiss. Hh-why?" Cephean asked, whiskers twitching furiously.

"Well," Carlyle said. "Well—it's because we are protected by the Guild. They enforce the regulations."

"Ssso. Hh-why?"

"Because if they didn't, people would take advantage of us." He didn't want to say that it was because riggers were . . . different. "We're the only ones who can fly starships, so they give us special protection."

"Hh-why h-only hyou ffly?"

"Cephean," he said with a flare of temper, "we're not like other people!"

The cynthian hissed and started pacing around the deck, muttering. Then he sat again and looked off in another direction. The riffmar hunched nearby.

Carlyle had to think about preparing for rendezvous with the tow. They were halfway across the solar system from Garsoom's Haven, but they were probably being sent the fastest tow ship available. So he should get busy making sure that the ship really was still space-secure.

Cephean was watching him with an unreadable expression. (But he sensed *scorn*.) Does he see this as another rescue—cause for "demise"? Carlyle wondered. Hope he's recovered from his suicidal urge.

The cynthian blinked and looked away.

Carlyle had been trying to understand his mood since the Flume. Cephean had been cooperative, but in a withdrawn sort of way. Does he regret having lived, is he anxious about landing on a human world, with slim chance of returning home? Cephean had refused to talk about it, and his "leaks" of emotion were more confusing than clarifying. He's young for a cynthian, Carlyle thought. Maybe he's plain scared.

The cynthian gazed at him darkly.

Carlyle gave up. "Cephean, I have to go check some of the systems down on the second level—below our quarters. Will you stay here? If you hear someone calling '*Sedora*' on the communicator, call me down below." He pushed several switches and pointed to the intercom. "If I don't answer, that means this intercom isn't working, and you'll have to come get me. All right?"

Cephean swayed from side to side. His tail flipped once. *"All right?"*

(Carlyle sensed *annoyance.*) "Hyiss," said Cephean finally.

He had been in the life-systems room for less than an hour, reassuring himself that all the systems were in fact working, when he heard his name. "Caharleel." He looked up. "Caharleel." The sound came from the intercom.

"Yes, Cephean."

"Iss khall."

What? "Is the tow calling?"

"Hyiss. Iss khall."

"I'm coming right up." He closed the inspection panel.

"Iss khall," the cynthian repeated.

The tow flew out to them on a high-energy Krans trajectory. When it appeared, it grew with astonishing speed and slid across the starfield to intercept *Sedora*. It was nothing but a flying I-beam with Circadie space inductors at either end, a crew blister in the center, and attachment locks on either side of center. The pilot called them on direct beam. "*Sedora*, are you ready to be taken in tow?"

"Go ahead, *Fitztaylor*."

Cephean watched the proceedings skeptically. His ears fluttered every few seconds, as though something were bothering him.

The tow blocked the viewport as it approached, then drifted down and to the side. It still covered about one-third of the view when it locked, with a bump, to *Sedora's* forward section. "Are you ready to relinquish control, *Sedora*?" the pilot asked.

Carlyle started to acknowledge in the affirmative but paused when he heard a low hiss from Cephean. The cynthian's eyes were dim and half lidded. (*Disapproval*, he sensed clearly.) He flushed angrily. "Yes, ready," he said.

"Are you in any immediate danger?" the pilot asked. He sounded bored but amiable.

"No immediate danger," Carlyle said. He still burned from Cephean's stare.

"*Fitztaylor*," he said, "we'd like to get in as soon as possible. It's been a rough ride."

"Do our best," the pilot assured him.

Far to each side of *Sedora*'s nose, the Circadie space inductors glowed golden, and then white; and the joined ships began to change velocity and drop across the solar system toward Garsoom's Haven.

After touchdown, when the tow ship detached and vanished back into the sky of Garsoom's Haven, they went out through the exit lock and into a transfer pod, with their personal baggage piled high on a robot porter. The pod carried them toward the spaceport terminal, performing decontamination procedures as it moved. Meanwhile Carlyle spoke by videophone with the RiggerGuild counsel. On his advice, Carlyle authorized release of *Sedora*'s log for inspection by the Guild and the Spacing Authority.

When the transfer pod slid into its bay at the terminal, the RiggerGuild counsel was there to meet them. "Rigger Carlyle, I'm Holly Wellen," the man said, shaking hands delicately and rather gravely. He was a tall, firm-featured man, probably in his late nineties; his hair was just turning gray, and his eyes were fatherly and full of concern.

Carlyle introduced the cynthian and riffmar to Wellen. He explained that Cephean could understand most spoken words telepathically, and could manage a fair reproduction of human speech. Wellen greeted them and suggested that they go set up quarters in the Guild Haven. They crossed the lobby and got on a moving walkway that ran the length of the terminal; Wellen pointed out the bay windows as they moved.

The city of Plateau edged the spaceport in a giant crescent, in the middle of a range of rugged and dark-forested mountains. Nearly all of the encircling mountains rose higher than the plateau. Over the edge, in the valley, was the lower half of the city, Deephaven; a part of it could be seen climbing up an opposing mountain. Further off in that direction, in the misty valleys beyond the settled region, lay the wilds—and deep in the wilds lived the koryfs of Garsoom's Haven.

Plateau was the largest city on this "stable frontier" planet, a world still untamed and sparsely settled—but sufficiently developed to provide for its own survival, some industry, and its own spacing capabilities. Like any planet, however, it depended upon the RiggerGuild to keep the rigger-ships coming and going with interstellar commerce.

Past the end of the walkway, they entered the privacy of the Rigger Haven and were shown to their adjoining rooms. The robot porter left their belongings neatly stacked in the rooms. Then Wellen said he would call them later, and they were left to rest and become settled.

They never did have the chance to go looking for a live koryf; the hearings into the *Sedora* accident began almost immediately. In the early sessions, the legal framework was established and the ship's log reviewed, along with autopsy reports on the dead crewmen. Carlyle sat in a small room in the Guild quarter with a woman counselor named Dial Jade, and together they watched a holo projection of the other participants: Holly Wellen, representing Carlyle and the RiggerGuild; Jon Pierce, a deputy administrator of the Garsoom's Haven Spacing Authority; Jules Tong, appointed by the Spacing Authority to represent the ship's owner *in absentia;* and various other experts and consultants. Carlyle was free to switch out of the session any time he chose, but right now he wanted to listen.

Deputy Administrator Pierce greeted him. "Welcome, Rigger Carlyle, and thank you for joining us voluntarily. We will be reviewing the log cubes from *Sedora,* and at the ap-

propriate time we'll ask you for your opinions and evaluation. Our first purpose will be to determine whether or not
failure existed on the part of the ship's owner and maintenance staff—or, in other words, to determine whether or not
the lives of your crewmates might have been saved."

Wellen spoke to Carlyle on a private channel from the
hearing room. "Don't let him worry you, Gev. They're really
just here to decide what to do with the ship and whether the
Guild should file sanctions against the owner. I've heard the
records myself, and there's no question about your own actions being commendable. And I have to say that I saw no
indication of negligence on the owner's part. Nevertheless,
they'll go over the whole accident at least five more times to
settle the claims between the Spacing Authority and the
owner. Unless you think otherwise, I don't see that the
Guild should make any claim beyond an award for you and
Cephean, and a settlement on behalf of the deceased."

Carlyle relaxed a little, but he was going to be nervous
until it was over and the incident was behind him. He
glanced at Dial Jade, beside him. She whispered reassur-
ingly, "This is just a lot of formality. Holly is sure that you'll
receive a commendation for bringing the ship in after the
accident. If they seem a bit stiff to you, it's just that they always act carefully when there's any chance of a problem
with the Guild."

"Will I be able to get a ship out of here when it's all
over?"

She nodded. "Don't worry."

"What about Cephean? I think he might want to go
home, but he hasn't told me."

"It would be good if you could talk that over with him,"
she said. "But he'll be taken care of as a rigger guest. Possibly the Spacing Authority will ask you to bring him to the
hearings to be a liaison between human and cynthian
worlds."

Carlyle pulled back. "I don't know if he'd go along with that. He doesn't even talk to *me* much anymore."

"If he doesn't want to, then that will be that," said Dial. She touched a switch to restore voice contact with the hearing room.

In the early parts of the hearing, he mostly listened, or spoke in asides with either Holly or Dial. Later he spoke to the group on possible uncharted hazards along the Flux route which *Sedora* had followed, but he was unable to make a definitive statement. Since he was out of the net at the time of the accident, he simply did not know whether the Flux abscess had been an external feature of the Flux or an aberration in his crewmates' vision.

Between sessions, he saw Cephean and explained what had gone on. The cynthian hardly seemed interested. He blinked his eyes and said, "Hyiss? Ssso?" and turned back to his riff-bud cultures, from which he was growing a handful of tiny ferns.

"Well," said Carlyle, "they're probably going to reward us for bringing in the ship, by setting us up with some arrangement to fly to wherever we want to go." He waited a moment, hoping that Cephean would respond. Then he said, "Cephean?"

The cynthian looked around. "Sssss?"

"Do you want to go home? To Syncleya?"

Cephean muttered darkly and turned away again.

"Do you want to speak to the panel? They've never met a cynthian before, and they'd like to talk with you." No answer. "*Cephean?*"

The cynthian looked around slowly. "Hhh-no," he said.

"Well, what do you want to do?" said Carlyle. He was trying to be patient, but why was Cephean being so sullen? Because he was alone on a human planet? "Do you want to keep flying with me, then?"

"Hhh-no," hissed Cephean.

Carlyle felt relief, but also guilt. Had Cephean said no because he felt unwanted? Did he *want* to feel wanted?

"Cephean—" he said. He wanted to say something soothing—or probing. "Are you all right? I mean, being away from your own people, being here with us, is that . . . hard?" He felt angry with himself for fumbling so, for being so awkward.

Cephean sat, staring at him with his copper-and-obsidian eyes. The riffmar were stirring about in the clutter behind Cephean, and one of them traipsed forward, dragging a syrup stalk. The stalk was wilted, but Cephean took it in his jaws and chewed it slowly.

Carlyle walked to the back of the room and peered into Cephean's wood-crate cache of food. "Hell," he said, "you're almost out of food." The Guild room steward had offered them provisions, but Cephean had refused; he probably was afraid of human food. But if his own supply was drying up, he might be suffering physically. Who knew what a cynthian's nutritional needs were? "Cephean, you're running out of food!"

Cephean's eyes dimmed with despair.

"Well, look. We can fix that, we can get you food. I know you don't trust our food, but if we do some shopping, we can probably come up with something like . . . odomilk . . . or your syrup stalk and whatever else you have. Do you want to go out with me and see what we can find?"

The cynthian blinked nervously. He inhaled and exhaled with a hiss, then fell silent. He started chewing his stalk again.

Carlyle looked around the room. The place was a mess, and despite good ventilation, it smelled. The cynthian did not use the human toilet but kept his wastes, rather sloppily at present, in a box which fed into the riffmar nutrient tray and the riff-bud culture tank. The floor was covered with little clots of black hair, and there were a few broken riffmar leaves lying about, suggesting that Cephean might have taken a few swipes at Idi and Odi. Obviously he was depressed, and possibly he was again becoming suicidal.

"Cephean," Carlyle said gently, "why don't we have this place cleaned up, and let's go out and see if we can find some food you'll like. All right?"

Again there was silence. Cephean seemed immobilized by fear. Is that it? Carlyle wondered. Fear? I can understand that—any rigger can. Some of us never go out into the outside world at all.

He reached out sympathetically to touch the cynthian—and stopped. How would that kind of gesture be taken by a cynthian? His hand trembled, and he felt ridiculous holding it out. Then he thought, go ahead—he's just a big, smart telepathic cat.

(*Irritation*, he sensed.)

Finally he reached all the way out and touched Cephean's forehead and pushed his fingers into the long, black fur between the cynthian's ears. Cephean's eyes widened, and his copper irises dilated to bright, skinny rings of fire around black pupils. (Carlyle felt ripples of . . . what? . . . *consolation . . . affection . . . condescension?* He couldn't be sure.)

"We have to help each other out, Cephean. We'll just go out in the city to some food shops. No koryfs. No trouble. All right?" He was tempted to suggest that they work out their problems together in the RiggerGuild dreampool, but he quashed that thought immediately. He patted Cephean's smooth, muscular shoulder. "All right?"

Cephean bared his teeth and worked his tongue around inside his mouth. Finally he dipped his head. "H-all righ-ss. Yiss."

Carlyle sighed gratefully. His heart was pounding. "Do you want to bring Idi and Odi?" he asked.

Cephean tossed his head in the direction of the riffmar, mulling. "H-no. Thake khair hriff-ffudss," he hissed.

Carlyle peered at the two riffmar. They were fidgeting

near the riff-bud cultures, taking care of the new "baby riffmar." Apparently they could manage without supervision. "Okay," he said.

They left by the main spaceport exit. Carlyle wore a magenta rigger tunic, which provided him with a measure of physical security but also made him feel self-conscious—wearing his rank, and implicitly demanding privilege. Cephean padded alongside, sniffing and staring about. He hissed in approval at the sight of ships arrayed on the spaceport field; but once they were in the general traffic, he began to mutter. Carlyle tried not to imagine that he was walking with a long-haired, panther-sized housecat.

The weather was sunny but cool, and Carlyle puffed up his windbreaker for greater insulation. They got on a shuttle which carried them two kilometers or so into the first shopping district of Plateau, where they got off and began prowling. There were no open markets with products visible from the street; here there were only small, closed-in shops. Carlyle went into the first one alone, since Cephean refused to cross the threshold. The store sold only synthetics, anyway, so he went back out. "Don't think so," he said. Cephean snuffled and hissed, and padded on.

The next shop looked more promising. "Hyou ssee," said Cephean indifferently, when Carlyle gestured toward the door. Again, Carlyle went to look.

The place was darker, cooler, and full of odors. He went back out. "Cephean, they have fresh-grown fruit and vegetables," he said. "Why don't you come in with me? There may be some things you'll like here."

Cephean sniffed.

"There are hardly any people in here now. It'll be all right."

Finally the cynthian followed him in. The air held dozens of smells, and Cephean sniffed and snorted suspiciously. "Come on toward the back," said Carlyle. The shopkeeper, at the rear, noticed them suddenly and came forward disapprovingly. "My friend is a sentient and a cynthian," Carlyle blurted defensively, trying to forestall any comment. He would have added that they were both under Rigger protection, but the shopkeeper had already noticed Carlyle's tunic and waved an unenthusiastic acknowledgement.

Carlyle looked over several open counters of produce and picked out a milk-bearing melon. He held it up for Cephean's examination. "How about this?" The cynthian's eyes glinted suspiciously. "Hmm." He put the melon back and picked up a yellow fruit. "How about this?" Cephean sniffed it, then took it in his jaws and bit deeply. "Yach!" he cried, spitting it out with a spray of saliva. "Whass sss iss?"

Carlyle picked it up from the floor where it had rolled and put it back in the bin where he had gotten it. He shrugged.

It occurred to him then that the thing to do was to have a whole assortment of foods sent to the spaceport and analyzed, and have a sample of Cephean's food analyzed, and see what came closest to matching. But they might as well try a few more items here. He showed Cephean the melon again, but the cynthian refused another trial bite. They went down the line, Carlyle holding each item for Cephean's inspection and the cynthian sniffing with disdainful disinterest. The floor creaked quietly as they moved, shuffling, toward the back. Finally Carlyle went to the counter and said, "I'd like two of everything, sent to us at the RiggerGuild Haven." The keeper looked at him skeptically but filled out the order and had Carlyle thumbprint it.

When they were back on the street, Carlyle said, "Do you want to go down into the valley, see the mountains?"

Cephean looked at him gravely. (*Alarm.*) "H-no. Noss wanss ssee k-k-horiff. Noss!"

"No koryfs," Carlyle promised. "They're all in the wild country, anyway—not near the city." At least that was how he remembered it.

"H-no," the cynthian insisted. "Muss gho vvack." (*Ur-gency. Urgency.*)

"Are you worried about the riffmar and the riff-buds?"

Cephean did not answer.

They returned to the spaceport.

Reluctantly, Cephean yielded samples of his dwindling food stock for analysis.

The answers from the specialists came back the next day. Carlyle studied the report in Cephean's room. The cynthian looked unkempt and ratty, with his fur matted to his body. "Hey," said Carlyle, "I think we can keep you from starving. All you have to do is eat the things on this list. Hope you like some of them." The closest substitute for odomilk, as it turned out, was the melon which Cephean had disdained yesterday. Or condensed valley-goat milk with nectar. There were a number of promising substitutes for syrup stalk, in particular celery soaked in Velan molasses, with vitamin and mineral supplements. For bramleaf, he would have to be happy with cereal grain products—perhaps thin flatcakes.

The cynthian's reaction was not enthusiastic, but at least he did not refuse outright to try the food. Maybe he's starting to understand that he has to adapt, Carlyle thought.

Cephean looked down at the crate of food which had been delivered by the shop. His eyes contracted, and the riffmar sprang into action. They scavenged through the box until they found the one remaining melon and, struggling, they lifted it to the edge of the box. It fell from their hands and thumped to the floor and rolled away. They scurried to catch it, and they turned it and rolled it toward Cephean, hissing softly with the effort. Cephean eyed the melon doubtfully, then mouthed it.

"Wait," said Carlyle. "I'd better cut that open for you." He went back to his own quarters and returned with a sharp knife and a platter. Taking the melon from Cephean, he placed it on the platter and carefully sliced it open. A yellowish milk spilled out, filling the platter. "You can try the milk, and you might like the inside of the melon, too," he said, quartering the fruit and placing the pieces to one side.

Cephean sniffed. "Iss noss ffoisson?" he asked cautiously.

"No, I'm sure it's safe."

The cynthian took a tentative lick, then jerked back and worried his tongue about inside his mouth. "Yach! Whass iss iss?" He hunched forward and took another taste. He shook his head jerkily. "Noss . . . noss . . . vvaddss," he sputtered. But he backed away and to one side and sat stiffly, glancing down at the platter and back up at Carlyle. "Fferhaffs, Caharleel, fferhaffs." He looked perplexed, and swiped nervously with one black paw at his unkempt fur. He looked thoughtful for a moment. Suddenly the riffmar shuffled forward and climbed up his fur and onto his shoulders, one on each side. They began to comb the fur on his head and neck, plucking out tufts that had been shed, and cleaning bits of dirt from his scalp. Their fern tops waved and fluttered as they worked. Cephean bent and licked at the milk again.

Carlyle left them and went for his final meeting with the Guild med and psych experts, and, after that, the hearing panel. The meetings went smoothly, though he never got over his feeling that somehow they were going to find fault with *him* before the inquest was finished. In fact, he failed to hear the concluding commendation the first time it was read, because he was too absorbed in his thoughts. Would he be blamed for the flux-pile adjustments he made just prior to the accident? Would he be judged unstable? Would he be blamed for bringing the ship to Garsoom's Haven instead of Gammon's Annex and putting the Spacing Authority here to so much trouble? *"Skan?"*

"What's wrong now, Gev? You're completely in the clear."

And Janofer: "You don't have to worry, Gev. You really don't."

"Will I be able to join you when I get back?"

"Get back, first, dear."

He glanced up and saw that every holo-figure was watching him. He cleared his throat.

Fortunately, Wellen stepped in for him. "Gev, the Board has found that you handled your station with more than the requisite care and skill, and it has granted you high commendation, with reward."

Carlyle turned, startled, to Dial Jade. She smiled. He began to feel giddy with relief.

Wellen continued, "When you decide what you want to do next, the Board will help you any way it can. You may remain with *Sedora* after she's been refitted, if you like, or you can take on a different ship."

"I want to go back to Chaening's World," Carlyle said, impelled by a rush of homesickness—for Jarvis, for *Lady Brillig.*

Pierce, the deputy administrator, said, "I'm sure we can arrange that."

Wellen glanced at Carlyle, then said to Pierce, "Fine. Perhaps we can work out a way to combine that with the monetary settlement for the riggers."

Hearing that, Carlyle wondered. A monetary settlement? Just for saving himself and the ship? Of course this was all standard procedure, as specified by agreement between the RiggerGuild and the Interstellar Consortium of Spacing Authorities. Skan was right; he should have expected all this. But he still felt peculiar about it.

"And your companion, the cynthian," Pierce said. "Can you tell us what his choice for the future might be?"

Carlyle frowned. "I think he'd like to return home, too, but I don't think he knows the way back from here. I don't think we *can* take him home."

"You will try to learn for us what we can do for him, then?" Pierce asked.

"Of course. I'll try."

The hearings were adjourned, then, and Carlyle went to be alone to think. He felt responsible to Cephean, but what did that mean he should do if he left Garsoom's Haven for Chaening's World? Should he just do his best for Cephean here and trust Wellen and the Guild to help him? Should he invite him along to Chaening's World? How would that benefit him? Cephean was so damned stubborn about not talking; but he probably wouldn't be such bad company if he would just open up.

Dial Jade met him as he was walking back to his quarters. "Holly asked me to tell you that there's a light courier ship available, with a cargo already cleared for Elacia V. If you'd like to fly that, the Spacing Authority will set up a floating command arrangement, and you can take the ship on through to Chaening's World or any other destination you can get minimum carryage for. That's probably the quickest way home for you, and it would serve as a long-term monetary settlement, since you would have command and a share of shipping profits. It can be flown as a one- or two-rigger ship. Would you be interested?"

Blood pounded in his head, and it was a moment before he could even think. Chaening's World! The images: bright, busy spaceport at Jarvis with flashing ships of all designs, the city of Jarvis to one side, and beyond it the gleaming sea. And . . . *Lady Brillig* poised to lift, and three long-awaiting friends.

Dial was watching him curiously, smiling, as he brought his mind back. "Yes," he said. "It sounds like exactly what I want." And he could fly either alone or with company; just what he needed.

"Good," said Dial. "Holly is down in the spaceport now, if you want to go look over the ship with him."

Carlyle grinned and bounded down toward the main

lobby joining the Guild quarter and the spaceport. Holly was there with Deputy Administrator Pierce. "The ship can carry a co-rigger, too, if you like," said Pierce.

"You mean Cephean?"

"Do you think he'd like to go with you?" Pierce clearly hoped so; it would discharge their obligation to Cephean with the least trouble to them. "We could modify the second rigger station for him."

Carlyle hesitated. "I haven't had a chance to talk with him yet, but—"

Pierce waited.

Before Carlyle could conclude his thought, Wellen suggested quietly, "Why don't we go look over the ship?" Carlyle agreed at once.

Later, after they had inspected the vessel, Wellen and Carlyle talked privately. "What do you think of her?" Wellen asked.

Carlyle gestured affirmatively. The ship seemed respectable enough. Its name was *Spillix*, and it was shaped like a long, thin seed. It seemed appropriate for its mission, which was carrying mail and/or valuable light cargo. "It's fine. It's what I need to get back home, and after that it won't matter, since I'll be rejoining my old friends on another ship." He had already told Wellen his plans for getting together with Skan and Janofer and Legroeder.

Wellen gazed at him with clear eyes. He tapped his cheekbone with one finger; he traced the line of his wide sideburn. "I hope that your expectations work out," he said. "But please don't become *too* hopeful. There are many uncertainties in the way things happen, and time goes by. I'd hate for you to become too attached to what is, after all, only a hope."

Carlyle looked at him. Confusion buzzed in his mind. Anger.

"Do you understand why I'm saying this, Gev?" The lines in Wellen's face deepened.

Carlyle felt dizzy, and his vision blurred. Yes, of course he knew what Wellen was talking about. Uncertainty. The uncertainty of the rigger. A part of his way of life—that time could play strange tricks, that in a journey completed something might be lost.

Nothing he didn't already know in theory. But to have it flung at him in a moment of hope, of vulnerability—and by the Guild counsel, a friend—was unkind. "I understand," he said tightly.

He understood. The fact was that for all the established dangers of rigging, there were others known only by speculation, by rumor and legend. The legend that a crew once sundered could never be rejoined. The legend that a rigger-ship and its crew lost something in passing through the Flux, a trace of substance, an unmeasurable bit of mass.

Legend only. There had never been established any loss of mass not attributable to pile or fusor conversion, or simple gas loss from the ship. But rumors and legends persisted. It was said that a rigger who plied the Flux long enough lost something of his body and of his soul and even became, in a ghostly sort of fashion, translucent. And that ships themselves, with their crews, became ghost ships. Legend only. No one Carlyle knew had ever seen a translucent rigger or a ghost ship. But . . . there was the so-called Dutchman legend, the legend of the ship called *Impris*, with her ghostly and immortal crew which had wandered the seas of the Flux for centuries and would continue wandering for all of eternity, doomed. Legend only.

But what Carlyle really feared was not legend but *change* —something which might stab at him out of the future's murk. A change such as finding his place on *Lady Brillig* taken by another . . . by someone who had shared nothing of Gev Carlyle and who cared even less . . . by someone who had rendered him unneeded, extra. His face burned with blood as the thought circled in his mind. He saw Wellen again, looked deep into his eyes. They were the eyes of a friend who knew the upset his words had caused, because he cared.

Carlyle's fear slowly dropped away, and though his heart was still fluttering rapidly he pushed his anxiety aside, and he said simply, "Yes. All right."

He was astonished to find Cephean's quarters tidied, at least by comparison with their former state. The floor had been cleared of debris, and the containers of food were now arranged neatly in two piles at one side of the room. The two riffmar stood under a sunlamp; their toes *sssk*'d deep in the rich-smelling nutrient bed.

"Good lord," he said.

The black cynthian studied him aloofly. "Hyiss?"

"Well. I hardly know what to say. The room looks good, you've been busy." Or the riffmar had been busy. "Anyway, I'm getting ready to leave on another ship, to go home. And you have to tell me what you want to do."

The cynthian turned away, feigning disinterest.

Carlyle looked around the room again. He wondered why the food boxes were piled in two separate piles. Sidling closer, he saw that a number of the boxes were dented and battered, and he wondered if the cynthian had thrown another rampage. But Idi and Odi and the riff-buds appeared unharmed. "Cephean, did you separate the foods you like from those you don't like?" he asked.

"Hyiss," whispered the cynthian.

Carlyle nodded. "Good. Well then. You can stay here if you like, and you'll be under the protection of the Rigger-Guild."

(*Scorn, revulsion* answered him, though the cynthian did not turn.)

"I can't imagine why you would want to stay, though. The people here probably won't be able to help you get home."

(*Irritation. Impatience.*) Cephean turned, and Carlyle

sighed. "Cephean, why don't you come along with me? I'm not saying that I can get you home, either, or that you'll like the next planet any better than this one. But at least you know me, and you won't have to make your way alone."

The cynthian's ears lifted slightly, but otherwise his gaze did not change. The sensation Carlyle received was a trembling contradiction of emotions. Probably Cephean did truly want to be alone; but he also wanted *not* to be alone. "How about it, Cephean? Will you come with me?"

Still the cynthian stared, copper-and-obsidian eyes blinking at second-long intervals. (*Fear. Killing anxiety.*)

"Cephean?"

Still the cynthian stared. And suddenly he cried out, "Hyiss, Caharleel! Hyiss!" He blinked rapidly, and his whiskers twitched with great agitation. (*Shame. Relief.*)

Carlyle held his breath with his mouth half open, and then, slowly, he smiled. "Okay. Start getting your things ready to go. Let's make a list of the food you have to order. And maybe some fertilizer for the riffmar beds?"

Stretching to his full length, Cephean leaped to all four feet and began pacing the room. "Hyiss. Yiss, yiss."

6

CHAENING'S WORLD

The sky opened to darkness and the stars. An hour later, the tow left *Spillix* in a fast ascending solar orbit and departed, and Carlyle applied his hands to the controls for the first time. *Spillix* was a light and maneuverable craft, a pleasure to pilot even in normal-space. As Garsoom's Haven dwindled behind him, he tested the net for feel; but it was not until *Spillix* reached the fringes of the Garsoom's Haven star system and left the system's major gravitational influences that he entered the Flux.

The journey to Elacia V went as easily as the Guild navigational library had described it. Carlyle intuited a long glide-skate ride along rolling cyan hills under a rose sky, *Spillix* flattened and shrunk into a small board beneath his feet, racing along half a meter above the ground. The hills unrolled, rising and falling and curving, but always spilling in a generally downward direction toward the lowlands in which he knew Elacia V lay, curled about the estuary of a glistening sea. *So easy! Am I riding on hope?* He didn't care; he was happy to be making homeward progress, and the future was his friend. There was no need to call Cephean into the net on this leg, and he left the cynthian to such privacy as there was on the small ship, joining him occasionally for a chat or a bit of play with the riffmar.

The trip took eight shipdays. Speeding into the Elacian

system, home system of the old Elacian National Worlds, he was picked up quickly by a tow and carried around the sun to the fifth planet. After they landed, Carlyle immediately applied to the Elacian Spacing Authority for courier and/or precious cargo to Chaening's World. While waiting, he studied aspects of the Flux route to Chaening's World in the Guild library, talked with a rigger who knew the route, and then went to the seashore and lay in the sun. He persuaded Cephean to come along and purchased a large hoop-handled basket for carrying the riffmar and the riff-buds. But while Carlyle enjoyed the ocean and sun, Cephean mostly just sat and stared enigmatically off into space, the only sign that he was not frozen in a trance being the occasional flutter of his black great-cat ears.

Carlyle's timing was excellent. Three days after landing, he received departure clearance for Chaening's World with a small precious-grade cargo and several fat courier bundles, well over the minimum carryage required to make the trip. They lifted at once, and half a day later *Spillix* and her crew entered the Flux bound for Jarvis on Chaening's World.

The flight from Elacia to the Aeregian Planets, of which Chaening's World was one, was much longer than the last leg—forty-three lightyears, normal-space. The topography was longer, also, and more varied. Carlyle tried and found pleasing an image of fluctuating forest landscapes: they sailed birdlike through silvery woods mazed by stuttering streams and ponds, blazing with sunlight by day and suffused by night with the glow of several moons; later, they drifted more slowly, a tufted airborne seed riding the breezes of a denser wood with undergrowth and blossoms of all colors; they crossed a violet marsh and later still followed a twisting river through meadow and forest. The scenery was natural for Cephean, as well; he flew with Carlyle and even seemed to enjoy himself.

Life aboard *Spillix* was relaxed for the three weeks of the flight. Carlyle was content with his expectations for the future, and though Cephean did not seem content he at least answered when spoken to, usually, and made himself at home despite the cramped space. The ship had only a small commons/galley and two private cabins for living space. Cephean had his food from Garsoom's Haven stacked neatly in the galley, and he was eating it and no longer complaining or making vulgar noises. He even tried several of Carlyle's packaged synthetics, and he used the fertilizer solutions in both the riffmar beds and the riff-bud trays. The young ferns were doing quite well; they were now about a third the size of Idi and Odi, though they were still fragile and not yet walking. Cephean, despite his snorts at them, seemed pleased.

Later, they rigged through more exotic scenes: a flaming forest, a sunset blazing through silver-leafed, blue-barked trees. It was a mysterious wood, with slinking creatures of the ground and swift, shy animals of the air. Brooks darted and cascaded from hidden sources. *Spillix* was a swift air-eel gliding and snaking through the trees, never pausing.

Carlyle grew more excited toward the end, and Cephean more perplexed. *Whass, Caharleel? Fsthraange! H-why hyou sso ssthraange?*

We're in Aeregian space, now, Cephean. We'll be coming into Chaening's World soon. If the image was strange and frenetic, that was because the Aeregian worlds occupied a strange and frenetic space, with many stars less than a light-year apart, and all of them inside the curled end of a thin, crimson nebula.

My home, Cephean. This image reflects my feelings. Excitement, mystery, and hope against danger; it was not so much a reflection of his actual world of the past, as of his fantasies of the past. Memories as they might have been. Memories of a past that might yet exist beneath reality's clouds. Visions of a world which orbited at the heart of this Flux image, visions of certain people.

Janofer, I'll be there soon. Skan? Legroeder? Have you kept my place for me?

Silence. They were not there, right now, to answer.

You haven't forgotten me? Not after helping me through with Sedora!

Still, silence.

Caharleel. Hyor frenss noss here?

No, Cephean, they aren't here. They never were, really. But they would be soon.

The forest became dreamy, with queer creatures peering out of hollows to watch the eel, *Spillix,* glide by. The sun grew bloodier and gloomier. Carlyle squinted and steered by instinct, and he laughed in a whisper at the evening animals in the treetops.

Ahead, the forest opened to a glinting terrain. Cephean, hanging way back in the net, whispered nervously, *Caharleel! Iss s-sea ssmell?*

Yes. The sea. Nothing symbolized Chaening's World to him quite so vividly as sunlight flashing over the coastline of the sea. They were very close, now. Soon they would withdraw from the Flux; and they would be at the edge of the Verjol star system. By normal-space they would proceed to Verjol's fourth planet, Chaening's World.

Carlyle was riding a crest of expectancy. Salt smell filled the breaking forest, and sunset turned into sunrise. The light grew whiter and the distant glitter became patches of water. His pulse quickened as he applied real muscle to the net. The forest fell astern—and the ship flattened into a wide board beneath his feet. He shifted his weight back and forth, testing his control, and then he loosed all restraint and rode the fastest winds toward the approaching shore. At once he peered for a sign of people along the seashore, people who might be waiting for a particular rigger. He saw gulls, tiny boats bouncing on the waters, clouds high overhead, sun beaming onto sand and sea—and there, at the base of a sand cliff, people watching the sky.

He banked perilously and skimmed lower, along the cliff. The people waved. Janofer blew him a kiss, and Skan watched him with hands on his hips, grinning. Legroeder glanced up at him and immediately looked out to sea, but with a twinkle in his gaze.

Coming! he cried.

They waved again, laughing, calling, *Gev . . . !* The rest was lost, but that didn't matter; Carlyle leaned into the board again and carried *Spillix* over the water and climbed for a towering view of the sea. Sapphire, as far as he could see, all the way to the horizon where it met the sky. And the sun, flashing and splintering with abandon on the swells. And the shore, sand tumbling down from the edge of the forest.

Delirious, he flew higher, higher, the sky darkening and the land shrinking . . . he took *Spillix* ever higher in the Flux, circling and spiraling. The glow of sea and land beneath him faded, darkened . . . and he was surrounded by stars.

Normal-space.

Cephean wheezed nearby as the net fell dark. Carlyle tilted his rigger-couch forward and activated the normal-space controls. He turned the ship for a view of Chaening's World's sun, Verjol, a blazing disk against jeweled space. The sight of that sun made him dizzy with emotion. So many times he had doubted—now he was simply overwhelmed.

"Caharleel. Iss thiss h-where h-we gho?" Cephean was peering at him, not at the view. (*Anxiety.*)

"This is it, Cephean. That's the planet. That's where my friends fly their ship from." He was so nervous it hurt. He had to get on with it before he burst with anticipation.

Chaening's World Spacing Authority responded after a short delay and told him that a tow ship was being dispatched.

Now it was just a matter of time.

* * *

When they came in under the power of the tow's Circadie space inductors, Carlyle sat like a fixture at the port. The Lacerta Ocean glowed deep to light blue along the coast; coming around on the leading edge of the planet was the continent of Aries, on the Lacerta coast of which was Jarvis. Scattered cloud cover made it impossible for him to spot the city, but he called Cephean to the view and pointed to where Jarvis must be underneath the clouds. "Yiss?" Cephean muttered. "Sso?"

"So that's where we're going!"

"H-we ffly h-another shiff f-from hhere?"

"Maybe. Maybe." He scowled and looked back out. The pilot was taking them through a powered, high-speed approach. The Aries continent disappeared behind them. "Look," he said, "I know you're not all that interested, but you might be surprised. You might like it down there. You might even like some of the people."

Cephean pawed his nose carefully.

Is he afraid of company, anything that might remind him of the quarm? Carlyle wondered. "Cephean, I think you should at least *try* to talk to people when we land this time. You can't just keep to yourself all the time. Will you try?"

The cynthian looked at him speculatively. The riffmar danced forward and retreated nervously. Cephean held his coppery eyes steady with Carlyle's. "Whass h-we do hon thiss fflaness, Caharleel?"

Carlyle thought carefully. Cephean wanted to know, really, what *he* would do on Chaening's World, and that was indeed a good question. If Carlyle rejoined Janofer, Legroeder, and Skan, it was not clear where Cephean might fit into the group. And if there was no place for him with Carlyle and his friends, what then? Could he find another ship, rig with another person? Live in the RiggerGuild Haven and become an alien curiosity? Carlyle's throat tightened as he considered the question. He couldn't be responsible for Cephean forever, could he?

What would *we* do on this planet, the cynthian had asked. Without Carlyle, Cephean would be friendless. And despite the cynthian's quest for solitude, he didn't truly want to be friendless. Did he?

Cephean was still waiting for an answer.

"Well, we'll check in, and if my friends are here now, you'll meet them, and—"

He was interrupted by a call from the tow pilot. "*Spillix*, we will be landing in approximately twenty minutes."

"All right, tow. Fine," Carlyle answered. He turned back to Cephean. The riffmar were now on his shoulders, combing his fur. Cephean seemed to have forgotten his question. Carlyle was happy to try and forget it, too.

They were back over the Lacerta Ocean now. It grew beneath them, and the coastline drew nearer. Swells moved in long lines across the sea. And then they were over land, and the attitude of the ship changed, and they settled downward. Finally they touched down with a bump. The tow broke its connection and lifted, leaving *Spillix* motionless on the ground.

Chaening's World!

Carlyle looked out across the Jarvis spaceport. Most of the ships were fatter and taller than his, blocking the view. But above two freighters he saw a passenger liner lifting gently under the ungainly framework of a tow ship.

"Cephean," he said faintly—and stopped. It was hitting him. His heart turned inside out. He couldn't see the tower, the city, or much of the field, but that didn't matter. He was here. That was what mattered. He was *here*. Chaening's World. Jarvis.

The cynthian padded over to look at him curiously. Cephean was clearly puzzled, and no wonder. Carlyle was radiating a welter of human emotions, and even he did not understand all the kinds of hurt he felt. "Don't ask me to explain, Cephean. I can't. But maybe if you stick with me you'll get to understand." He glanced at the board where the communicator was winking, and then back out at the space field. "Got to check in."

The cynthian snorted and walked toward the exit. "H-we kheef h-our ssingss hon thiss shiff?" he asked, turning at the doorway.

Carlyle paused at the board and looked back. "No . . . no, we'd better pack all our gear and take it with us. I'm not sure if we'll even be back aboard again."

Cephean hissed and left to pack. The riffmar trooped along behind him.

Carlyle shrugged and turned back to the board. "Jarvis Control, this is *Spillix* rigger Gev Carlyle. Checking in with courier and precious cargo." He was busy for about five minutes, and then it was time to head into the spaceport center and the RiggerGuild.

The transport pod slipped along a clear tube running the length of the field. Scores of ships lined both sides of the tubeway. Cephean hissed and looked every which way out of the pod while they rode; Carlyle was untalkative, preoccupied by a feeling that his future was coming upon him rapidly. He remembered Holly Wellen's warning about hoping too much; but the worst that was likely, he felt sure, was that *Lady Brillig* might be out on a flight, and he would have to wait for her return. In that case he would relax, and perhaps travel. Maybe Cephean would be interested in touring.

The tube looped, and for a moment they had a view of the entire field, and then they glided into the spaceport terminal. They were discharged into a lobby that was paneled with glass and cut stone and dark woods from native forests. Two enormous grinbey plants climbed in intricate patterns from either side of the lobby, meeting in an intermeshing arch at the far side, over the entrance to the RiggerGuild section. They passed through the arch and on into the Haven.

The Guild Haven was carpeted with indoor moss, walled with soft-finished wood, filled with plants, and trimmed with curtains and psychetropic tapestries. The corridors were broken by frequent arches and alcoves and were busy without being crowded. Riggers wandered about in various forms of traditional dress: some in all-magenta tunics or full uniforms, some in capes or robes, others merely with a rigger shoulder belt or emblem. Most of them could have been recognized as riggers anyway. There was something in the gaze, the expression of dreamy intensity. A few required escort through the corridors, so lost were they in their visions. And some wore the special blue-edged belts which denoted the riggers of passenger ships—the fastest and most capable of all riggers, but not necessarily the most stable; these select individuals always flew with delicately chosen crews, under the direction of a Guild Captain, who was a com-rigger, a space captain, and a psychologist all in one.

Carlyle felt strange—glad to be home, but not quite feeling at home. He kept a sharp lookout for his friends; he saw a few faces he thought he recognized but no one he knew. Does anyone recognize me? he wondered.

They first went to the main lobby and secured quarters, which they visited long enough to have their possessions stowed and the riff-bud cultures set up near a sunny window. Then Carlyle, anxious to check after his ship and his friends, urged Cephean to come along with him. The cynthian agreed, leaving the riff-buds but bringing Idi and Odi. They went back to the same lobby and into the subsection handling crew and ship assignments.

A Guildswoman waved him over to her niche. "I have my own ship, *Spillix*, to check in," he said, "and then I want to check on some friends of mine, to see if they're in port." He beamed at Cephean, who seemed bored by all the talking. The woman nodded and communicated at a touch with the Jarvis Spacing Authority. She recorded the pertinent flight information and credit exchange, based upon Carlyle's "lease-command" with a percentage recorded back to Garsoom's Haven. She asked Carlyle what arrangements he wanted for *Spillix*—immediate reassignment, short layover, or long layover.

"Is that my decision to make?" he asked.

She explained, "You've been assigned the ship indefinitely, in floating command, as long as you keep it in service with at least minimum profit, and no layover longer than forty days if carryage is available."

"Really?" he said in surprise. Now that he thought about it, he remembered that all this had been explained to him back on Garsoom's Haven. "I really don't expect to be flying her again, though. Not as long as I can sign back aboard *Lady Brillig*."

"Perhaps," she said, "you should request layover on *Spillix* until you find out about that. Then, if you don't want it, you can sign the ship over to the Authority. But you'll have it as a backup in case there are problems."

Carlyle looked at her skeptically, then agreed—mainly to avoid making a scene about something unimportant. *Spillix* had been a good ship, but she wasn't *his* ship. "Can you check on *Lady Brillig* for me now?" he asked. "And Janofer Lief, Skan Sen, and Renwald Legroeder?"

She nodded and started working. After a minute, she looked up thoughtfully, shook her head with a quick smile. "The three riggers you named were on *Lady Brillig?*" she asked.

"Sure, but—"

She held up a finger and went back to work, pressing a crescent-shaped headset behind her ear and working her lips silently. After a minute she stood up and said, "Could you come into the next room with me, please?" Carlyle beckoned to Cephean and followed. He didn't like this.

They went into a chamber which was furnished with several comfortable chairs and a curved desk. Seated at the desk was a man who reminded Carlyle instantly of Holly

Wellen. When Carlyle and Cephean and the riffmar were settled, the man retracted his desk about halfway into the wall so that it no longer stood between them, and he introduced himself. "I'm Walter Freyling. I'm pleased to meet you and your companion, Cephean—and both pleased and amazed to meet your riffmar." His eyebrows danced up and down while he studied the riffmar.

"We've gotten some of the information you asked about. It took us a few minutes, because the ship you knew as *Lady Brillig* is no longer registered under that name. It was sold about three months ago by Irwin Kloss, and the name was changed at that time. The Guild is not officially privy to name changes under such circumstances, so you would have to follow the rumor tree to learn what the ship's new name is. I think, though, that it is no longer operating out of Chaening's World."

Carlyle stared blankly at the man. He must have heard wrong—or they had misunderstood which ship he had asked about. *Lady Brillig* sold? Renamed? How was that possible?

The blow was hitting him slowly, picking him up and carrying him out of the present, out of anything which felt like reality. How could his ship no longer be here, no longer even exist for him to fly? If it had been wrecked, that would be one thing. But this? He had left her only four or five months ago. This was wrong!

The impact was deep in his gut, now, in some part of his body he had not known existed. He felt as though he were coming apart, flying apart in pieces. He stared at Freyling, not seeing him, seeing only the blurred figure of a man who had uttered some words. His blood was pounding so loudly in his head that he could hear nothing else.

What about Janofer and Legroeder and Skan?

"Can you hear me, Gev?" Freyling asked gently. Carlyle focused on the source of the words. A voice. Someone speaking. Freyling had been waiting for him to absorb the news. Now he spoke again. "We have some information on your friends, but not much, unfortunately. None of them are on Chaening's World right now, so far as we know. After the ship was sold, they broke up as a group and rigged out on separate ships. All we can give you right now is their original flight assignments—but I don't know if that will help you find them. They rigged out months ago."

Carlyle stopped listening again. He couldn't keep on; it hurt too much. His effort—gone, wasted. Everything he had hoped for. He had carried his hope all the way from the other side of the Flume—and now there was nothing.

Had they left no word, no explanation?

Beside him, Cephean stirred, transmitting feelings of a bewildering sort. It was beyond him to understand. His gut turned itself inside out, and all the blood seemed to drain from his head. And then he was aware of Freyling turning to him from the desk com.

"Gev," Freyling said. "There's a recorded message for you, from one of your friends. It's just been found. Would you like to see it now? I can leave you alone here for a few minutes—"

"What?" Carlyle came back to awareness with a jolt.

Freyling spoke to his desk again and pulled out a thin square of plastic. He placed it over a luminous square on the desk and said, "Just touch here when you're ready." He indicated a spot under the square. Then he rose and left the room.

Carlyle looked glazedly at Cephean, then leaned forward and touched the spot. The square brightened, and he sat back. A holo-image appeared beside the desk.

He breathed sharply.

It was Janofer. She was life-sized, and she was seated on the edge of a chair, facing just to the right of Carlyle. For a moment he thought that she had changed, or that his memory was faulty. But no—her hair had always been that silver-brown mixture, and her eyes always deep and intense. But they were troubled, sad; she had been crying. Her eyes looked out into the room, shifting, brushing his but not catching. No, of course they wouldn't. She was speaking to a holo-recorder—how long ago?

"Gev?" she said, her voice trembling. "Hello. And goodbye. I wanted to welcome you home myself—we all did. But this is the best I can do. You've read my letter, so all I can really add is to say how sorry we are about *Lady Brillig*. We all loved her, and we're as unhappy as you will be. We all wanted to be here to see you again, but we're leaving on our new berths soon. I'm leaving tomorrow, Legroeder's already left, and Skan will be off in about four days. So you'll be seeing this after we're gone. It's terrible parting like this, but we all must carry on, and this is our way. I've found a new crew, though I'm sure they won't let me fly for a few days, I'm so shaky right now." She stopped and leaned forward for a long minute, apparently thinking. Carlyle tried to shift his position so as to look into her eyes. She tilted her head, and her hair fell awkwardly, and her face strained as though she might cry again, but she did not. This was the real Janofer. When she spoke again, her voice was stronger. "So, Gev, good-bye. We all love you, and I love you. Good-bye." She tried to smile, and then she was gone.

Carlyle was unable to move. He heard Cephean's questioning hiss, but he could not answer. Janofer had reached to the deepest nerve of his soul, had grabbed, twisted, and wrenched—and now there was an emptiness which was like the emptiness he had felt on leaving his crewmates months ago, but deeper a thousandfold.

She had said something about a letter. What letter? He had been given only the recording, and Freyling had said nothing at all about a letter.

"Mr. Freyling!" he shouted, jumping up. "Mr. Freyling!" He gazed at Cephean in dismay. The riffmar hid behind the cynthian's front paws.

Freyling entered from the far side of the room.

"Where's the letter?" Carlyle asked, pacing. "What happened to the letter? She said that there was a letter I was supposed to read, and that was supposed to explain everything. Where is it?"

Seating himself again, Freyling said slowly, "Why, I don't know. Perhaps there's been a mistake." He turned and spoke silently into the desk intercom. Finally he turned back. "We're going to check again," he said, "but there doesn't appear to be any letter in our care. The recording was placed in safekeeping by Janofer Lief, and as far as we know it was the only thing she put in the box. Perhaps she made other arrangements for a letter, or perhaps she simply forgot to leave it here. Or, possibly, we have made a mistake in our finder coding."

Mistake? How could they make a mistake? But Janofer forgetting—that was something which might have happened. What other arrangements could she have made? Janofer . . . oh dear Janofer. It would be so like her to painfully write a letter, telling him everything, and to make a holorecording to make the letter more personal—and then to forget to deposit the letter. Lost in her own new dreams, perhaps, trying in vain to put her past behind her. And forgetting. Simply forgetting. Perhaps she had the letter with her even now, wherever she was.

This pain was like nothing he had ever known—it lanced straight to the heart of his soul. Why had they split apart? Why had *Lady Brillig* been sold? Why renamed?

He addressed Freyling hoarsely, the questions falling all out of order in his thoughts even as he spoke. "Don't you—can't you find out anything more about *Lady Brillig?* Isn't there anything you can do?"

Freyling looked at him kindly. "I'm afraid there really is nothing we can do, Gev. We have no control over what an owner chooses to do with his ship, so long as he meets Guild standards. They don't have to tell us their business arrangements, and that's why we only keep current status on record."

"But why would Mr. Kloss mind telling? He always seemed friendly enough." Carlyle stared in frustration.

Suddenly Cephean broke in, sputtering. "Whass iss hwrong, Caharleel? Whass hyor frenss ssay? Hi ssaw buss c-houldss noss hundersthandss."

"That was just a holo-image," Carlyle said miserably. "They've gone. All of them. And my old ship's gone, too. What am I going to do now?" He gazed helplessly at Freyling; he started to choke and almost to cry, but not quite. For a long while, he simply sat and stared through watering eyes, and thought about really nothing at all, and about everything; and though he wanted to release it all, he could not.

Cephean was breathing with a sharp hiss, and seemed increasingly ill at ease. (The emotions touching Carlyle from the outside were a blurry mixture of *confusion* and *scorn* and *sympathy* and *fear*.)

Freyling finally broke the silence. "Perhaps," he said, "if Mr. Kloss is, as you say, a friendly man—and I don't know him, so I'm only speculating—perhaps you could go talk to him and he would tell you something more about the ship, at least."

Carlyle thought about that. "Can you try to find out about Janofer for me? And Skan and Legroeder?"

"We can try, of course. But tracking someone who's left the system is difficult at best, and usually impossible without physically following the trail. You know how expensive and erratic Flux-modulation transmissions are, even with the nearby systems. That really just leaves the mail."

Carlyle scarcely heard. Suddenly he said, "We'll go to our rooms, now. I'm going to look for Mr. Kloss. And I don't know what else. For the letter." He looked at Cephean. "Ready to come? You have to go see to your riff-buds."

"Yiss, yiss," Cephean whispered. He seemed to be looking at Carlyle as though expecting something more—his ears were lifted though flattened outward at the tips—but when

Carlyle led without speaking Cephean simply directed the riffmar ahead, running in low, fast leaps, and followed Carlyle himself.

Carlyle's thoughts were already focused elsewhere—on the future and on the past, but not on the present. Not at all on the present. The cynthian following him provided the comfort of familiarity, but that was small and irrelevant comfort now.

7

LAKE TARAINE

Carlyle gazed at the cynthian in astonishment and looked down at the floor where seven baby riffmar staggered and squeaked. Cephean hissed with nervous satisfaction, his eyes bright.

"I'll be damned," Carlyle said. "Nice work. But Cephean, do you really want to go off? I mean, whatever you want. . . ." He tried to keep the melancholy out of his voice, but he couldn't.

Cephean looked at him nervously. Carlyle had just returned from a futile effort to have *Lady Brillig* traced through Spacing Authority registry. And now Cephean was telling him that he wanted to go away with the "new-born" riffmar, to take them to a forest where they could grow up properly.

Carlyle felt wretched and lonely.

Cephean tilted his head. "Hyou ffinds hyor shiff?" he hissed, his voice trembling.

Carlyle shook his head. Maybe that was why Cephean wanted to go off—because he found it impossible to bear the tortured emotions of a human being. Or perhaps he really did need to bring up the riffmar in forest surroundings. That would be how it was done at home.

"I found out where I have to go to see the man who owned my ship," said Carlyle. "There's nothing else I can do. So, if you want me to see you off to the nearest forest, I can do that before I leave.

"Will you come back?"

Cephean's whiskers trembled. "Fferhaffs. Hi muss theash h-riffmahr fforess hwayss. Fferhaffs h-we sthay."

Carlyle felt more pain than he'd have thought. Well, he'd no reason to expect the cynthian to stay with him. Why should the cat be interested in chasing around looking for a human's friends—especially if he might be abandoned afterwards? Not that he would be, but. . . .

The young riffmar were racing around like crazy. They were cute, but they'd surely be a nuisance running around underfoot. Better Cephean should take them somewhere else to drill, anyway.

"So. Well. I can help you get out to Ornipsee Park, which isn't too far. That way you'll be able to get back to the spaceport if you want. And you'll be able to stay here if things don't work out in the forest, or if you decide you want to fly again." Carlyle turned away, then, not wanting to show how angry he felt. He walked into the kitchenette which divided his room and Cephean's, and he started looking for something to eat. Enough of worrying about cynthian and riffmar; he had problems of his own.

When he touched open the cupboard, he found the shelves littered with torn wrappings where his stash of pressed Garsoom nut-fruits had been. His blood pressure surged, and he turned and shouted, "Cephean!" He closed his eyes and held them shut, but he couldn't hold the anger in. "Did you eat all my damn food?" When he had *offered* Cephean the nut-fruits, the reply had been a rumble of disgust. But today, it seemed, Cephean had changed his mind and torn through the entire stock. "Did you do this?" he cried furiously.

The cynthian looked around and hissed softly. (*Surprise. Annoyance.* Distant *pleasure.*)

"Well, jeesus, you didn't have to take it *all*, did you? You might have left a little!"

"Buss hyou hofferdss iss. Hi ss-ry iss h-and ate-ss iss."

"Yes, I see that." His fury was diminishing, but his exasperation was not. Hell. Now what was he going to eat? He'd have to send down to the supply room for a restocking.

And hope he could find something that the cynthian wouldn't develop a taste for.

Escorting Cephean to Ornipsee Park, which was at the edge of a large parcel of virgin territory to the east, took up the better part of a day. At first Cephean insisted that the baby riffmar should *walk* out with them, but Carlyle dissuaded him; the little ferns would be trampled underfoot. Finally Cephean agreed to carrying all the riffmar in a hand-trolley which Carlyle would personally push. A "slave-cart," keyed to the cynthian, floated along behind. Cephean was willing to entrust his supplies, anyway, to the slave. He would be taking it with him, and he wouldn't have to do anything except allow it to follow him around.

Once they were loaded in the car and airborne, Carlyle ran a thin chain around Cephean's neck, bearing a medallion which identified him as a rigger guest and carried a credit coding in case he needed to make purchases. "Just don't lose this chain," Carlyle cautioned. Cephean sniffed.

When they finally landed at Ornipsee Park, he introduced Cephean at the park headquarters and alerted the rangers there to the possibility that Cephean might require assistance from time to time, whether in obtaining food or arranging for transport back to Jarvis. Only when he was satisfied that Cephean would not be stranded did he go outside with the cynthian and the riffmar to say good-bye at the edge of a deep cedaric forest.

The riffmar danced madly, scuttling about over the carpet of fallen needles. Cephean hissed and radiated a melange of emotions, most of them so primally cynthian that Carlyle could not begin to understand them. But the cynthian's eyes sparkled brightly, and his whiskers and ears stood out alertly. "Caharleel," he hissed. "Hi gho h-now. Hyou gho findss hyor frenss?"

"I'm going to try," Carlyle said. "I might have to be away from the spaceport for a little while, myself, but I'll see you back there if you decide not to stay in the forest. I'll wait for word from you before I leave the planet, so if you decide you're not coming back, tell the people here, so they can tell me and . . . well . . . I hope you like the kind of trees we have here, and I hope the little ones like them, too." His stomach knotted.

Cephean twitched his whiskers. Carlyle squatted for a moment and held out a hand toward Idi and Odi. At first they simply danced in place, rustling; then, first Idi, then Odi shuffled forward shyly and brushed their ferny hands against Carlyle's. Their touch was dry and cool. They danced away, shepherding the little ones, and Carlyle stood up again. For a moment he thought to pat the cynthian also, but he held back, and he pursed his lips and said, "Well, Cephean, good-bye."

"Hyiss," Cephean said, his eyes pulsing. "Ghuudss ffy." He turned and padded into the trees, the riffmar racing ahead of him. (Carlyle caught, in the whirlwind, both *joy* and *sadness*.) Only when the cynthian was almost lost in the trees did he look back, and then just for a moment. Carlyle pressed his lips together tightly and hurried back toward the car.

His first destination back in Jarvis was the Kloss Shipping Company, downtown. Dressed in formal rigger attire, he boarded a skyrail shuttle and rode into the city on a great curving silver thread, cutting across and beneath the aircar lanes. The city of Jarvis was beautiful, and it hurt now to see that beauty. Jarvis was a new city, on a world which had only been settled for a hundred years. It was a city which graced its surroundings, partly because of its attractive design, and partly because the heaviest industries were located far out in space, orbiting. Huge Circadie ferries brought the manufactured products down to the planet, mostly to the Jarvis spaceport.

The skyline was silver and gold and deep brown, and the predominating theme in above-ground architecture was upward curving lines. Scarcely was there a straight or flat-featured building in the skyline, except to complement the dishes and helices outlined against the horizon. The skyrail swept in on its own curve and wound among the buildings.

Carlyle's shuttle set down in the middle of the city. It was only a short walk to the address of Kloss Shipping, but he hurried, feeling pressed. A part of his worry was still Cephean, but *Lady Brillig* and his shipmates were rapidly engulfing his mind. What would they tell him here?

The building was graceful but unostentatious. Kloss Shipping occupied only a few offices, marked by a small metal sign next to a reddish opaque-door. He touched the entry plate, and when the door paled he walked in.

A woman, probably in her nineties, slid her chair around to the front desk and said with a waxen expression, "Yes, may I help you?" She noted his uniform with her eyes.

"Well, maybe. I hope so," he said. "Is Mr. Kloss in right now?"

"No, he isn't. May I help you?"

"Well, I think I probably really have to talk to him. It's about a ship he used to own, that I used to fly," he said edgily. "*Lady Brillig?*"

The woman looked at him. "Yes?"

"Well, I'm trying to find out what happened to it. Her."

He tried to smile and felt as though his arteries would burst.

"I see," she said. "You'd have to speak with Mr. Kloss about that. Shall I make you an appointment?"

"Will he be in tomorrow?"

"He's gone for several weeks. The soonest I could make an appointment for you would be four weeks from now." Her face remained expressionless.

"Well, is there any way I can reach him?" Desperation was creeping into his voice.

"Let me see," she said, turning to a console and running her finger down the display. "Yes." She stopped, pressing her lips together. "But it says that only in emergency situations is he to be reached at this location. And I don't know—"

"This is definitely an emergency. Really it is. It couldn't be more of an emergency."

She pursed her lips and eyed his rigger uniform again. Was it his imagination, or did she shrink back a little? She nodded. "Well, in that case, he'll be at the Lake Taraine offices during the next two weeks, and if you want to call there and make an appointment perhaps he will see you." She finished on a firm note, and he knew the conversation was concluded.

"Well, thank you," he said, his heart still racing. "Lake Taraine. Thank you very much." He turned and left. Only when he was standing outside the building again did his heart finally slow down. He tried to walk unhurriedly and let the nervousness drain from him; he prayed that no one would try to speak with him.

Well, he had found out where Kloss was. At Lake Taraine. Now he had to find out where Lake Taraine was.

Back at the Guild Haven he went to the resources office. Lake Taraine, he learned from a travel adviser, was located north of Jarvis and inland a few hundred kilometers. There was an exclusive resort at the lake, in the midst of which were "branch offices" of a number of large firms. Carlyle asked if the Guild could arrange him transportation up there.

"How about flying up tomorrow morning?" the adviser said.

"Couldn't I get there sooner? Today?"

"We could get you there today, but I don't know that we could get you a place to stay."

"I don't have to stay. I just want to talk to someone and come back."

"I'm afraid," the Guildsman said gently, with a gesture toward the setting sun, "that it's probably too late for that today. You'd be better off seeing him at the offices tomorrow."

"Oh." Carlyle nodded and went back to his quarters to think. What should he say to Kloss, anyway? Perhaps he should be open with him—the man had seemed like a decent person when Carlyle had seen him, and he was one of the few shipowners who cared to visit his ships and meet their crews. Perhaps it was because he wasn't a really *big*time shipowner. He had been friendly when he came around, and that counted for a lot from a non-rigger.

Carlyle wandered into his kitchenette, then peered beyond it into Cephean's quarters. Mighty quiet, for a change. Almost too quiet. Cephean was probably taking care of himself quite well, out there alone in the woods.

He rummaged through the cupboard and found a package of nut-leaf cookies. Cephean must have missed them. He unzipped the package; the cookies broke under the pressure of his hands and crumbled to the floor. He stared at them maliciously. Then he kicked the pieces, threw the wrapper at the counter, and walked out of the kitchen, around his room once, and out. He'd eat in the Guild restaurant, or maybe even the spaceport restaurant. No, the Guild restaurant; maybe he'd see somebody he knew. And he didn't feel like facing outer society tonight.

In the Guild restaurant one could sit either in alcoves equipped with privacy-shadows, or in the more gregarious setting of a sunken central area, softly carpeted, with round tables. He chose the latter; he really didn't feel like talking, but neither did he feel like sitting in seclusion. What he wanted was to sit comfortably with friends. He looked around. Several of the other round tables were occupied, one by three riggers talking together, another by two riggers seated apart looking as though they wanted to talk. He'd watch for anyone he knew.

The menu glowed in the tabletop. He studied it for a moment, almost decided on stuffed highland ferns, then thought of Idi and Odi and changed his mind. He decided to have broiled Lacerta bladefish instead. A signal pulsed gently, asking whether he preferred automatic or attended service. He almost touched *auto*, then moved his finger to *attended*.

The waiter arrived just as Carlyle sighted three riggers crossing the far side of the room. His heart jumped, lifting him halfway out of his seat. Two men and a woman, and they looked like . . . they turned toward him, then, and he sank back. It was not them. He glanced at the waiter, who could not have helped seeing his convulsive movement. The waiter simply asked if Carlyle would like something to drink before dinner. "Mineral wine," Carlyle said, and waved him away. The first group of three now got up from their table, but others were coming in—still no one familiar. He kept looking, studying faces. The waiter returned with the wine. Another group came down into the central section and took a table.

He was hungry. He sipped the wine. It was slightly bitter, but lifting. He glanced to the side—and started.

There was a rigger he knew—a slender young man, walking by with another rigger. What was his name? Jenis, Jamis, something like that? He had known the man in training school. Not well, but enough to say hello to. He waited;

perhaps he could renew the acquaintance. As he watched, though, the rigger and his companion turned suddenly and vanished into one of the alcoves. A privacy-shadow went up. Carlyle frowned. Perhaps the man simply hadn't noticed him. Perhaps he *had* noticed. Carlyle shook his head as the waiter brought him his dinner.

An hour later, he gave up with a sigh. There was no point in staying. He could go to one of the lounges and have a drink, of course, but . . . no, tomorrow was going to be a difficult day.

He got up early and caught a shuttle downtown, and then a small commercial flyer to Lake Taraine. The city and its outskirts passed beneath the flyer, and then they were high over thickly forested land pocketed by russet meadows and glinting lakes. Overhead the sky was full hued, with flanking clouds.

Carlyle watched idly and nervously. This was his home-coming—but not the homecoming he wanted. No matter how hard he tried to enjoy this one bit of the past which had *not* changed, it just wasn't the same. There was a great emptiness between him and the feel of the land. He counted the passing kilometers.

Most of his fellow passengers looked like business people, and he scarcely gave them a second glance after making sure that Kloss was not among them. Halfway up the cabin, however, was an attractive young woman whom he looked at more times than twice, but she too looked like a business-woman, and soon he forgot her as well.

After an hour, the flyer began its descent. A clear lake came into view on the left, and Carlyle thought that that was Lake Taraine; but it passed behind them, and the flyer banked right, then left, and a longer and deeper lake broke into view. Visible at the end of this one were the buildings of the resort village. The flyer dropped quickly, and a few minutes later it landed at the settlement's edge.

Carlyle walked into the village and tried to get his bearings, but everything looked different from the holo-pictures he had seen earlier. Well, he would have to ask for directions—much as he hated to draw attention to himself.

A female voice behind him said softly, "Do you need help finding something, Rigger?"

Startled, he turned around. It was the woman he had seen on the flyer. He stared at her, embarrassed. She was about his height, taller and slimmer than the average on this world. Perhaps she was a native of a lower g planet. Her figure was graceful and lightly full, like women he had seen on Doerning's World and Gabril. She smiled at his stare, and came up alongside, saying, "Why don't you tell me where you want to go, and I'll see if I can steer you that way."

He nodded, feeling very nervous now that she was standing so close to him. "Actually," he said, "I may only have to go to one place, and if I get everything done there I'll just take the next flyer out."

"Oh," she said, "you shouldn't just leave. Stay and enjoy yourself. Go down to the lake, at least." She pointed. The lake shimmered blue and cool. From where they stood, a part of a long white beach was visible, and a small harbor full of sailboats and kiteboats and diving skates and canoes.

"I don't think I'll have time," he said uncomfortably.

"That's too bad, really," she said. "You know, we don't often see riggers here. But I don't see why you shouldn't enjoy it, too."

He reddened. This was not a rigger's place, not with all these business people here.

"I hope I didn't say anything . . . I didn't mean to offend you," she said, alarmed.

He shook his head.

"Good. Well, I didn't mean to pry. I just thought . . . anyway, where did you want to go?" She gestured to warn

him of a step; they had continued walking up to the main
pedestrian road.

"Kloss Shipping Lines."

She stopped in surprise. "I should have guessed! That's
where I'm going. Have you come to see Irwin? I mean, Mr.
Kloss?"

"Yes. I mean . . . yes, yes, I have." He looked at her
strangely.

"You must be the person who stopped in at the main
office in Jarvis yesterday," she said. "Judith told me some
one from the riggers was looking for Mr. Kloss." She stuck
out her hand. "I'm Alyaca Perone. Personal aide to Mr.
Kloss."

"Then you could take me to his office," Carlyle exclaimed.
"I—well, I didn't make an appointment. Maybe I should
have." Suddenly he realized that her hand was extended to
him, and he took it nervously in a very light handshake. Her
hand was slender, cool. He let go, afraid of holding it too
long.

Her face clouded. "I could, yes—except that Mr. Kloss
isn't here now."

"But I was told—"

"I know . . . that he was here. Unfortunately, he called
this morning to say he was leaving on a forest safari, and he
won't be back for at least four days, and possibly as long as
ten." She looked thoughtful. "And he really can't be
reached, except in extreme emergency." Her eyes were sym-
pathetic but measuring as they met his. "Is your emergency
extreme?" Her eyes suggested that nothing short of impend-
ing bankruptcy would be considered extreme.

"Wait," she said, before he could answer. "Would you
like to have a cup of roast, or tea, or something? We have a
very nice lounge in our offices, and it seems like that's the
least I can do, since I can't produce Mr. Kloss for you."

Carlyle accepted the offer, and they walked a block to a
handsomely towered wood building. Once they were seated

in the office lounge—on the top floor, with a splendid view—he explained his problem, or at least the part about the ship.

"You just want to find out what happened to *Lady Brilligi*" Alyaca asked. "Mm. I work with Mr. Kloss in other areas, mainly with transcontinental transport and that sort of thing. So I don't know anything about that ship, one way or the other. You'd have to find out from him—but he'd probably tell you."

Carlyle drank his roast quickly—and choked on it. He coughed until his windpipe was clear again. "Well," he grunted. "What do you think—"

She touched his forearm. "I think you should do what I said earlier. Why don't you stay here at the lodge and relax and wait for Irwin to return?" Her whole body seemed to shrug as she shifted in her seat. "Do you really have to go back?"

"Well—" and he started to say *yes* but thought about it. Why go back without information, if by waiting here he could get the information sooner? Except . . . how would he get along here in the open company of the public? A rather elite public at that—wealthy business people. Would he have to endure hidden stares and invisible abuse?

She perhaps read his thoughts. "I'm not trying to talk you into anything. But if it's that you think the arrangements might be a problem, I could help you there."

"Thanks," he managed to say. Her touch on his arm had made him edgy as hell. He stalled, thinking.

"What?" he said, realizing that she had asked a question.

She tilted her head toward him. "You never told me your name. I told you mine. Come on, now. Fair's fair."

"Right," he said. "Absolutely. Gev Carlyle."

"Rigger Carlyle. Pleased to meet you!"

"Hi," he said, bobbing his head. Then he stopped. "Uh. I—ah, what was your name?" He tried, dizzily, to listen very carefully.

"Alyaca Perone."

A-ly-a-ca Per-one. Alyaca Perone, he repeated silently.

"You can call me Alyaca if I can call you Gev. Deal?"

"Deal, Alyaca. Perone." He swallowed, trying to hide his embarrassment. Perhaps he wouldn't have felt so awkward, except for the fact that she was so attractive. Absurdly, he wanted to make a good impression.

She was watching him, with a grin playing at her mouth.

"Miss—I mean, Alyaca. Why—why are you going to all this trouble?"

"No trouble."

"But still, you're—"

"Does there *have* to be a reason?"

"No—*yes*. No."

"So—there we are. Would you like another roast?"

He nodded. For a few moments, while she went to refill their cups, he sat quietly and watched the boats kiting back and forth across the lake. She set a fresh cup before him and sat down again. They watched the lake together, until he realized that she was watching him. He blushed and started to look her up and down, then caught himself and turned his gaze quickly back to the window. He concentrated very hard on a bright blue kiteboat which was skimming above the water, and hoped that she hadn't noticed. "That looks like fun," he said inaudibly.

She was relaxed, sipping her roast. He tried to conceal his agitation. "Hey, really," he blurted. "Why?"

"Why what?"

"You know. Why are you going out of your way to be nice to me?" No outsider was ever like this.

She thought for a moment before answering. "Well," she said. "If there has to be a reason, let's just say that I had a friend, and he left to become a rigger. That was a long time ago. But I thought, well—maybe it would be nice for me to be nice to another rigger." She looked at him, and this time he thought *she* was embarrassed. "That an okay reason?"

"Sure," he said. But it sounded fictitious. She did not look to him like the kind of person who would have been involved with the kind of person who would have become a rigger.

Involved? he chided himself. She just said he was a friend. Now don't start making it something—

"Gev."

"Yes?"

"Do you want to stay? Because if not, you should be going now to catch the flyer. I wouldn't want you to miss it on account of me."

"Oh no, no, it wouldn't be on account of you. Anyway—" He looked at her and looked at the window. It was quite clean, but when one looked carefully, one could see a few small haze marks right down near the bottom, where perhaps someone had put his foot.

So did he want to stay or not? Conflicting urges knotted in his gut until he thought, well, he didn't want to get up this very instant and go running to the flyer, and it couldn't hurt anything to stay for the day. If he got lonely and depressed here, would it be any better back at the Guild quarters?

"I could show you around a little if you'd like to stay."

Impulsively, he grinned and nodded.

"Good! Now I have to go up to the office for a few minutes, and you can call the lodge from there and see about getting yourself a room." She put her cup down and got to her feet and, quite unsure of what he was doing, Carlyle followed.

While Alyaca was in her office, Carlyle called the nearest of the two lodges. Unfortunately, their accommodations were filled, and were in fact reserved for the next three weeks. Disappointed, he called the other lodge. They were less popular; they were only reserved for the next nine days. He signed off gloomily. Well, it wasn't as though he had planned to stay here in the first place, so he wasn't really losing anything. He could take the evening flyer back to Jarvis.

The gloom inside his head was so deep he couldn't see out. He didn't even notice Alyaca standing in front of him.

"Gev?" she said, for what must have been the third time.

"*Oh!* Hi," he said disconsolately.

"What's the matter?"

"No rooms."

She looked perplexed for a moment, then said, "Okay. Wait just a second." She disappeared back into the office. A minute later she came back and said, "All set. I've gotten you one of the Kloss guest rooms at the Taratelle."

"Is that all right?"

"Sure," she said, her eyes twinkling. "Irwin keeps three suites there—all the companies do that—and none of them are in use now. Don't worry, Irwin won't mind. He has to pay for them anyway."

He could hardly argue with that, so he went with her over to the Taratelle, which was a luxurious structure near the lake. Alyaca left him, saying that she'd be tied up for the next couple of hours. So he went up to see his room, which turned out to be a dazzling suite of three rooms. Dazed, he came back down and went out to see the lake and the beaches.

The late morning air was mild and the sun bright, and the sky deep and clear. The front terrace gave way to a stretch of twine-grass lawn, and then cream-colored sand sloping to the water's edge. He walked along the sand toward the boathouse, on a lagoon connected to the lake. A sailboat was moving out of the lagoon, past a kiteboat, which was heeled over at an impossible angle. That kiteboating looked interesting, he decided. He wondered if Alyaca would go with him.

Questions sprang into his mind with that thought. Such an attractive woman—just "being nice to a rigger"? Why? With what motive? Was it just possible that she found *him* attractive? His blood rose to his skin. Alyaca with a rigger? With him?

The notion was absurd.

Hold it, Carlyle, he thought. She was only being friendly. She had merely been courteous to him, and certainly there was nothing wrong in that.

He let the question wash over him for a minute, and then his real troubles rushed back. He had gotten nowhere in his efforts to connect his future with his past, and really he should be back at the Guild trying to see if anyone had a lead on the whereabouts of Janofer or Legroeder or Skan. He should be *doing* something.

He went to the lodge and found a call booth. It took him three minutes to get Walter Freyling on the phone. "Hello, Gev. I heard you were out at Lake Taraine. Are you having any success?"

"Not yet." He explained his situation to Freyling and said, "What I was hoping was that you might have found something on Janofer or Skan or Legroeder by now." His hope rose as he spoke. Surely something had been learned by now.

Freyling gave just the slightest nod to acknowledge Carlyle's hope, but his words were a gentle let-down. "No, I'm afraid I don't know anything more than the day before yesterday. So far we've come up with nothing beyond their original departure assignments. The only other thing is that I've issued a request for any staffer or rigger who knew your friends to come see me, but that hasn't turned up anything either." Freyling's eyes moved away from the phone for a moment, then he nodded and looked back at Carlyle. "Nothing on that missing letter, either. It seems fairly certain that Janofer Lief did not leave the letter on deposit here. Do you think she might have simply forgotten to leave it for you?"

Carlyle nodded reluctantly. It was all too possible. "I'm staying here for a few days, then, until Mr. Kloss comes back. Taratelle Lodge. Could you send out some of my clothes? And call me if—if—"

"We will," Freyling said. "Good luck, and enjoy yourself. Good-bye."

Enjoy himself?

By the time Alyaca met him, he had become so edgy he found himself wishing that Cephean were here to complain and be temperamental.

She apologized for being late as she steered him into the restaurant for lunch. "That office is *supposed* to be just a front for vacationing, but there's always something coming up anyway. Did you get a good look around the place?"

"Uh-huh." He hesitated. "Do you know how to sail one of those kiteboats?"

"Sort of," she said. "Do you want to take one out?"

He shrugged. "Looks like it could be fun, if you know what you're doing."

"Oh, they're fun even if you don't."

"Does that mean—would you want to do it?"

She nodded with that grin playing at her lips again. Then she changed the subject and got him to order lunch, and they talked throughout the meal. Afterwards they went down to the boathouse and signed out a kiteboat.

The cockpit was just large enough for two people in fairly close quarters. In the vertical position they were riding about a meter and a half above water, with the feeling that nothing was holding them up. The keel-strut which bound them to the submerged tie-anchor unit was completely out of sight from inside the cockpit; and though in fact the keel-strut and tie-anchor held them down rather than up, that fact seemed like a lie when one watched other kiteboats gliding past. The levitators which actually held the boat in the air were mounted beneath the cockpit.

Alyaca got in first and took the front seat. "You can do the piloting," she said.

Carlyle looked up at the kite-sail buffeting over his head, freewheeling on the mast, and he picked up the lines which controlled the dump flaps at the top of the sail. The boat, he knew, was controlled primarily by shifting weight in the cockpit and changing the heel angle of the sail and strut, but the flaps presumably did something, too. He shook his head. "No." He handed the lines to Alyaca. "You drive. And show me how to do it." He couldn't help being embarrassed (a star pilot, afraid to handle a two-meter kiteboat?), but he was sure that he would only capsize them, and that would be a lot more embarrassing.

"All right," she said. "But we have to switch positions." They shifted, Carlyle tensing as she brushed close to him. "Cast us free," she said to the attendant. Before Carlyle had a chance to protest, they were drifting away from the dock. "Remember what I said," she cautioned, "I don't know exactly how to do this. So hang on."

That wasn't quite the way he remembered hearing her say it, but he kept his mouth shut and hung on. The wind shifted suddenly, and the boat pitched backward. "Lean back!" Alyaca cried. He scrambled up on his seat and leaned out over the bow. Alyaca hunched forward and pulled the flaps, and slowly the boat leveled. The wind surged and pitched them forward, and they both scrambled to shift again, but the wind had them, and they kited very fast toward the lagoon bank, the tie-anchor causing only a slight drag at its angled position just under the water surface. "To the right a little," Alyaca said, playing the flap lines uncertainly. Carlyle leaned right, but it was instantly clear that she had meant *her* right, not his. They slewed, and finally Alyaca got them into a right turn, which was what she'd wanted; heeling perilously, they sped through the channel and out into the lake.

"Damn!" he said as they cleared the end of the channel. His fingers were clenched onto the edge of the cockpit. Alyaca grinned and shifted her weight experimentally, trying to gain more control over the boat. They were heeled forward and flying fast, the wind in their hair, a vibration reaching them from the strut and tie-anchor rushing through the water—but now they had clear space ahead of them. Carlyle decided that they were moving correctly, though it felt more dangerous than dashing past the light-years. "Are we doing okay?" he asked.

Alyaca fiddled with the lines, squinting up at the sail, and nodded. "To the left, not too much. *My* left."

They slowly rolled and came around to the port, to a more windward heading. The wind was at their beam, now, and Alyaca took a lever beneath the gunwale, which Carlyle had not noticed before, and moved it back a few centimeters. She explained, "That controls the swivel of the sail at the mast. You have to really hitch it around when you're sailing close into the wind—otherwise you'd never get home."

At that moment they both leaned too far to the portside, and the cockpit rocked over as though on a wheel. They threw themselves to the starboard to compensate, and the cockpit hesitated, then heeled suddenly to the starboard, and Carlyle yelled, "We're going over!" The starboard gunwale dipped close to the water, and he hung on desperately, sure that he would fall—and Alyaca was hanging on, too, except that she was shrieking with laughter—and the moment that the boat hung there on its side seemed an eternity to him, but slowly, slowly it lifted up and righted itself. The kite-sail swung madly back and forth, but it, too, stabilized, and then the boat pitched *forward*, and Carlyle was straining to avoid falling backwards over the bow, and they were thundering forward at top speed, Alyaca laughing like a lunatic.

"What . . . !" he shouted. He gulped, grabbed, and shouted again, "What's—so—funny?"

She leaned back, gasping, until he was ready to plead—he was *scared*—and then she cried, "Don't worry! We can't go over!"

"What?"

"We can't go over! The levitators will keep us up!

They'll—" Then their balance went off again, and water was rushing dizzyingly past Carlyle's head—and suddenly he too was laughing uncontrollably, though he was nearly upside down.

When they reached the far end of the lake, Alyaca—with some effort—got them turned on a reverse tack. Carlyle made a cautiously sarcastic remark about the likelihood of their getting back, and she nearly dumped them in reply. Their return took an hour and a half and many zigzags, and they decided to quit while they were ahead.

They docked the boat and spent the rest of the afternoon walking. They walked through the cedaric groves bordering the east shore of the lake—which immediately made Carlyle wonder about Cephean—and they sat on a ledge by the shore farther up, and they talked. Carlyle got to thinking about Janofer and all the rest, and that made him moody, and after a while Alyaca prodded him into talking about it.

He had already told her about his most recent voyage, but this was the first time he had talked about his life on *Lady Brillig.* "We were very close friends. It was just the flying of the ship that we couldn't quite get together on. *I* couldn't, I mean." That wasn't too clear to Alyaca, but he couldn't explain it easily. It was the intimate blending of fantasies and memories and real abilities which was the elusive goal. "Sometimes you can manage that better with people you're not so close to, so personal troubles don't get in the way." But that wasn't what he wanted; that wasn't the ideal.

"What about that other ship?" she asked, turning to face him at an angle, the sun glowing on one side of her face. "You did all right on that one, didn't you?"

"*Sedora?* Yes, but those men weren't really my friends in any close way. And then later, with Cephean—god, that was more battle than cooperation."

"He sounds very interesting." Her eyes were golden brown, fixed intently on him.

"Who, Cephean?"

"Mm-hm."

"Well—" He shrugged, then said, "Yes, he's interesting. I like him, but it's hard to feel just one way about him. Anyway, I don't know if I'll ever see him again, or if I'll ever get to really know what goes on in his mind."

Her eyes closed and opened, still intent. "You're interesting, too," she said.

He swallowed. "You know, what really gets to me, though, is that all of them left. All three of them. Not one of them stayed behind to meet me after *Lady Brillig* was sold. And Janofer, with that letter she said she wrote and then she didn't even leave it for me!" Blood was rushing through his temples, beating. He shouldn't be spilling all this to someone he hardly knew. But she was interested, and he felt better talking about it.

"I guess," Alyaca said, "they all had to carry on with their lives. Maybe they thought you'd want to stay with your new crew."

His throat stopped up on that. It was probably true, what she had just said. But, he thought, I told them I was coming, they knew all along. They even helped me fly the ship so I could make it back!

But they hadn't. His fantasy-memory of them had, but they hadn't.

Suddenly he began trembling, first at the elbows and the back of his neck, then in the shoulders, and finally through his entire body. He started choking quietly.

"Gev—"

He couldn't answer. He didn't look at her.

"Gev. Hey, it'll be—" But she didn't finish. She leaned forward and touched a slim hand to his shoulder and massaged him gently; and when that didn't comfort him she took his hand and held him by one hand and one shoulder. He felt foolish—sure that she didn't really understand why he felt this way—but her touch was soothing, and he began to laugh sadly. He saw that her eyes were wide and serious, and then his vision blurred for a moment with tears from his laughter. He blinked and focused on the sensation of her touch. Strangely, her face seemed to come into clearer focus now—eyebrows crunched around peering eyes, lips not quite closed, hair falling forward throwing shadows over her cheeks—a face he could almost fall in love with.

If only she were a rigger-woman.

They spent the evening quietly in the lodge, dining late. Alyaca had met him in the restaurant, after changing. She now wore a gown of tan and pastel orange wrappings, cut low on the left side and across part of the back. She was so beautiful he was almost afraid to be seen with her. He wore simple light pants and a maroon-trimmed tunic with its cowl pushed back. They sat in a quiet corner of the dining room and looked out at the night, at the lake gleaming under stars and the pale light of the smaller of the two moons, and mostly he listened as she talked. She mentioned that there had been a RiggerGuild strike several months earlier, shutting down all traffic into and out of the Verjol system. He had heard nothing about it at the Guild Haven; but that was not entirely surprising. The Guild policy was to command a strike swiftly, in need, and to forget it as swiftly after amends had been made. The causative party in this case had been a company based in a neighboring system; but it had violated Code in dealing with riggers shipping into Chaening's World. Carlyle felt awkward learning about this from Alyaca, especially since she worked for a company which probably was hurt by the strike, but she assured him that from what she knew the strike had been justified.

She talked about herself, too, telling him that she had grown up on Opas III, the sun Opas being a star of southern Aeregian space. But after leaving home at the age of twenty-five, and traveling to several planets, she had come to Chaening's World, found a job which she liked, and stayed. When Carlyle asked her if she had really had a friend once who became a rigger, she said that it was true; but she had lost touch with the person completely. "So I've always wanted to know someone who really was, is, a rigger," she said, edging about in her seat, smiling.

After dinner, they went outside and said good night by the corner of the lodge. She lived in a Kloss-owned residence around the corner. "See you?" she said, looking at him in a peculiarly penetrating fashion.

"Sure," he said, nodding twitchily. He swallowed and turned, but not before he saw her eyes flickering in curiosity; and he went back inside the lodge and slowly, wanderingly, made his way up to his room.

The suite was so large that it made him uncomfortable. He paced through the three rooms, mulling over the day. Finally he settled into an easy-g chair in the bedroom, enjoying the floating feel of its reduced gravity field. He was tired but still wide awake. Alyaca went through his mind, and Janofer, and even Cephean. Clacking his teeth, he got up and went to the entertainment console. He flicked on the holo-screen and sampled the channels and storage cubes, but he found nothing that he liked, so he switched that off and turned on music instead, with lighted flo-globe. He went to the bar and drew himself a sting brandy, then returned and sat and listened to a windsong symphony. And kept thinking about Alyaca. And when he wasn't thinking about her, he thought about Janofer, and that hurt so much that he started thinking about Alyaca again.

He considered switching on a mood sparkle-pattern, but before he could make up his mind the door signal quavered. So he got up, wondering who it could be, and answered the door.

"Who is it?" he said cautiously.

"Don't you trust me?" It was Alyaca.

He started to pale the door, then remembered that it was a solid wood panel. He opened it, and Alyaca smiled, blushing a little. For a moment he just stood, his heart cutting off his windpipe, his arm blocking off the doorway. Finally she said, crunching her eyebrows together, "I got lonely. May I come in?"

8

ALYACA

He stumbled over his feet backing away to let her in. Suddenly he felt dizzy, thinking, Why has she come to see me?

She was inside and had the door closed before he recovered his footing, and she was pulling him toward her before he could begin to find his lost thoughts. His feelings blurred, and he succumbed to her embrace and to the warm pressure of her lips, and for a very long few moments he felt that this was all he needed, it was what he had needed all along, to be kissed like this by a lovely woman—and why had he kept himself in torment by such worries and fears?

Alyaca disengaged herself gently, with a caress to his cheek. She walked into the suite, across the room to the half-silvered picture window, and looked out. Then she turned back to face him, her eyes tracing a curious line about the room before coming back into contact with his. She smiled, letting out her breath with a little laugh. He laughed, too, uncertainly. Suddenly he was wondering what was coming, and whether it was something he wanted to do, ought to do, or could do without losing what was left of his equilibrium.

He wished that his heart would stop beating as though it were going to bound right out of his chest.

She came to him and touched his hair, and then she walked to the bar and drew herself a sting brandy. He recovered enough to pick up his own glass, and when she returned they clinked their two glasses together. "To things working out," she said.

He agreed with a nod, wondering just what she meant. He could not speak.

"Are you glad I came?" she asked softly, sipping her drink.

He nodded again.

"Were you expecting me?" She didn't wait for him to answer; instead she peered at him over her glass and shrugged. "I really wanted to come, and when you didn't ask me I decided to ask myself." She grew somber and said, in a lower voice, "I really was lonely."

He sipped nervously. The brandy was potent, drilling straight to his head, mixing with adrenaline. He really couldn't think of anything to say. He was in shock, and he didn't want the shock to end, for fear that if he started thinking he would understand all the reasons why he shouldn't be in a situation like this with a non-rigger, especially someone he hardly knew.

She was standing very close to him, looking at him; and her perfume, musklike and dizzying, seemed to be affecting more than just his olfactory organs. The room seemed very hot. Her eyes were warm brown, and her mouth . . .

. . . she pressed to his, soft and warm and moist and giving. He breathed very hard when they stopped kissing this time, and he kept his arms around her. Her eyes flashed and closed—what am I doing? he thought—and her lips parted warmly against his—why? she's not—and her hands stroked his neck and his hair, and he was totally compelled by the kiss, surrounded by her warmth, and he surrendered and his doubts were lifted away, forgotten.

She gently broke the kiss and looked at him, obviously pleased by the effect. She was flushed, and her eyes communicated arousal. She stepped back silently, and fingered a fastening at one shoulder of her gown. The fabric loosened, and the end fell back over her shoulder. She pulled away a swath of cloth and tossed it lightly to the floor. Both shoulders were bare, now, as was her left side down to her hip. Two tapered stretches of cloth angled to cover the lower right halves of both breasts, leaving exposed the rounded tops of the breasts, semicircles of dark aureoles, and a glimpse of the nipples. Her breasts rose and fell gently with her breath.

Carlyle swallowed with difficulty. He tremblingly reached, thinking to touch her shoulders, wanting to touch all of her body, all the way down . . . but thinking—she isn't . . . isn't. . . .

She sank a little and drew herself to him.

He tumbled first to the polyfluid bed. As she slid across toward him, the rest of her gown dropped away, leaving her nude. With her hair falling, breasts bumping over him, firm and alive, nipples hard, she pulled off his tunic and pants, kissed him teasingly, and then slid lower to bring him to full erection with her hair brushing over him, her breath and lips warm and moist. When he was groaning, penis filled with blood and straining and bobbing against her cheeks, she moved back up, kissed his neck gently, and parted her legs to straddle him. Her breasts moved enchantingly over him, and her breath was hot and uneven against his face. The dark hair at her crotch brushed wetly against the swollen head of his penis, and then she had him centered and sank slowly onto him, swallowing him in her heat.

He slid his hands along her back, following the curve of her hips, then rubbing softly at the fascinating dark fuzz between her thighs, and moving up along the gentle roundness of her belly and the abrupt roundness of her breasts. He

caught her eyes, wide and sharp, and held them wonderingly, his thoughts tugging at hers, trying to know what she
was feeling. She caught her breath as he, and then she,
began to move. . . .

Her back went rigid, and he clasped his hands and fore-
arms to her sides and held her as she swayed, struggling.
Moments later she bent toward him again, her face rubbing
wetly against his. He closed his arms over her back and held
her tightly. He had already come, and he was shrinking
now, starting to pull free of her. Holding her close, warm
and solid against him, he tried to make it last. He did not
want to speak, did not want the moment to end yet. . . .

How can she know me, how can she understand? Why
have I done this? And does it matter?

"Did you enjoy making love with me?" she whispered,
inches from his face, her fingers stroking his cheek.

"Yes," he whispered back, probably inaudibly; and he
nodded against the pillow, almost imperceptibly. But you
are not a rigger, he added silently. And that must make
some difference—

A little later, as they lay still together, he gazed at her
forehead and the fringe of hair behind it, while she studied
his chest. She said, "Are you thinking of your friends?" She
looked up.

Startled, he avoided her eyes. Yes, he had been, especially
of Janofer. And what of Janofer? Had he been disloyal to
her?

"That means 'yes,'" she said. He could not tell how she
reacted to her own statement. "Well. I guess you would be,
of course." She rolled back, looking up at the ceiling. She lay
still like that for a moment, then turned back to him and
pulled herself close. His feelings rushed dizzyingly as he
held her, stroking her shoulders and hair, stroking, stroking.

Attraction to Alyaca, longing for Janofer (for the Janofer who was, and for the Janofer who might have been; which Janofer was he thinking of now?). Fear. Fear of this woman, of loving her. What would she want of him, what could he ask of her?

She pressed her lips softly to his neck. "Good night," she murmured.

He stroked her and lay awake wondering.

During the days following, they swam together at the beach and hiked in the forest. They piloted a diving skate into the lake's depths, and they rode in the gondola of a balloon over the lake and the surrounding area. Carlyle told her something of rigging and the way of life it created, and the difficulties it entailed in the net of a starship; and he told her some of the legends of the riggers, some of the tales passed down through the centuries and across the worlds, some from before the days in which rigging first superceded the old *foreshortening* starflight, the sailing ship making obsolete the high-powered shell. The legend of *Impris* interested her particularly. "It's called the Dutchman," he said, "because in ancient times on one of the home worlds there was a sea-going ship called . . . *Flying Dutchman*, I think. *Impris* is supposed to be like that other ship, sailing eternally, lost in the Flux. She would be a ghost ship even if she returned, according to the legend. Of course the ship may never have existed. No one has found irrefutable evidence that a ship named *Impris* ever existed and then disappeared, but it's said that the records were deliberately destroyed to discredit the legend, because it was thought to be too frightening a prospect to allow riggers to believe." He chuckled. "Anyway, the legend is probably a couple of hundred years old."

Alyaca asked him if he believed in the legends himself. "Well, that's hard to say," he said uncomfortably. "I think some of them might be true." He was glad, at least for the moment, that she was interested in these stories. It kept them from more painful personal topics, and made him almost believe that their affair together might last.

During their third night, however, Alyaca asked him to tell more about Janofer. The pain rushed back as though it had been building, waiting for a trigger.

"Do you still miss her that much?" she asked, sounding incredulous.

"It's hard to explain." His throat was very tight.

"Why? How long were you lovers?"

"We hardly were at all," he said. He dropped his face into the pillow. He lay that way, breathing through the hyperexpanded puff, not wanting to say another word. It wasn't fair that he should be tormented by thoughts of Janofer, here, now, while he was having trouble enough accepting Alyaca. It just wasn't fair. He looked up finally, to see her staring at him, waiting for him to make sense. "Well," he said, "we were. But it didn't last; it didn't work, even right from the beginning." His pulse pounded in his temples. The more he thought about it, the less he wanted to talk; but there seemed no way out—he would have to talk sooner or later.

"Gev?"

"Uh?"

"How can you be so hooked on her if you really weren't even that close?"

The pounding increased: you don't talk about this with an outsider—

—but she's not really an outsider; after all, she's in your bed—

—but she's not a rigger, either—

"We were close," he said tightly. "Close friends." How could he explain how desperately important that was to him, to a man who had grown up so lonely he had not even *realized* how lonely he was? "She was my first real friend—" and she was a rigger. "I thought it would always last—"

He dropped his head lower again, staring at the pillow.

Should he tell her what it was like growing up on Alcest IV, a growing frontier world where the unrelenting demand was for practical-minded people, for civilization builders? Should he tell her what it was like growing up an odd dreamer in a family of settlers and engineers and designers? What it was like as a child walking and playing endlessly through waking dreams, and failing in the goals set for him by others, and being thought curious—until someone, a friend of his father's, not even a member of his own family, had recognized the rigger in him?

"It was hard for me when I was young," he mumbled.

It was not that riggers weren't well thought of, not respected, not needed. But that didn't mean that his family wanted one of their own. Truthfully, he did not even recognize the emptiness until later. Even when he was sent to train—eventually off Alcest IV altogether, to other Aeregian planets—he was taught mastery of his dreams and mastery of the mechanics of space; but who needed companionship then, with dreams so attractive and so highly approved of? When they had taught him that rigging required the capacity for intimacy, for empathy—and when his needs finally awoke of their own accord—it was very nearly too late.

But how could he explain that to Alyaca?

"When I found Janofer," he said, "I already knew how much I needed her. And the others, too—Skan and Legroeder." He turned his head, biting his lip, and looked at her. Her eyes were dark, her hair tousled, her bare shoulders hunched together. "Does that make sense to you?"

She pulled her hair back, in frustration, from her eyes. "I understand, sure. She filled a need."

She doesn't understand at all—

"It's the same with anyone. But you have to let go when the time comes."

Not a word. How could she possibly know what I'm saying?

She gazed full into his eyes with what seemed too much

like raw curiosity to make him comfortable. Then she reached over him, her breasts hanging oddly before him, and she adjusted the sparkle-pattern in the darkened room to a more erotic setting. When she slid back down, her thigh touched his bare penis and he started slightly. He felt naked, vulnerable. And then he felt embarrassed.

In a sudden confusion of impulses, he buried his hands in her hair and pulled her close, pressing himself against her hip and the top of her thigh. Her eyes flickered and she responded with her own movements, rocking him and entwining her legs around him.

The erotic ringlets of the sparkle-pattern flashed about the room, distractingly.

When they stopped moving, a little later, Alyaca drifted off to sleep, but he did not. She slumped close to him, and when she rolled over he encircled her loosely with one arm, closed his eyes, and pretended to sleep. Though they had completed their lovemaking, he felt that he had been a failure, or that it had been wrong.

Alyaca, still rising and falling slightly on the fluid bed, sleepily moved her arm up to cover his.

Over the next few days, he began to think how ironic it was. The more he felt the distance between them, the more he was enchanted by her body, her beauty, and her company, and the more determined he was to continue the affair regardless of painful consequences.

But the future was growing slimmer. He wondered what Alyaca thought she was getting out of the relationship, and if her continuing interest wasn't just some distorted impulse to "know a rigger"—any rigger. She was having to spend most of her days in the office, and one night she was recalled to Jarvis and did not return until the following afternoon. But she got a Kloss aircar the evening she returned and took Carlyle out to a spot known as Gloander Bluff, a hill of exposed bedrock which was considered one of the best scenic viewing spots in the area. They missed the sunset but watched the stars come out in the sky over a shadow-deepened land.

"They're out there somewhere, aren't they?" she asked pointedly. The words sent a stab through his heart. That was about all he knew, based on the latest word from Frey-ling and the Guild; his friends were out there somewhere. It would be a long trail for him to follow, if it came to that.

But why had she asked that question, here and now? Was she deliberately trying to hurt him? Was his pain of an alien sort to her?

She looked at him intently, her brows furrowed. She shiv-ered and moved closer to him, touching him. "Are you going to go looking for them?" she asked in a low voice, not quite an accusing voice.

Can she care that much about me? Does she love me, or does she just not want to lose the rigger she's finally found? He cleared his throat and shrugged slightly. "I might have to, yes." He was acutely aware of her body close to his, and he began to ache and tremble, wanting her. What was he doing to himself? He looked up, and the stars pulled at his soul. He looked at her, and she pulled at him, too.

"Well," she said, disguising what might have been anger or just disappointment, "I'd like to meet your friend Ceph-ean, anyway, before you go." Her face was dim and beau-tiful in the starlight.

Is she trying to make me fall in love with her?

"I don't know if I'll even see Cephean again myself," he said uncomfortably. He could see Cephean standing beside him right now, hissing and muttering, and he felt a strange sorrow that the cynthian was not *really* here. He was also filled with desire for Alyaca—or for somebody—and he was sure that she knew it. *Janofer, what am I doing here?*

To his surprise, Janofer came, peering wonderingly at him. *Gev, what's the matter? You want her, don't you? And she wants you.*

How have I gotten myself into this?

Into what? She's attractive to you, and she wants you in her bed.

But—

What? She's not a rigger? So?

She doesn't understand. She doesn't know why I have to come looking for you.

Well, ease her down. Don't ruin it. Why not stay with her for a while?

I have to get back into space, or I'll lose your trail—

"Gev?" Alyaca was prodding him. When he focused on her, she slid her arms around him and kissed him. "What's wrong?" she whispered.

He shook his head. The curves of her body pressed against him, bringing him back to the present.

"Go back now?" she asked quietly. He nodded.

They returned quickly, touching one another in the car as they flew back. Soon enough they were in his suite, in his bed, halfway under the drift blanket. Alyaca's eyes glinted wetly as she rocked sideways and forward and back over him, her hair brushing his face as she bent to kiss him, preparing to straddle him. Janofer lowered herself over him, and he cried with pleasure at the sight of her. But—it was Alyaca, not Janofer, sinking down upon him—and for a moment he was confused and dismayed, and in the next moment he was coming in quick, spastic spurts. It was over before he was even completely inside her.

She smiled, breathing hard, and kissed him and stretched out full length against him, hiding her disappointment if that was what she felt. But he was flushed with shame—not so much for his premature climax as for his confusion. How could he have confused the two? How?

Alyaca whispered urgently that it was all right. But it was not. Though they tried again a little later, he could not achieve another erection.

* * *

Two days later, she called him at the lodge to tell him that Kloss had returned and would see him in his office. He hurried over, hoping that he could get into Kloss' office without having to face Alyaca. He was ashamed to face her and certain that she considered their problems of the last two nights a sign of waning desire on his part. And he was not altogether sure that she was wrong.

Alyaca was quiet when he arrived, but he felt her eyes following him as he went into the inner office to see Kloss. Kloss was a portly gentleman, who beamed at him when he entered the office. "Rigger Carlyle! Haven't seen you since I visited the old *Lady*—when was it? Have a seat! Make yourself at home! What can I do for you?" He spoke so quickly and effortlessly that it took Carlyle a second to catch up with his words.

He sat, uncomfortably. "Well, it's about *Lady Brillig*, actually."

"Fine ship. I was sorry to have to give her up." Kloss leaned back in his swivel-rest and rubbed his bushy temples with both hands.

"That's what I was wondering about—well—you see, I've just returned on another ship and I was expecting to be coming back to *Lady Brillig* and my old crew who were running her. And then I found out that *Lady Brillig* had been sold, and the crew broken up, and the Guild didn't know anything else, not even who she was sold to. And I thought maybe you could tell me. Maybe you know where the ship is now, and why you sold her, and—"

"Certainly! Now I see why you came all the way up here looking for me. Not often that anyone from your department does that, you know. Usually it's just my creditors." He chuckled. "The truth is, though, that I can't tell you very much. At least not about your friends, though I appreciate your loyalty to them. And to the ship.

"But I can tell you where I sold the ship, anyway—that's no secret. She went to the Guenther Shipping Express Lines in a security sale sort of arrangement. That means it's possible I might get her back in the future, depending on a number of things. But they took her to Delta Aeregiae, and they were intending to use her on the outboard Aeregian cluster shuttle. So far as I know, that's what they did."

"You might get her back?" Carlyle said breathlessly. He hadn't expected *that* kind of hopeful news.

"Well, I can't promise anything now," Kloss continued. "But we hope to get her back, yes."

"Why did you sell her?"

Kloss chuckled humorlessly. "Well—I hate to make this sound personal. I mean it wasn't any problem with the crew or anything—I didn't mean that kind of personal—but the RiggerGuild called a general strike because of something some slipshod outfit from Triax did, and it just came at the wrong time. We lost a couple of important contracts, and this and that happened, and by the time the strike was lifted, it was most advantageous for us to sell the ship. Hated to do it, though."

Carlyle reddened.

"Now I'm not saying the Guild wasn't right, though I do think they were a trifle hasty. The Spacing Interests Association would have moved on the matter, they just weren't aware of it soon enough. In any case, it's water through the spillway, and I know it certainly wasn't something you or your friends wanted. In fact, I'd be glad to have you running on any of our other ships."

Carlyle nodded uncomfortably.

Kloss leaned forward, clucking thoughtfully. "Tell you what, though. If we do reacquire the *Lady*, I'll give you and Skan and the others priority preference in running her for me. If you'd like."

"That'd be wonderful," Carlyle said dizzily. "I don't know if I can get them back together, though." He was talking more to himself now than to Kloss. "I'm having a lot of trouble tracking them down."

"I can see that'd be a real problem," Kloss agreed. "Wish I could help you, but I don't know there's anything I can do." He leaned back again, swiveling from side to side. "Listen, as long as you've come all the way out here, though, the least I can do is to show you some hospitality. I'll speak to my assistant and have her arrange for a place for you to stay at the lodge, and maybe she'd like to take some time off to show you around a bit."

Carlyle tried to disguise an intense blush.

Kloss eyed him. "Hmm?"

Carlyle's voice trembled. "Well—actually she's already done that."

"She's done which?"

"Both." He cleared his throat. "We met earlier."

Kloss grinned wickedly. "I might have known. Alyaca's usually a good hostess."

Carlyle's thoughts swirled darkly for a moment, then he said, trying to edge away from the subject, "She's very nice. She was very helpful." Was that what she was being? "Helpful"? Was she "helpful" to every visitor here? He bit his lip to stop the train of thought.

Leaning far over the top of his desk, Kloss extended a hand and said, "It's been good to see you. Not many of you folks come around my way. Be sure and let me know if there's ever anything I might be able to do for you—and if we get our ship back and you want to run her, let me know about that, too. Okay?"

Carlyle nodded. "Okay. Thanks." He touched his fingers to Kloss' hand, turned, and hurried from the office. When he was back at the lodge, he called Alyaca.

She sounded bewildered. "What are you doing over there? You ran right out of the office."

"I wanted to think. Mr. Kloss was very helpful."

"Did he put you onto the trail of your friends?"

"No. But he tried."

"What did he say?"

"He told me about the ship, and he said that he might be getting her back, and if he does he'll let me and my old crew rig her again, if I can get them all together to do it."

There was silence for a moment. He moved to where he could see her face in the phone screen. "That's better," she said resentfully. Then she brought her expression carefully under control, in a businesslike manner. "So. Does this mean you'll be leaving in pursuit of your friend? Friends?"

"Yes. Today. Or tomorrow." His head was spinning; he hardly knew what he was saying.

Silence again. Then Alyaca said, "Don't spend an extra night here on my account." Her face was curiously stony, as though she did not know whether to maintain the expression or not. Then anger began to creep back into her eyes as she tilted her head. "It's not necessary."

He began to reply but never got the words out. His diaphragm was lurching in spasms, and air convulsed against his stuck windpipe. "I—" he croaked, and he cleared his throat angrily. The anger came up in a rush; it was anger with himself, and with Alyaca, and with everything else. His face was very hot, and his eyes hurt, and he could not even begin to think straight.

She looked at him darkly—but oddly. He was sure that she was about to demand something. But she said nothing. Her expression said all that she had to say.

He tried to answer. He wanted to say that he would spend the night, and they could try to end their affair gently, with a last time together which they both would remember with pleasure. But he could not. His heart was already elsewhere. He couldn't face her again, and he couldn't be passionate even if he did, and without that he just didn't know how he could even speak to her without being humiliated.

"I'd better . . . leave now," he said hoarsely into the phone. "Right now." And I've enjoyed it—it's been something I've enjoyed. But it just wasn't meant to be, and it hurts too much to think about it now, and I'm going to run. Run!

"Right now?" she said in disbelief. She looked confused and offended, and at any moment she would become furious. How could he be this way, so abrupt, so callous? he knew she was thinking.

He couldn't face her anger. He just couldn't. "I have to leave, so—so—good-bye." He clenched his eyes shut, trying just to hold himself together, never mind understand what he was doing.

"Gev!" she cried furiously.

He switched the phone off, trembling, crying suddenly with tears leaking out of his shut eyelids. I'm not callous like you think. Really I'm not.

The tears came out faster, and faster.

9

BEGINNING THE SEARCH

The landscape hurtled beneath his window, blurred. The flyer back to Jarvis was more than half empty, so he was able to feel alone and relatively, in some sense, secure. He tried hard not to think about Alyaca and what he had done to her—and what she had done to him, exposing him to such anguish—because every time he thought of her his eyes began to ache with terrible pressure. But right now his eyes were dry, grittily dry.

So he had to carry on, after all, despite a feeling that he'd had something in his grasp which he had lost through blindness or ineptitude. But you didn't, he thought angrily. You knew all along that it wouldn't work, and you got yourself into it, anyway; that was stupid. But Alyaca had seemed like *she* knew what she was doing. Hadn't she seen how it would turn out? Or had she also known and carried it through regardless?

He lapsed into a time-stretching misery, which shimmered into dream visions: enormous collapsing structures, and dark plains under a smoky red sun caving into a subterranean abyss. There were people on the plain, and they too collapsed under their own weight; their faces sagged and crumbled, limbs stretched and ran flaccid, and sexual organs dropped away altogether, leaving dark wounds. The sky trembled and cracked. The sun loomed closer and darker overhead.

Stop it! Stop it!

If he indulged himself in visions like those, he might find himself producing them in the rigger net—where they could mean a quick end both to himself and to his ship.

The flyer arrived in Jarvis suddenly; he was astonished at how lost he had been in his internal world. He left the flyer and took another car to the spaceport, and soon he was back at the RiggerGuild Haven. How could the trip have been completed so fast? So little time to think!

He hesitated a moment before the door to his quarters. Entering that room would be putting a wall between himself and the last week. Was he ready?

He paled the door and walked in. Then he stopped. There was a certain amount of litter on the floor, and the doorway to the adjoining room was open. Cephean padded to the doorway and gazed at him, eyes flashing out of his black face.

"Caharleel!" he hissed.

"I'll be damned!" Carlyle said. He was at a loss for words. "I'll be damned!" He stared at Cephean. "Cephean! I'll be *damned!* I sure didn't expect to find you here!" He started to grin, and to laugh.

"Hyiss, Caharleel. Hi heff hre-turnss hyesterdays b-hefore hyesterdays. H-where were hyou? Hi thoss hyou were g-honss." The cynthian stared, blinking, and turned his head slightly to the side with what seemed almost to be a grin of his own. (*Relief. Pleasure.*)

"I'll be damned, Cephean," Carlyle whispered. He was ready to cry again. He looked around the room, at the food wrappings scattered on the floor, and back up at Cephean.

"H-where were hyou, Caharleel?"

"Well," he said, "I was off speaking to the owner of *Lady Brillig*, trying to find out what had happened while I was gone. He doesn't know where Janofer and Skan and Legroeder are now, but he might get our ship back, and if I can get my friends together we can fly her."

"Yiss?" Cephean replied, watching him curiously. "Thiss iss whass hyou were do-hing?"

"Well . . . most of the time," Carlyle said. He fought back a wave of pain. Time enough to explain all that later. "Anyway, how was your forest? The riffmar! Are they all right? Are Idi and Odi all right?"

A train of riffmar scuttled out of the doorway past Cephean. One, two, three . . . Carlyle counted nine altogether. Nine—that was the right number. And two of them were a little larger and less fluttery—but when those little ones got bigger he wouldn't be able to tell them apart from Idi and Odi!

"Hyiss," said Cephean. "Ff-sun h-and-s fforess h-were ff-very ghoods. Ssthey g-hrow hwell."

"They look great," Carlyle said with real admiration. He hesitated, then asked hopefully, "Are you going to fly with me again?"

Cephean's black tail looped over his head, behind his ears. His whiskers quivered. "H-where h-we gho, Caharleel?"

Carlyle grinned and said, "How would you like to help me try to track down my friends? Maybe the five of us could fly *Lady Brillig*. I mean, since you don't really have any other plans, probably, right now. Do you?"

"Hiss h-woulds vee hintheresthing. Hi noss wanss sthay hin foress. Men-ss noss hleave hriffmar ands me halone." His copper and black eyes flashed dangerously.

Carlyle wondered what Cephean's response to the men had been. He decided not to ask. Cephean had been wearing (he hoped) his rigger-friend medallion, so he should be covered if there was any trouble. "Okay, Cephean. I'll start making the arrangements today."

First he checked back with Walter Freyling to see if there was any word on the whereabouts of his friends. One message had come through—that Legroeder was known to have left the northern Aeregian territory, bound for a planet called Charos. That was in the general direction of Golen space—which could be ominous news—although there were plenty of respectable outworlds located in that direction, also. As for Janofer and Skan, there was nothing definite. They had left Chaening's World separately, both bound eventually for circuits of northern Aeregian space. That could mean any of twenty or thirty systems, but at least Carlyle could start looking for all of them in the same radius of a half-dozen light years.

The second thing he did was notify the Spacing Authority, through the flight assignments desk, that he wanted to lift aboard *Spillix* as soon as a cargo could be cleared for any of the northern Aeregian worlds.

The third thing was to apply for proper rigger certification for Cephean. The RiggerGuild registrar, it turned out, was reluctant to issue the decree, not so much because Cephean was an alien as because he had not graduated from a recognized academy or passed an evaluation. Carlyle went to Freyling, who said that the registrar was correct in refusing Cephean full status, but perhaps something could be arranged. The next day Carlyle received a message telling him to return to the registrar. He went.

The registrar blinked at him and said, "Oh yes, we've taken care of your friend, the cynthian. Did you bring him with you? We need him to take holos and prints, and so forth."

Carlyle went back to get Cephean, who came along hissing and grumbling. He had insisted on bringing the entire group of riffmar with him, and they followed along in a train, Idi and Odi bringing up the rear. "Whass iss thiss?" Cephean sputtered at the registrar when the man motioned to the recording devices.

"For the files," the registrar said. Cephean hissed. The man arched his eyebrows only slightly and went on, "We are giving you the certification of Special Provisional Apprentice Rigger. You'll have a medallion to wear, and you'll be accorded all the normal Guild privileges, except for voting. You'll only be allowed to vote when you're given normal status, and you'll be eligible to apply for that in one local year or one point two years standard."

Cephean blinked and canted his ears. "Whass hhe means, Caharleel?" The man fiddled with the instruments, making clicking sounds.

"It means you can fly *Spillix* with me. And you won't have to stay with me if you don't want to—you can go to any RiggerGuild Haven and stay as long as you want."

Cephean sputtered something vaguely affirmative. By that time, the registrar was finished with what he had been doing, and he moved around behind the instruments. "Wait here," he muttered, and went into the next room.

He came back a few minutes later and held something out for Cephean to take, then shrugged and handed it to Carlyle. It was a medallion similar to the rigger-friend medallion which Cephean already had. "Lower your head," Carlyle said. Cephean reluctantly obeyed, and Carlyle carefully fitted the medallion to the cynthian's forehead and secured it in place with a cleverly designed harness made of a thin gold chain, which clung to the back of Cephean's head. The medallion at once changed from a flat gray color to luminous gold. A smoky pattern in the gold changed shape slowly and continuously.

"It'll only do that when you are wearing it," the registrar said with a certain mixture of nonchalance and pride.

"Not bad, Cephean," said Carlyle. "It sets off your fur

very nicely." He pointed to a wall mirror, and Cephean turned.

"Ssssss," he muttered. "Yiss."

Next they went to the flight assignments section and checked with the Spacing Authority dispatcher. Minimum carryage for *Spillix* was available for a flight to Rinesindrum IV, seventeen lightyears north and counterclockwise out, which was at the extremity of the area Carlyle wanted to search. Carlyle considered, then decided to wait and see what else developed.

That night he dined alone in the Guild restaurant. Things were on his mind—one of them Alyaca and one of them Janofer. Alyaca was a sharp hurt; when he thought of her he was flushed with feelings of inadequacy and anger and regret. But they carried less deeply than the slow burning in his chest each time he thought of Janofer. Janofer, Janofer. He tried to call her for a conversation, but she did not respond. He ate little, and did not much enjoy what he ate; but the longer he thought, the more anxious he was to lift ship and find his friends.

Next morning came a call. Courier baggage had just been checked for Gladstone Port on Dani III, thirteen lightyears almost due north. Gladstone had been Legroeder's first port after leaving Chaening's World, and it was also quite likely a stop on the northern Aeregian tour which Skan had reportedly intended to rig. They could lift off that day if they hurried with the arrangements.

"Caharleel," hissed Cephean. "H-we khann ffly tzugethsser?" (*Uncertainty*, shimmering with *anticipation*.)

"Well—" Carlyle said, startled, "of course. Are you worried that we won't be able to?"

"Sssssss." The cynthian swallowed his words, mumbling. He batted a riffmar idly.

Carlyle thought hard. What if they *did* have problems working together? "Look. Tell you what. We can have a small dreampool generator installed in the ship's commons.

It wouldn't be as nice as the one on old *Sedora*, but it will help if we start to have problems."

"Hyiss," Cephean said. And that startled Carlyle almost as much as the original question. So willing? Was Cephean beginning to miss his quarm, perhaps?

He put in the order, though, and by midafternoon *Spillix* was ready for flight—cargo, provisions, and all.

The Lacerta Ocean fell away beneath them, a shimmering blue ocean edged by land. Chaening's World. He would want to return. But now was the time to get away and be on with things. Overhead was the tow, her broad wings and Circadie space inductors glowing fuzzily against deepening darkness. Chaening's World shrank quickly as *Spillix* and her tow sped across the black emptiness of the Verjol system, accelerating continuously. Five hours later the tug broke company and dropped away into the distance; and half a day later Carlyle dropped *Spillix* into the Flux.

Cephean joined him in the net but did little actual flying. However, he muttered and ffumff'd and occasionally remarked on their progress. *Ghoods foress ffor hriffmar,* he said as Carlyle pelted *Spillix* in a zigzag fashion through an autumnal forest which, as it happened, was filled mostly with evergreens. He was bound for winter.

I expect it would be. He didn't want to say that it would be getting cold in this forest soon; and he didn't know for sure, but he suspected that the riffmar would not do well in a winter climate. But winter was in his heart, and he thought that the safest way to handle that feeling was to choose a winter scene which he could control and make safe. *Would you like it for yourself, too?*

Yiss.

Are you in the mood for snow? That's what we're going to see soon. Do you want to help fly?

Sssssnoh?

Light fluffy stuff. We'll make it good and powdery and

dry. Hanging off the trees nicely. The image followed quickly on the thought, and *Spillix* flew among snow-laden boughs. The ground was covered deeply with the soft stuff.

Caharleel—hi kann noss ffly hhere!

Of course you can—you did it before on Sedora, *just before the Flume. Remember?*

Yiss, buss hi kantss now!

Instead of abandoning the landscape, which he should have done, Carlyle tried to encourage his crewmate. *Give it a try, Cephean, all right? We can do it together.*

Cephean tried. He strengthened his presence in the net and gave the ship an extra kick. Carlyle called to the cynthian to stay close, so they wouldn't lose each other in the powder.

Yiss, Cephean answered, but he seemed unsure of himself. In an effort to keep up he actually slid back along the shimmering ghost that was the net's outline. His hind paws dragged in the snow, and he slipped and skittered—as *Spillix* careered past a tree. *Hhae-yae-sss!* Cephean howled. He pulled himself in as Carlyle readjusted their flight path.

Cephean, wait!

But the cynthian withdrew to the inner safety of the net, and there he remained. Damn! Carlyle muttered. He felt terribly alone. He thought of Janofer and Alyaca, and flushed with unhappiness.

Spillix pitched downward, with his mood, and exploded into the powder. The net went white—then *Spillix* erupted beneath the snow and winged into a cavern system where the walls and ceiling were ice split by crevasses, and the only sun was a bluish glow bleeding in from the outside world. Carlyle shuddered and flew with every nerve in his body. It was a damn-fool place to be: stalactites groaning above them and ceilings quaking, threatening collapse, and treachery in flying fast through a deceptive maze.

Where am I going? I don't know the way out!

Fear closed over him, icy and blue. Imprisoning. *Ceph-*

ean, I need help! No, wait—if he's nervous in snow, he'll be a disaster here. *Cephean, just let me know if you're there!*

What's happening? Why am I saying this?

A wall jutted from the left. Frightened, he veered and skirted close to the right-hand wall. That wasn't good, either; he banked closer to the center. *Cephean! Cephean, I'm scared. Are you there?*

Whassss? Cephean crept a little closer to him in the net.

I shouldn't have gotten into this place—I have to get us out. Can you come closer and stay with me while I find a way out? A vision of cataclysm entered his mind against his will: tumbling walls of ice, earthquake-loosened, smashing *Spillix* like a tin balloon.

H-nno!

No no no! That's not going to happen! It just—

But the cry was in vain; Cephean had pulled out of the net instantly, in alarm. He was completely alone now. And he was flying at perilous speed; there had to be a way to slow down, to get out. There had to be a way. A new image —that was in his power—all he had to do was imagine a path of escape for the ship (but I can't do it alone!) and not panic because he had fallen into a dark fantasy, fear fear fear—jeesus, a thought of a woman got him here, so why couldn't a thought of a woman get him out? A woman who knew the way. Janofer would know—and there she was now, at the far end of the cavern, waiting for him up there by the tiny little light which must be the exit; if he could just fly true and clear, he could reach her.

Janofer laughed, and her face lit the way, and the tiny little piece of light was now a bright piece of sky. It was easy, after all, it was nothing to sail right out through the hole in the ice ceiling—and suddenly they were free in the air, with open sky over tundra. Janofer sang, and kissed him once, and was gone without having spoken a word.

Wait! he cried. But it was no use. She was gone, and

maybe she'd be back when he needed her; but it didn't seem that she'd be around when he merely *wanted* her.

The sky turned to pure threaded gold, and he locked the stabilizers and got out of the net.

They were a week late getting into the Dani system, due mainly to Carlyle's getting lost in an endless and winding brackish-water glade. He had started taking things more slowly, rigging only when he could maintain images satisfactory to both Cephean and himself. As a result, he charted a longer course than he had intended. He fretted about the delay. He wanted to get there, to find a trail if there was one, and to move on quickly if there was not.

"Cephean," he said, "let's get this ship straightened up before we come in, all right?" The commons were littered with spillover from Cephean's room; he was not keeping the riffmar on the job of housekeeping.

"Caharleel, whass hwe dho hhere?" Cephean asked, rather than answering the question.

"We're going to the port of Gladstone, on Dani III, and I'm going to ask for news of my friends. Probably we won't be here long; probably we'll be trying another planet."

The cynthian studied him, whiskers twitching. His eyes were slits with a glint of copper. He looked at the litter on the deck, looked back up at Carlyle. He seemed to be trying to decide if the effort was worthwhile. Then he turned and went into his quarters, and Carlyle heard the rustling of riffmar at work.

After two weeks of flight, they left the Flux. The Dani III tow met them and took them into a landing at the Gladstone spaceport. This was an urban port, with the gray buildings of an industrial city forming a skyline beside the space field. Carlyle had never been here before and he was not sorry, now that he saw it. The Guild Haven was adequate, however, if not lavish.

He left his shipmates in the bar and went to the Guild offices to see what he could learn.

What he learned was something, but not much. Legroeder had passed through here a couple of months ago. But he had not returned from Argos II, which was to have been his next port of call. There was no information at all about Janofer or Skan. It was suggested to Carlyle that he might spend some time in the bar, talk to as many people as he could, and hope for news or rumor from other riggers who had been traveling in this region.

Glumly he returned to the bar. He looked around for Cephean, and couldn't believe his eyes. The cynthian was seated at a bar table, on a large cushion which someone had evidently placed on the floor for him. Several of the riffmar were up on the table, swaying slightly in time with the sensory light show coming from the rear of the bar, and the rest were clustered under the table. But what most astonished Carlyle was the cocktail bulb in front of Cephean. As he approached the table, two of the young riffmar picked up the bulb, pointed its jet into Cephean's mouth, and pumped it gently. Cephean lapped at the stream, spilling half of it; and then he pulled away, blinking and sputtering.

Carlyle slid into a seat. "When did you start drinking cocktails?" he asked, examining the contents of the bulb. It looked like a rum-fruit cocktail. "Did you order this yourself?" He noticed now that there was another bulb on the table, squashed flat.

Cephean licked his lips and pawed at his whiskers. Was he tipsy, or was that Carlyle's imagination? "Ghoods, Caharleel," he sputtered. "Mans bross iss." His whiskers twitched to the left, and he emoted *satisfaction*.

From the shadows on Carlyle's right, a man approached the table. He looked rather old and pale, he wore an oversized rigger's shirt, and he squinted in one eye. "Name's Jolson. I was sharing a couple of drinks, here, with your friend."

Carlyle gestured, and Jolson took the opposite seat. "I'm Gev Carlyle. And this is Cephean."

"Ah, Cephean. So that's your *name*. I wasn't sure." Jolson glanced back and forth between the two, grinning. "We talked a bit, earlier—or mostly I talked. But we had a little trouble making sense."

Cephean's eyes moved liquidly from Carlyle to Jolson.

"Where are you from, Jolson?" Carlyle asked.

"Oh, lots of places," Jolson said, waving vaguely across the table. He coughed. "Just in on a long haul from the Dreznelles. But that was actually the first time I rigged in that particular direction. Usually I work the northern Aeregian lanes—I like to take slow floaters and duel a bit with the dragons along that mountain route to Lexis and Venice." Jolson caught a waiter's eye and procured another bulb.

Carlyle asked for a beermalt, in a glass. To Jolson he said, "You haven't been around a planet called Charos, by any chance?"

"Charos? Why sure. In and out of there quite often."

Carlyle lifted his eyebrows and glanced at Cephean. The cynthian was watching them both impassively, in apparent contentment. Carlyle accepted his glass and sipped at it. He braced himself for the next question. "You haven't come across a rigger by the name of Legroeder, have you? I heard he was bound for Charos, some time back."

"Oh, then, that's another matter. He could be anywhere. What was his name? Magroder?" Jolson squinted harder.

"*Legroeder*. Small man, dark hair, sort of dark skin. He was a stern-rigger when I was with him."

Jolson squirted a stream from his bulb and swallowed it. "That name does sound familiar, and so does the description. But I'm not sure I could put the two together and make it stick. Let me think about it for a bit." His eyes narrowed and followed the passage of two female Narseil riggers across the bar. They were glistening, almost humanoid amphibians; the Narseil were rarely seen so openly in human company.

"Well, how about a couple of other friends of mine? Janofer Lief, a woman with long silvery hair." How many times would he have to go through this before he finished? How many times could he? "And . . . and Skan Sen. Light skin, solid facial features, faintly oriental eyes."

There was a quiet slurping noise—Cephean taking another swallow of his drink, then licking his lips. Jolson struck the table with his fist. "Skan! Yes, by damn—by damn, I did meet a Skan. But not at Charos. It was—where was it? It was, I think it was at Andros. That was it. By the Wall of the Barrier Nebula. Near Golen space." He took a long pull from his bulb.

Carlyle gulped his beermalt nervously. The lightshow flickered against the side of Jolson's face, making him look even paler than he had before; there seemed a hint of translucence to him (or is that my imagination?).

"Golen space," he muttered.

"Uh-huh," said Jolson, peering at him. "You ever been there?"

Carlyle shook his head. "No, but I've heard." Pirates. Flux abscess. Many lost ships. Golen space began with the fringe outworlds, and became more lawless and politically unstable the further one flew. There were rumors of hostile aliens, as well.

"Most of what you've heard is true—in essence if not degree." Jolson snapped at the waiter for another bulb. His voice was softer, now, and Carlyle leaned forward to pick out the words. Cephean crooned softly to himself, apparently not listening. The riffmar squatted on the tabletop, looking as though *they* were listening.

"Did you talk to Skan? Did he say what he was doing there?"

"Well, no," answered Jolson. "Not exactly. This was some time ago, you understand, before my Dreznelles haul. And I don't believe I actually spoke much with him myself. But I do seem to recall hearing that a ship was taking on riggers heading for one of the Golen space worlds—I think one of the more civilized ones. He may have gone on that ship."

"But you don't know?"

"No," he said, shaking his head. He squirted from his bulb.

Carlyle's hand trembled as he lifted his glass. He drank quickly, spilling beermalt down his chin. The thought of Golen space chilled him straight to the marrow. But if his friends were there, he had to go.

But . . . Jolson didn't know.

Jolson's eyes were flickering closed. He blinked them open again and looked at Carlyle with a start. "I'm tired now. Need sleep. And I really did want to talk some more with your Cephean friend." He sighed, finished his cocktail, and dropped the flattened bulb on the table with the others. He started to rise. "Perhaps if you'll be here tomorrow, we can speak again." He fought back a tic in his left cheek; his face seemed almost bloodless.

"Legroeder," Carlyle said urgently. "Do you remember anything about Legroeder?"

"Who?" Jolson said, touching his brow.

"Legroeder."

"Legroeder? No, I don't believe I ever met a Legroeder." He smiled politely. "I wish I could help you. But there—you see? I can't. Good night."

Before Carlyle could think of another word to say, the man disappeared into the shadowy wing of the bar. Carlyle looked at the cynthian. "You all right?" he said softly. Cephean hissed faintly. His eyes were slits, with a sliver of glinting liquid showing in each. Carlyle sighed. "You're drunk. Let's go get a room."

Carlyle checked with assignments and records again the next day but learned nothing. He spent much of the day in

the Guild bar; and when he got tired there he went over to
the spaceport bar, which was busier, noisier, and a lot more
ramshackled. There were few riggers there, however, and he
could not manage to initiate a conversation with any of the
regular spacers. Eventually he went for dinner, and then returned to the Guild bar. Cephean came with him this time,
after recovering from the effects of a hangover.

Jolson was nowhere to be found. Carlyle went around
hesitantly asking people—riggers and rigger-guests and
staffers—if they knew anything about Jolson (or Legroeder,
Janofer, or Skan—none did). Eventually he found a waiter
who conceded that he was familiar with Jolson's habits.
"He's probably in the city, sir. I don't know that I should
say too much more—I wouldn't want to infringe on his privacy. I hope you understand."

"Then he's in and out a lot? Are most of his space stories
true, usually?"

The waiter bit his lip.

A rigger sitting nearby, who looked as old and eccentric
as Jolson, spoke up in a tone of friendly derision. "Good
friend of mine, Jolson. We've rigged together—he's a fine
rigger. He's also crazy as a Zebreedy lunecock. Don't believe
a word he says. Say, waiter, could I have a sprite inhaler?"

Carlyle looked at him with an odd feeling. "How exactly
do you mean that—'Don't believe him'? Do you mean he ex-
aggerates a little, or do you mean I really shouldn't believe
him?"

"Thank you, waiter." The man held a small inhaler to his
nostrils and sniffed deeply. He smiled. "What's that? Jolson?
Well, like I said, he stretches the truth here and there, and a
lot of stories he makes up altogether. But then again he
knows more than most three riggers put together, so you'd
do well to heed him." He sniffed again from the inhaler.

The odd sensation in Carlyle's gut got worse. What was
he supposed to believe? "Listen," he said earnestly, "do you

know if Jolson has really been rigging recently out of Charos, or out near the edge of Golen space?"

"Oh, sure," said the man. His eyes were becoming hard, his pupils contracted to small dots. "Sure, Jolson's been out that way. And most of what he tells you about it is true, too. You can believe that." He glanced around the bar. "I believe I want to see a young fellow over here—good day!" He moved away, mumbling.

Carlyle grunted and turned to Cephean, who had sat silently through the exchange. "What do you think?" he asked, really meaning it rhetorically. But—perhaps Cephean had gleaned some insight telepathically if he had been following the conversation. "Should I believe what old man Jolson told me?"

The cynthian blinked. His whiskery eyebrows bunched together as he said, "Fferhaffs, Caharleel."

"Or did he make it all up when I gave him Skan's name?"

The eyebrows relaxed. "Fferhaffs." Cephean switched his tail and looped it up behind his head.

"Cephean, you're an enormous help, do you know that?"

"Hyiss. Sssanks hyou."

"I guess we'd better stay here and look for more rumors."

But they did not hear more rumors that day, nor the next. In all, they stayed at the Gladstone Haven for five days without learning anything new; so, when Carlyle was offered a mail cargo for the Ettebes system, of which Charos was one of the planets, he accepted at once. As soon as Cephean was sober, they boarded *Spillix* and returned to space.

10
GOLEN SPACE

The flight to the Ettebes system took ten days, shiptime. They stayed in the system for a total of four weeks, checking all possible sources and traveling from one planet to another within the system. They delivered mail shipments to Deirdre (Ettebes VI), and then to Centrix (a minor planet between the orbits of Deirdre and Ettebes V), and to one of the moons of Charos, and finally to Charos (Ettebes IV) itself. At each of these stops, Carlyle asked through both official and unofficial channels after his friends. At the first three ports he learned nothing except that the city Charos on planet Charos was considered the best place in the system to look for anyone of the wandering sort, or any kind of information or rumor where either spacers or riggers were concerned.

Upon arriving at Charos itself, he learned from Guild sources that Legroeder had been on the planet ten weeks earlier but had left, bound for Deirdre. However, on Deirdre there had been no record of him. Either the records in one place or the other were faulty, or Legroeder had changed destinations enroute. Of Janofer and Skan, there was no official word.

On advice of several Guildsmen, Carlyle looked further in the city. The popular bar for riggers at this port was not the Guild bar, as was customary in most places, but a bar downtown called the Rogues', Thieves' & Spacemen's Tavern. There Carlyle spoke with a shuttle spacer introduced to him by a peculiarly gregarious rigger. The spacer claimed to have met and known Janofer on the second moon of Deirdre. She had talked of leaving the system soon, and this had been many weeks ago. He didn't know where she'd been planning to go, but he had a hunch that she might have had the Andros system in mind. Carlyle was skeptical of the story (why no record of her with the Guild? were there *no* accurate records kept in this star system?), but he had nothing else to go on. And: *Andros*. That rang a bell; hadn't Jolson back at Gladstone said something about Andros? But that was Skan he'd been talking about.

They stayed in Charos a few extra days. It was a colorful and brawling city—and Cephean liked the Rogues', Thieves' & Spacemen's Tavern, probably for the large number of interesting aliens who frequented the bar. The cynthian seemed to enjoy watching the aliens and listening, while he himself showed off his riffmar and ignored various people's attempts to converse with him. Finally, though, Carlyle learned that there was carryage available to Andros II, and he committed them for departure.

The flight to Andros was rather long in lightyears but fast in terms of shipdays through the Flux. There was mainly barren space between the two systems—and long, steady currents in the Flux. They were in the Flux for only seven days, shiptime. While Carlyle flew, he conferred with Janofer and Skan, hoping for encouragement. They talked over the difficulties he was having, and the two suggested that perhaps it would be better if he abandoned his search. *I'd*

*love to see you again, Gev, you know that—but you have to
think to your own life,* said Janofer.

I couldn't consider it, Carlyle said adamantly. *You're too
important to me, and I want to fly with you—and that's all
there is to it.*

Well, Skan admitted, *I do have similar feelings myself,
and, even though I think you're crazy, I'm glad you're doing
this.* And Janofer looked secretly delighted by both of them,
despite her own remark.

But before he could ask them the most important question
—where they were—they waved and departed from the net.
And so it always went, in their conversations.

When *Spillix* arrived at Andros II, Carlyle found it an
unspectacular planet in a spectacular parcel of space.
Andros II was a dry world, rocky and sparsely vegetated.
The spaceport sat on a huge bluff overlooking one of the
small seas of the southern hemisphere, and the plain which
bordered that sea was practically the planet's only developed arable land.

But the night sky was the world's drawing attraction, at
least during the summer season. Carlyle stood outside with
Cephean the night after their landing and gazed up. The
sky was dominated by the Wall of the Barrier Nebula—a
broad, luminous plane which angled upward from the horizon and seemed to curve outward like a ribbon, away from
the zenith. It was a gaseous emission nebula, actually just
one end of a nebula which reached far out into unexplored
space. It glimmered with a pale cyan and red sheen, hovering like a ghostly stage curtain before the mysteries of the
far regions of the galaxy. The dark track of a dust lane
meandered across its face, obscuring a part of its glow; the
dust lane extended beyond the far end of the Wall, smudg-
ing the view of stars, there—in Golen space.

Golen space. They were virtually at the edge of it now,
standing on a bluff on Andros II, looking up into a part of

the night where the stars . . . well, they looked the same to the naked eye as stars in any other space, but they didn't *feel* the same to look at—and to Carlyle, to any rigger, it was the feeling which counted. He wondered how much of his uneasiness at the sight was due to years of rumor, and how much to a real intuitive sense of strangeness nearby. Beside him, Cephean was silent (but radiated *disquiet*). Was that Cephean's reflection of Carlyle's fear, or was it Cephean's own rigger-intuition?

If Golen space is where we're going, Carlyle thought, we could slip right up alongside the Wall, straight as an arrow, and off. Off the Wall and straight into . . . the heart of madness.

Why would they have gone in there? For what conceivable reason?

He shook his head. He needed to imagine, yes—but he had to control it.

Gev, have you found where you're heading yet?

Stupid question—even coming from Janofer, who ought to know better. Of course he didn't know where he was going; he didn't know where *they* were. But he had a terrible feeling.

You'll be careful, won't you—if you go out there?

He stared into space and shivered suddenly. "Let's go," he said to Cephean. As they turned he heard Janofer calling, asking him to tell her please that he'd be careful. *Later*, he thought angrily. *Talk to me later.*

Never, in all the years he had known her, had he cut off Janofer like that—and he hated himself for it.

They went inside the spaceport Haven and Carlyle went asking for information, as usual. His initial inquiries yielded nothing, however, and he decided to wait until morning to do anything further. He was weary—not of the day's activities but of the search itself, or of the seeming futility of it. And when he said good night to Cephean and closed the sliding door between their quarters, he wondered if he really had the right to drag Cephean on an endless, fruitless chase.

But his weariness vanished early the next morning when he was awakened by his phone. The caller was a rigger, but seemed afraid to give his name. "I overheard you asking around last night—and I don't mean you to think I was eavesdropping, but if I can help you I thought it would be better for me to call than just to keep quiet. So you don't mind, do you? If—"

"Please," Carlyle interrupted, shaking himself awake. "Do you know something?"

"Well, I heard you mention the name of a rigger you were trying to find, and since you said you'd been all over trying to locate her—"

Her!

"—I thought since I did know something about her—well, at first I wasn't going to say anything, since it's none of my business—but then I figured—"

"What do you know about her? Do you mean Janofer?"

"What?"

Carlyle shouted, "Janofer! Is her name Janofer?"

"Well, yes, of course. That's who you were asking about, wasn't it?" The man sounded hurt.

"Yes. Please—what do you know about her?" Carlyle cried. He was about to explode, talking to this little pictureless phone in his room.

"Well, I can't actually tell you anything about her myself." Carlyle's heart dropped. But the man added, "What you need to do is go downtown to a technics wholesale place, name of Gabriel Merck. M-e-r-c-k. Just ask for Merck's. They'll be able to tell you."

"What?" Carlyle asked anxiously. "Why?"

"They'll know. You just ask for Merck's. And then you go see Gabe himself. I've got to go now—"

"Wait! Can't you tell me anything—?" But he was talking to a dead phone. He slammed the desk top and paced the room. He stopped pacing and put his hands on his hips and stared at a hole in the wall near the door where the composition panel was flaking apart. The hole had a crumbly edge, with partition space showing inside. Carlyle longed to grab the edge of that hole and rip out another chunk of paneling, and to rip and keep ripping until he had torn a hole large enough to climb through. He could feel the sensation in his fingertips: the strain of pulling against the compressed, grainy material—the sudden give, and the handful of dust and chunks of crumbled material spilling to the floor.

Instead of doing that, he went and got Cephean. Then he called the Guild service desk. "How do I get to Merck's?" he asked. "Gabriel Merck's—a technics place?" Three minutes later, he had his directions. He told Cephean to wait for him, and he went out looking for a cab.

The cab ride took thirty minutes. It was a human-operated aircar, and the driver had some difficulty in finding certain key streets in the wholesale district; but eventually he stopped at the correct address. "Please wait," Carlyle asked. As he stepped toward the building at Merck's address —there was no name sign—the cab pulled away with a swoosh.

Carlyle held his breath angrily, then exhaled sharply and went into the building. He stepped cautiously around a seemingly built-in obstacle in the doorway, a tall mechanical device of uncertain function. A light on the device glowed as he passed. The shop was dim and crowded in front and seemed to extend for a considerable distance to the rear. Carlyle saw a movement among the vertical warehouse racks. He hesitated and then called out, "Mister Merck? Gabe Merck?" There was no answer, but he saw a movement again in the rear, something shadowy moving back and forth across a darker shadow. "Mr. Merck!" he called.

His eyes were beginning to adapt to the gloom. The place barely had a storefront; crated and uncrated technics products were stacked high on both sides. The counter was unusually low, and open in the middle. A glow from one corner far to the rear suggested a work area. "Mister Merck!" he called anxiously. He wondered if his "tip" had been a practical joke.

The storefront lights suddenly came up halfway. There was a hum and several clicks from the rear, and something came forward down one of the aisles. Carlyle stepped to the counter, feeling uneasy. The storekeeper emerged into the light. It, or he, was a cyborg. Riding in a hovering life-support system which boasted several manipulator arms was a Thangol, a humanoid with high, bony features and a mop of reddish brown hair around the back of its neck and over the back half of its skull. Or rather, it was the head and upper abdomen of a Thangol; the rest of his body was missing. He still possessed his right arm but only had a stump for his left.

"Gabriel Merck?" Carlyle asked.

"Yes," the Thangol answered in a gravelly whisper. Carlyle wasn't sure whether or not the whisper was a normal Thangoli tone. "Just one moment, if you please," said Merck. His cyborg body carried him humming around the end of an aisle.

Carlyle realized suddenly that Merck's voice had come from the mechanical unit, not from his lips.

Merck stopped near the end of a rack of shelves. He tilted his head back to look up, and his eyes searched the upper shelf. A leg suddenly telescoped from the bottom of his lower unit; Merck rose into the air on his hover unit, apparently balanced rather than supported by the leg. When he was at the level of the top shelf, he extended a mechanical arm and took a package in its grip. Then he descended, his leg retracting under him with a long sigh, and he hummed back around to where Carlyle was waiting. "Now then, may I help you?" he whispered. His mechanical arm held the package snugly against a shelf built into the front of his lower unit.

"Well, yes," said Carlyle. He hesitated. This was ridiculous. What would Janofer have had to do with a place like this? Unless . . . she had been injured somehow and—

Just because the shopkeeper's a cyborg doesn't mean his customers are!

"Yes," he said, trying to push the train of thought back into motion. "Have—you had a customer in here recently who was a rigger? A female human? Her name was Janofer Lief."

"A customer?" whispered the Thangol. "No, I do not recall a rigger being one of my customers."

Carlyle cleared his throat. "Well, perhaps not a customer, but here for some other reason."

The Thangol looked at him oddly.

"Perhaps you used the services of a rigger? Perhaps you own or lease a ship and arranged for riggers to fly it? Perhaps one or more of them visited here? Does any of this approach truth?" He was very tense, very nervous. Was he imagining a rise in hostility from the Thangol/cyborg?

"Yes," said the Thangol, "it is possible that I operate a ship for business reasons, and of course I would employ riggers such as yourself in flying the ship, if I had one. But the employment of riggers is customarily arranged by the RiggerGuild, is it not?"

"Customarily, yes," said Carlyle. "But there are exceptions. I don't mean to pry into your business practices at all —my only interest is in tracing a friend of mine, a rigger named Janofer Lief." Carefully he drew forth Janofer's holoprint and showed it to the Thangol. Merck studied it for a moment, holding it in his fleshy right hand. He returned it to Carlyle.

For a moment they exchanged stares. Then Carlyle prompted. "Do you recall seeing this woman?"

Merck rubbed the two thumbs of his right hand against the opposing three fingers. He studied the activity as though it belonged to the hand of another. "I can tell you that I might remember seeing someone who looked like her," he said finally.

Carlyle closed his eyes and took several slow breaths. He opened his eyes again. Normally he might be intimidated by the Thangol's appearance, by his cool reserve, by the fact that he could undoubtedly crush Carlyle with a single one of his mechanical hands. But Carlyle was tired of feeling intimidated. "Could you please be more specific?" he said quietly. "I am asking for my own personal information. Nevertheless, I am asking as a good standing member of the RiggerGuild. I had hoped that you would try to help me. As a member of the RiggerGuild."

The Thangol stared at him with both eyes wide and unblinking. Whether Merck interpreted Carlyle's statement as a threat or as formal protocol was not clear. But finally he whispered, "Yes, I think I can safely say that the female rigger you asked about was here."

"And did you engage her services? Or the services of Skan Sen, or Renwald Legroeder?" Carlyle showed the Thangol holoprints of the two men.

Merck waved his right hand. "No," he whispered hoarsely. "Neither of these two men."

"And the woman? Janofer Lief?"

The Thangol hesitated again. Carlyle lightly rubbed the rigger embroidering on his tunic, almost unconsciously. "Yes," said Merck at last. "I engaged her as a rigger on one of my ships."

"How long ago? Where were they bound?" Carlyle squinted, his anxieties multiplying.

"About two months ago."

"Local months?"

"Yes, local."

That was about a month and a half standard. "Where were they bound?" he said.

The Thangol stared at him for a long moment, then said,

"Good day!" and turned to float back to the dark recesses of his shop.

"One minute!" Carlyle barked. He was astonished by his own tone of voice. The Thangol/cyborg turned slowly and looked at him. "I said, where were they bound?" He waited, glaring. How far an implied RiggerGuild threat would carry him here he didn't know. But he had nothing to lose.

The Thangol held his silence but moved half a meter closer. Carlyle slammed his hand upon the counter. "*Where were they bound?*" he demanded.

"Denison's Outpost," whispered the Thangol. He spun and hummed out of sight down the aisle.

The lights in the storefront dimmed. Clearly Carlyle was being invited to leave. He stood thinking for a moment, then went outside. The door clicked locked behind him, leaving him isolated on the deserted street.

It took him half an hour to get another aircab, but he had plenty of thinking to do while the time went by. Denison's Outpost, he thought, was somewhere in Golen space—but he wasn't sure. There was a Dennison's Hardship, also, and a Denizen's Haven. And he couldn't remember for sure which ones were located where. But he had a bad feeling.

When he returned and checked in the Guild navigational library, his fear was confirmed. Denison's Outpost was located deep in Golen space. That was why the Thangol had been so reluctant to talk. Whatever shipment he had been making to that planet—if he had told the truth—was at least partly illegal. Nearly *all* shipments into Golen space were partly or entirely illegal, because so many of the planetary laws within that space were confused, contradictory, and repressive. But because most of the laws were unevenly enforced, illegal traffic proliferated: illicit drugs, high-energy weapons, psycho-active technics, slavery (both human and nonhuman), and "unsafeguarded" robots and organic computer cores—i.e., those lacking certain restrictive programmings which would protect human operators. And with the illicit traffic went banditry, piracy, and other more uncertain dangers.

The nonreturn rate for ships entering Golen space was five times that in any other outworld section of space. It was for this reason that sixty standard years ago the RiggerGuild had called a broad strike, demanding protection in Golen space. It was the only Guild strike ever to have failed—not because the combined spacing authorities had not wanted to establish controls over Golen space, but because they had been unable to do so. In rescinding the strike, the Guild had declared Golen space a "protection-free" zone. Riggers flew there only at their own risk, by their own independent arrangements, and without benefit of the Guild's protective umbrella. Under no circumstances could a rigger be required, regardless of contract, to enter Golen space; and all riggers were strongly discouraged from doing so.

Yet some did. Always some did. Some for adventure, for escape, for reward; some for perverse reasons, to satisfy self-destructive urges; some for the feel of exploration, for bravado. The reasons were as varied as the individuals who went. Some were simple, some complex; some were good, some bad; some carried hopes of success, others carried none.

But why would *Janofer* have wanted to go? A rigger who could have chosen almost any crew, any ship, any destination—what attraction would those forbidding spaces have held for her? Had she felt that desperate, that despairing?

And what of Skan and Legroeder? Carlyle had information, however unreliable, tracing both men to Andros II. And Andros II was a natural jumping off point for Golen space, though it was in and of itself a respectable enough port. But there seemed no way to be sure where they had gone. The Guild office advised Carlyle delicately that no records were maintained of riggers entering the protection-free zone. True, they could find no record of either man arriving at Andros II; but they had no record of Janofer's arriving, either, and Merck would hardly have admitted seeing her if she had not been on the planet. So the Guild's recordkeeping here was less than exemplary.

Perhaps all three were in Golen space.

"Cephean," Carlyle said, since he had decided for himself without even allowing debate, "will you fly with me in Golen space? It could be very dangerous."

"Sssssss," muttered Cephean. He flipped Odi into a somersault and stared at Carlyle with apparitional eyes. "H-all righ-ss."

"Good," said Carlyle. "We'll leave tonight. No cargo except light goods in case we have to barter."

Carlyle tried not to dwell on certain feelings of guilt about the ease with which he had persuaded Cephean. The cynthian almost certainly did not appreciate what it was he had agreed to. And neither, perhaps, did Carlyle.

The Wall of the Barrier Nebula loomed intimidatingly against one half of the universe. As *Spillix* coasted out of the Andros system, Carlyle set his course as carefully as he could, considering how little he knew of this region. The Guild navigational references about Golen space had been sketchy. He decided to skim close to the plane of the Wall, or whatever its Flux analogue would prove to be. Later they would turn outward to angle across to Denison's Outpost.

Golen space. Was he certain that he wanted to do this? He could be pursuing a phantom, a lie. But did he have any choice?

When he took *Spillix* down into the Flux, he decided to keep his navigational imagery similar to the actual normalspace view; this should render him less susceptible to surprise, to sudden change growing out of his own imagery. But it would slow their flight, since he could not use daring imagery to abridge their course or to speed them faster through the Flux. At present he just wanted the security provided by that huge, glowing nebula on his right.

Cephean, let me know immediately if you sense anything strange, anything that doesn't seem right. Okay?

Yiss. Whass hwill hi ss-see?

Don't know. I've never been in this space before.

Iss ff-sthrange? He was jittering around in the stern-rigger station, not yet as scared as Carlyle was.

Maybe. Maybe not, he answered reluctantly. *Bad things have happened in Golen space, like I told you. But I think we're in about the safest section of it.*

They flew a while in silence, then Carlyle said, *Why don't you take more of a hand in flying, Cephean? It's going pretty smoothly, now, and I think it would be good if we practiced together. In case anything comes up, you know?*

Cephean edged further into the net. He seemed more relaxed with this "realistic" imagery than with Carlyle's more personal landscapes, but still he did little except use his balance to help steady the ship. He held his tail straight out astern like a long black kite tail.

The Wall moved slowly past on the right, its pastel fuzziness mottled by areas of varying density, some brighter and some darker. The dust lane angled downward, like a sinuous and ghostly guardrail. They flew steadily, with only short breaks, for fifteen hours; and then they left the ship on stabilizers and slept for seven.

Later, they picked up essentially the same image, but Carlyle was aware of subtle changes. They still flew alongside a nebular wall, with a universe full of stars and the occasional dust cloud in all other directions; but the Wall was dimmer, more ghostly and greenish, and the open space was also changing. Some of the stars faded slowly from visibility, and others grew rounder and fuller, like fuzzy teardrops. They were entering the actual territory of Golen space. Carlyle was unnerved to think that the space itself could influence his images this strongly. He did not resist the changes in starscape, but he sought to be aware of all of them.

In the fourth day of flying along the Wall, they were joined in the net by Legroeder. Carlyle was taken by surprise—though it was his own mind producing the illusion of Legroeder's presence—but he was pleased to see his friend. Legroeder had not joined him for quite a long time, and it was good to have him back.

Legroeder smiled mysteriously in greeting but spoke not at all. He took up the mid-rigger post, which on *Spillix* was merely an area of continuity in the middle of the net.

Legroeder, do you know this area of space very well?

Legroeder nodded and hummed a little harmony to some unheard melody. Carlyle felt Legroeder's influence less as a physical assistance than as a strengthening of his own self assurance. Legroeder was unobtrusively giving guidance and confidence, which in a ship this small was probably the best possible form of assistance.

Cephean hissed and sputtered, and Carlyle asked him if it was all right to have Legroeder in the crew. *Hyiss, yiss,* answered Cephean. *Yiss.* But he seemed to keep a more careful eye on things. Did he distrust Legroeder? Carlyle wondered. But Legroeder wasn't real, here, and Cephean understood that—so how could he distrust the man?

Well, it probably didn't matter. They flew, and Carlyle listened to Legroeder's quiet humming and tried to guess what really was in the man's thoughts; and the ship drifted alongside the Wall like an unpowered balloon. Wondering if there was some way of speeding their progress, Carlyle asked Legroeder, *Do you know an image that can move us faster, but won't get us into trouble?*

Legroeder went right on doing what he was doing and gave no sign of having heard the question. And then, as Carlyle was about to repeat himself, Legroeder spoke.

Would you like another image? He hardly stopped humming as he spoke.

Well, yes. I'd like to get where we're going sooner. But I don't want to take chances, either. I don't know this region at all. For a moment, doubt crossed his mind and he cautioned himself not to get carried away by his fantasy, but the doubt shimmered away and the caution was lost. The image was already changing.

The Wall's luminosity dimmed to a ghostly greenish sheen. Most of the stars in surrounding space turned muddy and disappeared, as though obscured by intervening matter. It became difficult and confusing to judge the ship's movement along the Wall.

The net glimmered very faintly, as did the Wall. So, now, did a few undefinable patches, or areas of vision ahead, above, and to the left. Below was darkness. Behind was . . . Carlyle did not look behind. The spots off in space were like smudges on a glass, or light aberrations in a holograph, or lights in the distance in the underwater realm of a nighttime sea. And that, he knew now, was the image—nighttime under the sea.

The sight was not comforting. But there was a feeling of mystery which he found exhilarating. He hoped that "Legroeder" knew where they were going and would steer by the same intuition which had created the scene. To circumvent worry, he talked while he flew. Maybe he could learn some useful information. *Do you know what has become of Janofer and Skan, Legroeder? I've caught rumors of where they've been—and you, too—but here I am flying off to Denison's Outpost, and I don't even know that Janofer's there.*

The best way to find out is to look, Gev.

Yes, but haven't you heard anything? At least you've seen them more recently than I have, and maybe you've bumped into them at some port somewhere since you all split up. He started to ask why they'd split up—but this wasn't the time.

Legroeder muttered something in reply to the original question, but Carlyle couldn't make out what he said.

What?

Legroeder muttered again and did something to realign the ship. For a moment Carlyle thought, as he turned his attention back outward, that there was another movement—as though something were abeam of them, paralleling their course. Almost certainly it was his imagination. But he listened carefully for signs of other life, since another ship *could* make a disturbance like that. The probabilities of chance meeting with another ship in space were vanishingly small, even when ships followed common currents in the Flux, though, and he was reasonably sure that he had witnessed either some emanation from his own state of mind or a turbulence in the Flux itself.

Cephean, how are you doing back there? he asked.

Silence.

Cephean, are you still there?

Silence. Then: *Yiss.* Whispered. Carlyle thought he detected fear in the reply. Instinctual fear. Why would Cephean be afraid?

The ship glided smoothly in the night sea. The glimmering Wall was textured with fuzzy undulations, as though covered with vast, pale anemones, their flowering fingers alive and seeking in the night. The ship swayed with a fluid and relaxing movement. The current carried them forward and down along the Wall.

There was that shimmer again, of movement out to the left.

Perhaps it was one of the lost phantom ships, he thought wryly. *Devonhol,* perhaps, or *Atlantis.* Or even *Impris* herself, queen of all the legendary Dutchmen.

He envisioned a silvery leviathan emerging from the mists, her prow aimed across the course of *Spillix* like a cruiser intercepting a launch. The seven minds of an infinitely weary crew spotting him on collision course and broadcasting warning. Or laughing with deadly mirth, and deliberately cutting the smaller ship in their wake. Or perhaps not noticing *Spillix* at all.

Carlyle, cut it out.

He steadied his grip on the net. He had come very close to actually creating the scene he had been imagining. A good way to destroy themselves that would be.

Legroeder looked at him with an odd expression, which was about the nearest Legroeder ever came to laughter.

He banished the images and the worries, and concentrated on flying. The worries didn't stay banished, though—especially when the sounds began.

The first sounds were rolling sea sounds, more relaxing than unnerving. They reverberated as the gentlest conceivable disturbance in the Flux. Carlyle wondered if he was listening to the lapping sounds of sea against shore, or of currents bumping objects together in the depths. The sounds were rhythmical, a continuous bumping and sucking of water.

And that movement was real out there. A shape, a silhouette against pale light in the darkness. A ship, a creature, or an enormous shoal against a ghostly luminosity in the further depths. *Legroeder, do you see that?* he asked.

Silence. Except for the bumping, the bumping and sucking of water.

Legroeder? But he already knew the answer. Legroeder was out of the net, gone.

Cephean, are you still there? He was beginning to feel nervous, terribly nervous. *Cephean?*

Yiss. Soft, scared. Cephean didn't like what was happening here.

Stay close, all right? Pull in tight on your side of the net. The cynthian complied without answering.

On the left, in the distance, the light grew a little stronger. The shape which shimmered was a ship, a ship pacing them through this fantastic ocean in the night of space, a ship outlined like a shadow against a kind of light which made him shiver from the spine.

Was it real? What was it doing there? Was it possible that it really was a phantom ship?

Cephean, we may be headed for some kind of trouble—but I don't know. We both have to be ready. Please don't leave the net. Please!

Cephean hummed, hoarsely.

All right, Cephean?

H-all righ-ss, Caharleel.

He watched for a clue to what this thing might be. It was not an artifact of his mind, he was sure, but he didn't know if that was good or bad. Now there was a thrumming sound, thrumming as of great ancient engines. A sound of formidable power. Growing. Coming closer.

Khanns we noss chahange, Caharleel? Cephean whispered imploringly.

Carlyle thought hard. *No. I'm afraid we might lose our way if we change now, too suddenly.* He was tempted to send out a distress call on his long-space F-m communicator; but he was afraid. This was Golen space. Sending out a cry could be like an injured fish thrashing in a shark-infested sea.

The ship was approaching *Spillix*, now. The light against which it showed itself grew stronger, colder, and the ship's silhouette grew darker. The thrumming reached *Spillix* like a heartbeat, and there was a hiss, now, and a mutter of voices, many voices. The voices, which were indecipherable, seemed to echo against the Wall on the right. And the Wall was changing, bulging outward ahead, its bulge full of flecks which indicated possible turbulences, possible gravity wells. He had to steer left to stay clear of the Wall. Left, toward the mysterious ship.

He banked and hoped for a current to carry them swiftly ahead, more swiftly than the other ship was moving. But his effort was in vain. If the steerers of the other vessel were deliberately seeking to intercept him, they knew where the currents ran and where shoals lay hiding. His stomach felt as though it were crawling about inside him. His control of the net faltered.

The mutter of voices escalated in pitch and in volume.

Colors exploded about him in space. Drums boomed, boomed, reverberating.

The ocean was suddenly alive with scrambling life in a frenzy of feeding, with lights popping which glared and blinded against the turbidity of the night. It was hard to see the Wall, and the other ship was invisible against exploding paint splashes of color. *Spillix* trembled through her net, bucking. There was no longer any question: they were under attack.

He had no idea what to do. Attack was a danger which riggers were not supposed to have to face. The voices growled and shouted at him.

Caharleel, hyor frenss! cried Cephean.

What? What? Are they coming? Did Cephean want him to bring them to life again?

H-no! Hyor frenss! Hi hhear hyor frenss!

Are you mad? Cephean, we've got to pull this one out ourselves!

The ship was buffeted; the voices shouted. And suddenly he knew what the cynthian was hissing at him about.

He heard Legroeder's voice in the babble from the attacking ship.

11

RAIDERS AND GLASSFISH

Legroeder!

Was this—? No. *No!* This was not a memory-fantasy; he knew the real voice of Legroeder. His friend was aboard that ship—and he knew now what kind of a ship it was. It was a Golen space raider. A pirate ship.

And it was closing fast. Coronas of light flamed around it, but the ship remained dark, black, swallowing its own light. Carlyle found himself staring as though hypnotized—staring—staring—and suddenly realized that *Spillix's* net was slipping from his control, was starting to bend around like a comet's tail and stretch outward toward the raider. Carlyle fought to hold the net tight.

Caharleel! Whass? H-why? cried Cephean. (*Fear! Confusion! Anger!* spilled through the net in waves.) It was obvious that Cephean felt betrayed.

These people aren't friends—they're enemies! said Carlyle, in torment. *I don't know what Legroeder's doing there.*

The marauder-ship's corona bloomed with tentacles of flame which reached outward and around, as though to encircle *Spillix*. The raiders obviously meant to grapple *Spillix* and haul her out of the Flux, to take her back into normal-space where she would be helpless to repel boarders.

Whatever else, he had to keep *Spillix* free of the grapples.

The ocean was filled with flashes of light refracting weirdly. Carlyle banked *Spillix* desperately hard to starboard and down, away from the marauders and into the stroboscopic glare. *Cephean—hard into the tail! Hard!* The cynthian kicked, giving the ship an extra lurch away from the enemy—but the momentum was not enough. The arms of the marauder's net curved closer. Carlyle streamlined his net still further in a futile effort to gather speed.

Who were these raiders? Why was Legroeder with them?

The voices in the Flux were a kind of terrifying music, now. He could no longer identify Legroeder's voice. Perhaps he had been mistaken! Perhaps Legroeder was not there, was not a pirate. But no—even Cephean had distinguished the voice. And if he was there in the raider's net, Carlyle had to let him know who it was that he was attacking. Surely Legroeder could stop it if he knew!

The method of attack was an astounding overplay of the raiders' Flux imaging and Carlyle's own. It should be possible to reply in kind, if he had the power—but he was being hammered, and he was dizzy, and he was confused, and he could hardly think or breathe. Discordant chimes struck him in the face—backed by a bombardment of drums, booming drums, tribal undersea drums of terror and doom.

Whass iss thiss, Caha-harleel? Cephean cried in anguish.

Doom, doom, doom doom doom. . . .

Pirates, Cephean! Raiders! They're after us and our ship! Whass he-we dho? (*Anger! Terror!*)

Doom doom doom doom doomdoomdoom. . . .

I don't know! But he did know; he had to try to reach Legroeder. *Cephean! Create the old image—the nighttime image, the dark! Black out these lights! Muffle the sound!* They were being assaulted by sight and by sound; they were being wracked through their bones. God knew how many riggers they were combating in the other ship, or how much amplifying power in the raider's flux-pile. But they had to subdue this insanity to project a message through to Legroeder.

He felt Cephean clawing and spitting against his fear to create quiet, to regain the old image—to find the Wall to the right, and oceanic night all around. Lights flashed randomly about them, generating confusion, lights out of synchrony with the doom doom doomdoomdoom. Carlyle focused on night . . . night . . . night deep night . . . and what conceivable image could tell Legroeder that it was Gev Carlyle out here? *Try, Cephean, try!* And he thought and thought, and the lights flashing and drums dooming became a little darker, a little less distinct. He doubled his effort with Cephean; and for a moment, flickeringly, they held an image of night with a ghostly wall, with a phantom ship silhouetted treacherously against a pale and evil light.

Carlyle flashed out an image: Deusonport Field, Janofer and Skan and Legroeder crying farewell.

Night swallowed the image—and then came thunder booming and the coronal lightshow of a rigger net blossoming entirely around them. They were losing the battle; they were surrounded.

Again, Cephean, again! I have to get through!

Cephean sputtered, and the light darkened smokily, and again they were in a night sea moving inexorably on the current toward the other ship. The thunder receded.

Carlyle flashed forth another image: *Lady Brillig*, bold and gleaming against an evening sky.

Madness shattered the image. Tentacles of fire encircled them and joined, welded, and drew inward. They were captured. *Spillix* fell sideways in the current toward the raider.

Carlyle cried out against the bonds, and terror reverberated between him and the cynthian. He struck vainly against the tightening web of fire drawing them in.

*   *   *

There was a change in the Flux. The raider was beginning to climb with *Spillix*, out of the Flux toward normal-space.

Cephean! Deeper! Dive deeper!

Sssssss! cried Cephean frantically—and for a moment the cynthian's terror overwhelmed the total power of the enemy. Carlyle joined him fiercely, twisting downward, and *Spillix* like an enormous hooked fish dragged the raider deeper into the Flux. Night spilled like ink through the deadly light of the raider's net.

They succeeded for a few moments. But then the surprise and the momentum were lost, and the raider's superior power began to tell against them. The two ships again moved upward through the diminishing layers of the Flux.

Suddenly a shaft of light, just out of phase with the rest, spun from the raider and struck full into *Spillix*'s net. It blazed and then darkened in its center, and with a jump in focus Carlyle found himself staring down an enormous barrel toward the raider. Swirling energies in the tube wall held it solid, sealed against the outside.

Show yourself! demanded a voice, reverberating.

Carlyle jumped, startled, and peered down the bore. He could see nothing; it might have been the pirate's leader shouting, but he had to take the chance. He drew himself to full size in the net (whispering to Cephean, *Be ready! Be ready!*), and he bellowed down the tunnel: *This is Gev Carlyle! You show yourself!*

Christ, Gev—what are you doing here? roared Legroeder.

Carlyle stared, dumbfounded, up the tunnel. Finally he found his wits.

What am I doing? he cried. *I'm looking for you and the others! What are you doing with pirates? And why didn't you warn me?*

I just found out it was you! Wait—

There was a change, and *Spillix* seemed to be resisting the raider's pull more successfully.

I'm feigning difficulty with the others. I can't keep it up long.

Why didn't you warn me an hour ago, when we were flying together? Carlyle cried frantically.

What? What are you talking about?

When you . . . and suddenly he remembered, that had been a fantasy-construct of Legroeder . . . god, he was losing his grip . . . *never mind. What's going to happen to us?*

You're in trouble, Gev. The man doesn't take many captives. If I'm going to help you we've got to move fast.

What are you doing *here, Legroeder?*

No choice. And no time—and I don't know why you're looking for Janofer and Skan in Golen space, of all the—

They came this way.

What? Well why did you—?

Lady Brillig, Legroeder—so we can fly her again!

For that you—christ, Gev, our chances aren't worth—wait —wait. . . .

The moment seemed to last an hour, and they were drawing very close to normal-space now. Then the pounding of the drums faltered. Legroeder shouted, *Gev! Go!*

Beneath *Spillix,* a ribbon of the raider net broke free and trailed away, exposing a window of ink-black space. A window for escape.

Carlyle hesitated. There was so much to say! And Legroeder. . . .

GEV, GO! THIS IS IT!

Caharlee!!

The escape window was closing. The drums picked up and thundered, booming.

The cynthian didn't wait for Carlyle's decision. Yowling, he kicked, clawed his nails deep into the Flux, and dove downward with *Spillix* on his tail. Carlyle swung, gasping, and almost cartwheeled out of the net, stomach reeling—and he dove, hung onto Cephean, and focused on keeping *Spil-*

lix's net as small and as hard and as dense as he could. *Spillix* flew like a stone. Wind and drums and screaming voices rushed in his ears and somewhere among them was Legroeder shouting farewell. Carlyle clenched his eyes to keep the tears in, and they dropped through the hole in the raider's net just before it sizzled closed, and vacuum hit them with a thunderclap.

Around them was only darkness . . . and receding, receding screams of anger. Cephean kept the ship hurtling, spinning. So fierce was his desperation that he paid no heed to Carlyle or to the pursuing raiders or to direction, except to plunge back deeper and deeper into the Flux.

The Wall wheeled into view, a shimmering cloud, curling away to the left. *Keep diving, Cephean!* The cynthian didn't answer. Carlyle held his breath, and the Wall grew before them, covered with enormous hungry anemones, and *Spillix* arrowed straight through the ocean night and into the soft surface of the Wall, through billowing luminous clouds. The night was lost astern, and so was the raider, and so was Legroeder.

They were swimming in eerie chambers of cloud and flowing vapors. *Steer clear of the high density areas,* Carlyle warned as he finally took up his own reins in the net, with Cephean. *They could be Flux abscess.* Chamber opened into chamber, with walls of streaming pastel vapor. The densities he referred to were embedded like curious cysts in the fluid walls. *Spillix* drifted steadily through the system of chambers.

Good job getting us out of that, Carlyle said sadly, thinking of Legroeder. Odd shudders rippled through his spine. He stretched nervously through the net, glad for the cynthian's presence to keep him from dwelling on Legroeder. Cephean, too, was tired and nervous, and they both kept looking around for signs of pursuit. Carlyle felt that they were safely clear of that danger, but they were also clear of Legroeder. The time had been so incredibly short—so many things unsaid, unasked, unanswered. They had come so far looking, and now he was gone.

But Legroeder was a changed man, different from the man who lived in Carlyle's memory-visions. So abrupt, so forceful, so forward. Even in an extreme situation, that was not the man Carlyle knew or imagined. Never mind that he was a pirate. Probably he had risked his life for Carlyle's. It was doubtful that he could have concealed his actions from the others in the raider net. Would he return to *Lady Brillig?* Would he even be able to try?

Doubts crowded into Carlyle's mind. Even if he found Janofer and Skan, what new people—and new realities—would he discover?

Caharleel, h-where h-are we? Cephean whispered.

The present intruded again. *I—why, I don't know.* Their surroundings were eerily beautiful, whatever they represented. But though he assumed that they were somewhere within the analogue of the Barrier Nebula, Carlyle had not the slightest idea of their bearings or position. They would have to be extremely cautious until they learned more about the nature of this space. They might avoid one kind of abscess or queered gravitational effect, only, perhaps, to be taken unawares by another. And, there was no reason to assume that other outlaw ships did not fly or lie in wait in these peculiar clouds, though why any raider would expect innocent traffic in these clouds he couldn't imagine. Unless they maintained a base. . . .

Cephean, we must steer very carefully through here. I don't know what to expect.

Glowing clouds passed to the right, to the left, above and below them, like the system of some living, gaseous sponge. Carlyle shaped the spiderweb traceries of the net into sails and vanes, which were extensions of his own arms and legs; and he encouraged Cephean to use his tail as a rudder. The cynthian cooperated, but Carlyle sensed a certain tension from their close call with the raider. He wanted to say something, to apologize, to excuse the behavior of his fellow humans, but he really could think of nothing to say. He was stunned and bewildered himself. Later. Perhaps later they would both understand.

Legroeder—what will happen to you for setting us free?

If only he could have done something to help his friend in return. The price Legroeder would pay might be his life. And probably Carlyle would never know.

The Flux current moved smoothly, gently. They passed several dark regions of coalescing matter, giving a wide berth, and then they saw no more such hazards. In time, the mists thinned and edged out into the center current until there was no clear passageway, not even fuzzy boundaries between cloud and space. Now there were just varying intensities of mist, and they steered through the lesser. The current slowed, dissipated by its broadening, and eventually it was difficult to tell whether or not they were even still moving.

Carlyle studied the surroundings: pale illumination in all directions, but mostly in areas of obscurity, lemon and rose fog banks. They were in a doldrums area; he could detect no current at all. This was probably a good place to rest. He set the stabilizers and set alarms to summon him in the event of significant change. *Cephean, would you like to pull out for a while and rest?*

Ho yiss, whispered the cynthian—and he was gone from the net.

Carlyle joined him.

Four shipdays later, they were still in the doldrums zone. Carlyle really wasn't even sure that they had moved since entering the zone. They were trying to decide whether to continue waiting the situation out (while who knows how many days went by in the normal-space universe), or to change the image to something shiftier and probably riskier.

"I really wish I *knew* what we should do next," said

Carlyle. He watched the cynthian poke idly at the smaller riffmar, who were clustered raggedly about him on the floor of the commons. Carlyle reached out and tickled the leaves of Odi (at least he thought it was Odi), who was standing nearby with his back turned. The riffmar quivered and sssss'd gigglingly. Carlyle changed his touch to a stroke, and the riffmar relaxed.

But what Cephean had wanted to know, Carlyle thought, was what they were going to do *later*, if and when they made their way out of this area, and assuming that Carlyle could reestablish his bearings with respect to navigable space. They had made an intuitive judgment to remain in the Flux rather than leave it, because they would probably only confuse themselves more by emerging blind somewhere inside the Barrier Nebula. Better to go with intuition and go with the Flux.

Did Carlyle intend to continue on the uncertain trail of Janofer and Skan? He wasn't sure. But Cephean had made clear that *he* was sure of something: he wanted nothing more to do with pirates or raiders.

"We'll just have to see. Legroeder didn't think Skan or Janofer were even in Golen space—but that Thangol told me that Janofer flew to Denison's Outpost." If she made it, he thought worriedly. Legroeder probably didn't make it to wherever he was going—probably captured by raiders himself and impressed by them. What chance that he's even still alive? So do I keep looking for Janofer and Skan?

His goal of reuniting the *Lady Brillig* crew seemed more bitterly distant now than ever.

"Cephean, we'll do all right—especially now that we have some experience in this messy stuff," he said. He was trying to voice more conviction than he felt; but Cephean wouldn't be fooled.

"Fferhaffs, Caharleel," hissed Cephean. *Odomilk*, he directed the riffmar. He suddenly sat stiffly upright, his eyes wide and glazed. (*Sorrow. Pain.*) There was no odomilk; he had exhausted his supply long ago. *Melon*, he directed the riffmar sadly.

Twice more they rigged, and still there was no visible sign of progress. They decided to rest longer this time, and Carlyle, against his better judgment, downed a couple of ales and mixed a cocktail for Cephean. They both felt better, if slightly fuzzy in the head, afterwards.

That was when the alarms went off in the bridge.

Carlyle stumbled into a moving mass of cynthian fur on his way to his station, but after a minute of confusion they were both in their places, stretching their senses out into the net. *Caharleel!* exclaimed the cynthian expansively.

Yes, I see, said Carlyle, pleased and awed. The ship was moving, and at a rather good speed. The mist ahead was spinning, breaking up. There was an accelerating current moving into the vacuum left by the parting mists. And now he saw a dark spot of coalescing matter ahead, and that was apparently the primary force drawing the current. They had gotten into the net none too soon, if they didn't want to be drawn into that vortex (perhaps a sun being born in normal-space?). *Bank left, Cephean—we have to skirt this whole area*, he said, trying to clear his head of ale.

Cephean complied sluggishly, and Carlyle bent his own vanes to the task, and they swept to the left at a steadily increasing speed. They spun past the dark core at a safe distance and picked up still more speed in the process. Soon the turbulence of the abscess was behind them, and they sailed free through a luminous space with only distant landscape features for visual reference. It was a crystalline, watery space—an ocean, but a sunlit and amniotically warm ocean. It cleared Carlyle's head, and Cephean muttered grudging approval. It was somewhat like *Sedora's* dreampool.

Carlyle was glad to see the change but was uncertain of what it meant. Were they clear of the Barrier Nebula, or were they simply in some inner quiet zone and due shortly to encounter new features, new difficulties? And what direction were they traveling?

They could see for quite a distance, as through clear tropical water, except that the water was the color of pure sunshine. The features in the distance appeared to be some kind of reef, and they were growing larger as the current carried *Spillix* forward.

Caharleel, hi ffeel ssome-ssing-s. Ssome-whon-s.
Eh?

Reefs were passing by to the left and to the right, but none of them close enough to seem dangerous. They were peculiarly shaped, with frail supporting members intricately twined together, and upper mound-shaped structures which looked far too massive to be borne by the fragile midsections. The entire reef rested on a "seabed" which simply faded into the clear luminous sea. *Spillix,* guided by only gentle control from the net, drifted slowly and steadily and was now passing through the last of the reef congregation.

Something in the reefs, Cephean?
H-no. Noss hin reefss. H-aheads.

Carlyle cast his gaze far forward, beyond the reefs. If Cephean thought enough of his feeling to speak up, it was almost certainly something significant. Ahead, now, he saw what appeared to be incredibly huge kelp beds. Despite their distance, he could already distinguish individual fronds. Apparently they were in for a change of scale ahead; perhaps they and their ship would be as a tiny sea creature passing through a vast seaweed labyrinth.

Quickly enough, they crossed the empty sea between the reefs and the kelp beds; and his guess proved correct. The water became slightly hazy with plankton, and the floating fronds curved high above them and far beneath them as the ship approached, riding the continuing current. *In here, Cephean? I don't sense anything yet. Do you still sense it?* They glided above a curving frond and beneath another,

overhanging, and on through into the interstices of a seaweed cluster.

Yiss. Hi ffeel iss. Noss hhere.

Where? Do you know?

H-no.

Riggers? Raiders?

Ssssss. Hi don'ss h-know.

Clucking thoughtfully, Carlyle shrugged to himself—and
flew, with Cephean's help, along a convoluted passageway
through the kelp. There was really nothing much he could
do, except to be alert and ready for trouble.

A strong and ethereal sun filtered through the sea from
somewhere beyond his vision or knowledge. The light
streamed down in fluted rays, cut and blocked and reflected
by alternating fronds and open space in the regions overhead. They were gliding in silence through a cathedral of
the sea. The fronds twisted and floated through the angled
sun rays, gleaming here with velvety beads of silver, glowing there in golden-green sunlight, gloomy in another place
with shadow. Together with the fronds, there were spidery
holdfasts anchoring the plants and lilac-colored "blossoms"
and round, slick "grapes." *Spillix* drifted on the current, and
the two riggers kept her stable and straight, and watched
and waited.

They did not wait long. The current took a downward
turn and slid through increasingly dense kelp. Downward
they moved, downward. And the direct rays of the sun became scarcer and scarcer and finally nonexistent; they descended through a realm of gloom lined with dark but
faintly glistening fronds.

Hi ffeel iss h-more, Caharleel. Ssome-whon-s.

Down there?

Yiss.

The gloom deepened, and the space grew tight for maneuvering. Carlyle was nervous; these were not ideal circumstances for meeting a stranger—but the current was too

strong for turning back. Ahead was an inky cavity in the kelp, and that was where the current pulled. The ship glided into that darkness and emerged into a vast black abyss. Shadows of stars shimmered in the distance without illuminating. And—directly before them, turning to stare—were three transparent creatures which looked like luminous fish from the depths of an incredible alien sea. They were enormous, many times the size of the little starship.

Caharleel! (*Disbelief.*)

I see it, Cephean. I see it. But he wished he hadn't. These were surely the entities Cephean had sensed—but what were they? *Did you create this image, Cephean?*

H-no! Bvroil-damns ffish-ss!

I didn't think so—but I didn't, either. There was a powerful sentience emanating from those creatures; and he and Cephean were being carried directly toward them by the current. *They look like*—and he remembered an aquarium on Argyl, near the rigger-school—*like enormous Argylan glassfish.* But these fish were not in the deep abyss of any Argylan sea; they were in space, in the deep abyss of the Flux.

Whass?

Deep-space glassfish. That's what they are. Or what they should be. Deep abyssal fish—on an incredible scale—with transparent, glassy bodies glowing faintly as though in black light, and eyes which changed color as they moved. Floating against the jet blackness of space, they were figures of awesome and terrible appearance. They turned and stared at the approaching rigger-ship, their eyes a dark, shimmering red.

Carlyle felt the current slowing but rocking with some turbulence as it did so. Could it be that these creatures were stopping the current? He tried to put a confident face forward, but he shivered as he met the gaze of the nearest glassfish. (Cephean, he sensed, was distrustful and uneasy, but not overtly frightened. Good. That was good. *One* of them was not overtly frightened.)

A flower of light erupted from the glassfish. The flower blossomed, rose and violet and clover, swelling into the blackness in a crinkly, jerky fashion. Jets shot out of the flower past the rigger-ship. And then one exploded directly toward *Spillix*.

Carlyle braced for a shockwave.

A sheet of fire blazed in the net and charged it with spinning energy. He was dazzled and stunned, but the wave passed and left him unhurt. *Something is watching*, he whispered instinctively. He felt cautiously for Cephean's presence and found him unharmed but indignant, lashing his tail back and forth in the net, and testing his claws. Carlyle blinked, and the net fell dark. He again looked across the void at their adversaries—if that was what they were.

The glassfish let their bodies turn slightly as they floated; but their eyes, luminous and unblinking, remained focused upon *Spillix*. They made no other move. They hovered and watched intently.

12

CONTACT IS MADE

Spillix drifted dead in space. Carlyle expanded and contracted the net on one side and then the other in an effort to move the ship. But although she rocked and yawed in place, the ship did not move from her position. Apparently the glassfish controlled the current or were able to hold the ship directly.

The glassfish watched.

Carlyle waited for another shockwave, or some sign of aggression; but none followed. He wondered uneasily what the glassfish were seeing as they stared at him. A terrible sense filled him that somehow he and Cephean and *Spillix* were being probed, examined in detail by those powerful eyes. He felt *touched* . . . as though the glassfish were seeing him from the inside and making him as transparent as they were.

Cephean, what do you feel? he whispered urgently.

Bvroil-damns ffish! hissed the cynthian in fury.

Yes, whispered Carlyle. *But what else? Do you think they*

live here in the Flux? And are they . . . touching . . . you?
He felt chills flashing through his spine; the net shimmered
in response.

Sssssss, answered Cephean, his voice like static from
space. *Bvroil-damns ff-ffish-ss.* His tail was stilled, but he
glared across the void at the glassfish.

Carlyle started to repeat his question but changed his
mind; he would do better to focus his attention on the
glassfish. How could he speak to them?

Already, he felt, they were prying into and learning his
thoughts with those deadly eyes. He felt lightheaded, as
though layers of shielding were being lifted. Perhaps he
could speak to them directly. He focused his vision on the
glassfish, and he thought of *curiosity*, and he tried to probe
consciously and reach with his thoughts toward them.

An electric charge touched him, making him tingle.

He sensed . . . truculent curiosity from the glassfish. For
no clear reason, he felt that they were not planning to physically disturb their captives . . . at least not yet.

The charge touching him grew stronger. It electrified the
cells of his memory as it paralyzed him. He felt the insulation between cells, between subconscious and conscious,
sparkle with dancing bits of fire and then evaporate in
a glitter.

Caharleel! he heard.

No! he cried.

H-no!

Memories, long repressed, swarmed up like electrified
particles . . .

—home on Alcest IV, and his father betraying disillusion
in a son who failed to be part of his hopes, of his world—

—shame and joy mingled, leaving home, leaving never to
return—

—rigger school, Argyl—

—dreampools and drugs opening his mind, hypnotic training to release visions—
—leaping into brilliant fantasies, towers and fishes and
birds and galaxies of color—
—discovering the terrible truth of human loneliness—

. . . shimmering memories, swarming . . .

—fragments of the quarm on Syncleya, bowed cynthian
heads and joining thoughts—
—crafters moving through the forest with riffmar and
roffmar—
—smells and goodnesses of the world, odomilk and bramleaf and syrup—
—harrowed by the closeness of others, feeling abnormal,
frightened—
—failing to meet minds with a mate, not wanting to—
—Corneph insisting, pulling into the suffocation of the full
quarm—
—flight—
—disaster, and a peculiar alien, a human, a worthy creature but prone to excitability—

. . . remembering further . . .

—first love with a woman who left on a ship and never returned, and was never a friend—
—humiliation outside the rigger community, longings un-
fulfilled within—
—friendship with Janofer, and then Skan and Legroeder,
and flying *Lady Brillig*—
—loss—
—a long and uncertain quest to regain a security never
possessed—

. . . memories flickering up as though in an invisible cyclone; but he could see where they were going, flying in a great golden stream of lost secrets to the glassfish. Impulsively he stepped with a part of his mind into the eye of the cyclone and leaped with one of the memories—with *Lady Brillig*—and rode it in an arc across space to the glassfish.

And he entered the glassfish's mind.

The gestalt of all their minds. They call themselves *Mu-Laan,* he discovered.

He saw the Mu-Laan inspecting this small creature which dared, with smaller creatures inside it, to enter their realm, their dream-turbulent home in the world of ever-shifting realities. It was a peculiar world of the Mu-Laan, which Carlyle saw. The gestalt was of more than the three; there were other minds at work, linking and joining and crossing over incredible distances, meaningless distances to form the merged identity, the gestalt.

Distance meant nothing; it was an artifact of a limited mind.

He huddled, terrified of losing himself in the gestalt. But he peered out through the mind of the Mu-Laan, and he saw over fabulous distances, scenes as far away as the other galaxies, as near the internal organs of the glassfish. He viewed through other eyes, he touched other riggers, human and otherwise; he glimpsed creatures which dwelled in the glassfish universe, in the Flux.

Perhaps he could focus: he glimpsed the Hurricane Flume through the eyes of a rigger passing in a ship. No memory this—it was a vision different from his, a vision of another being. And here: the Wall of the Barrier Nebula, from outside, and just at the edge of the Flux. A rigger somewhere in Golen space, diving deeper. Thoughts and feelings of riggers fluttered across his senses. The touch of a pirate ship, a raider—and the paranoia and fear of the riggers who drove her. Legroeder! Had he touched Legroeder? The sense fluttered away before he could isolate it from the blur.

But he understood now what had happened to Legroeder; he had caught that in the flurry. Legroeder had been captured and impressed by the raiders, as he had guessed. And, he felt sadly, Legroeder would never be seen free and alive again by his old friends. He was sure of the fact, though he did not know how he knew.

The pain made his resolve quaver, and for a moment he was aware of his own frailty here; he was split in two minds, and he looked out of *Spillix* at the glassfish even as he looked out of the Mu-Laan mind at the Flux universe.

But if he could see so far and so clearly—

—couldn't he touch Janofer and Skan in the nets of their ships?

Mind whirling, he squinted and focused.

Stratified mists. Janofer looked at him curiously across the lightyears, the meaningless lightyears which did not even exist in the Flux. She looked at him but did not see him. She flew in the net of a ship—where?—in Golen space, flying speedily back toward protected territory. His astonishment was so great that it erupted joyfully out of his breast and echoed across the distances. And at the sound of joy ringing through space, Janofer widened her eyes; and she saw him and cried out in recognition.

Hope and amazement and bewilderment and loving desperation reverberated through the void between them. A part of the feeling was his and a part of it Janofer's, and he felt himself joined to her by tears and wordless emotions.

Janofer! How could he call to her, speak to her?

Janofer! Was it possible, after searching for so long?

She tossed her head against space. Her eyes gazed at him with delight and wonder, through the shimmering reality of the Mu-Laan vision. How could he know that she was real? He had spoken and flown with so many Janofers, so very many of her. Janofers who were constructs of memory and fantasy, Janofers who had touched him and cared for him and tried to help him love another, Janofers who had saved him in the net. Janofers who had vanished when his fantasy-sequences had ended.

There should be a difference.

The Mu-Laan consciousness grew restless around him. But the glassfish seemed gruffly interested in the mental knot he was struggling with—and so far they were refraining from aggression. (But Cephean, the part of him still on *Spillix* saw, was stirring with belligerent outrage.)

Janofer, what should I do? he cried out in desperation. And he wondered why he had cried out so.

Gev—it's you!

Yes! Janofer!

How are you reaching me? Her eyes were tearful with wonder. *I never expected to see you again! I've been thinking so much of you, and worrying!*

Janofer! This really was her; no doubt could remain; the others would not have been surprised. *I've been searching for you—I want you to come back and fly* Lady Brillig *with me!* His mind was shaking with joy. *And Skan! Is Skan with you?*

Confusion touched him, and he knew suddenly that Janofer was not flying with Skan. But he needed to reach Skan, as well. Impulsively he sent his vision lancing out through tangerine space, focusing dizzyingly, to wherever it was that Skan right now must be.

Skan gaped in astonishment. He squinted at Carlyle with one eye, blinking furiously, while with the other he jockeyed the silvery rig of his ship toward an approaching star system. Janofer caught the image, too, and cried out in delight —and Skan forgot his flying and stared at them both with both eyes. Carlyle swam in an ocean of Mu-Laan powers and prayed desperately that he would not lose the image or lose his anchor in his own reality, in the ship where his physical body lay slack in a rigger-station couch. (*Cephean, are you there?* he cried from his split mind.)

(*Sssssssss! Ff-ff-ish-ssssss! Bvroil-damness-kh-khill!*)

(*Cephean, don't try anything yet! Hold tight for me! Don't do anything!*)

Skan! Skan! Can you hear me?

I'll be damned, whispered Skan. *Am I mad?*

Skan, we're real! Please listen! pleaded Carlyle. *Please!*

I am mad. Dark despair.

No, Skan, Janofer cried. *Listen to him. He's touched me, also, from where he is.*

Skan blinked, and nodded. Carlyle quickly cried, *Skan, will you come back to Chaening's World? Fly* Lady Brillig *with us! Janofer's coming.*

Janofer started to protest—but she choked herself off. She peered anxiously. *What about Legroeder, Gev?*

Carlyle flashed a convulsive image of his meeting with the raiders. He said tearfully, *I'm afraid for him. But you'll come, won't you, Janofer? Skan?*

Gev, you are the one who's mad, said Skan, shaking his head unbelievingly. *It will never work. If it didn't work before, why should it now?* He seemed to study Janofer very thoughtfully; then he said, *But Gev, you've always been mad, haven't you. I don't know how you are doing this—but all right. I'll try. Even though we all know it won't work.*

Back to Chaening's World, Carlyle repeated.

Skan blinked in alarm. *And now I have a ship to bring in.* He vanished.

Me too, Gev, said Janofer. She shimmered, looking paler and more tired than Carlyle remembered her.

Janofer, wait! Can't you—?

The glassfish moaned, an eerie echoing groan of impatience or boredom or anger.

Janofer shimmered to a blur. *I'll try. Good-bye.* She was gone.

* * *

Carlyle stared at the memory of her. The Mu-Laan rocked him roughly in his pain, as though determined to dislodge him from its mental processes. *What are you doing?* Carlyle thought at the glassfish. He looked out through their tangerine vision and saw *Spillix* caught like a silver fly in the clear syrup surrounding the glassfish. For a moment he was content to watch, to think of the glassfish still scrutinizing him and Cephean in the net; and then he realized that his mind was dangerously split, and if he did not rejoin himself quickly he might never be able to. He gazed at the glassfish in black space/he gazed at *Spillix* in tangerine space.

The glassfish still had their thoughts locked musingly on the creatures in the ship's net. Leaping, Carlyle skated on that thought-link toward his ship. His own net rushed like a warm mist around him, and suddenly he was whole; and he gazed with a whole mind at those awesome, luminous glassfish hanging in the depths of space.

How little he had learned about the creatures themselves, though. Or had he learned so little? They lived their lives in the Flux—lives of millions of years of normal-space existence (he thought)—or did the comparison have meaning? They were somewhat scornful of, somewhat intrigued by, the occasional intruders which wandered their way from another reality.

Caharleel! growled Cephean ominously.

Cephean. I'm back.

H-now h-we gho!

Cephean, these creatures are powerful. I don't think we can escape—we have to communicate, to make them understand that we want to go.

H-no, Caharleel! Ff-ffish! Noss h-afraidss ff-ffish!

Carlyle reshuffled his thoughts frantically. The cynthian was angry, more angry than Carlyle had ever seen him. More angry than even the raiders had made him. *Cephean, I don't know—*

Sssssss!

From the stern-station flashed out an incredible series of enormous white daggers—teeth! The daggers gathered at the periphery of the net, poised to strike at the midsection of the nearest Mu-Laan glassfish.

Cephean!

Shsssssss!

Carlyle was stunned. The sight was both terrible and comic: three ethereal creatures of deep space—no, of the Flux—being threatened by an astonishing array of teeth, by the jaws of an incredible and otherwise invisible cat-creature. The teeth hovered and gleamed. And Cephean meant to strike.

Cephean!

Quiessssss!

Consternation blasted out from the glassfish and left the net shaking, reverberating. But Cephean, if disturbed by the warning, did not let it show. His remained aimed, glowing, threatening.

The nearest of the glassfish backed off slightly, and the other two jockeyed for different positions. Colored luminous spots glowed along their dorsal surfaces, and their transparent bodies shined with a fuller light against the blackness of space. There were no linking thoughts between *Spillix* and the glassfish, now, and Carlyle began to feel a chill in his portion of the net, and in the deepest nerves of his spine. Fear seeped through his body like alcohol, first to his stomach, then to his fingertips, then to his head.

Cephean was going to provoke an attack, then; he was sure of it. And if he couldn't dissuade the cynthian, he had to back him. Even if it meant death for both of them.

He strengthened the sinews of the net and watched the three glassfish.

The shockwave from the glassfish seemed to move slowly at first. It was an expanding spiral of light, blazing torchlight, and it first hit the array of teeth, exploding it to bits— and then it speeded up radically as it spiraled outward. It collapsed the front of *Spillix*'s net—Carlyle's own nerves absorbed the impact—and it swept through the net seeking the center of leverage for the ship. It gathered power and carried the ship and its two riggers, helpless as a chip on a spurting stream, outward, outward on the front of the spiral. The black ocean of night was gone, and in its place a watery cathedral of sunlight, and then smudges of dust and swirls of cloud and confusing flickering light, and then fog lashing against the ship and sucked away by vacuum. Carlyle was dizzy and scared, but he held the net together tightly until he felt loss of consciousness . . .

. . . which lasted, he thought, for only seconds. But when his senses cleared, *Spillix* was alone and drifting quickly upward through ascending layers of the Flux, spiraling on momentum. Pinpoints of lights sprang up against blackness.

Cephean!

Yiss. Weakly.

They were in normal-space; and they were clear of the hazily glowing Wall of the Barrier Nebula by at least a lightyear. Somewhere deep within that Wall, in the Flux reality corresponding to the inside of that nebula, three deep-space Mu-Laan glassfish floated serenely, presumably pleased to have disposed of the latest intruders. Carlyle guessed that they were, by rigger-travel time, a good three to four days' journey from the location of the glassfish, and perhaps more, should they have wanted to return.

He did not, nor did he think Cephean would.

Cephean, it worked. You did it.

Yiss. Hoff khorss.

Carlyle made no other remark. He turned the ship for a navigational fix; and he began plotting for the fastest possible course back out of Golen space.

13

A REUNION ON
CHAENING'S WORLD

The glassfish had thrown them to a position not far from the civilized border of Golen space. Flying the most direct route Carlyle could envision, they made it back to the Andros system in just two days of rigging through the Flux.

They were weary, still shaken, and relieved to land finally on Andros II. But they rested only briefly. Both Carlyle and Cephean were anxious to continue the journey—Carlyle to return to Chaening's World, and Cephean to put as much distance as possible between himself and Golen space, raiders, and glassfish. As soon as a mail cargo was offered to Fetzlen III, they lifted from Andros II and continued on their journey with the mail.

Traveling in stages, they worked their way back into northern Aeregian space, stopping at each port only for as long as necessary to sign on new cargo. Not quite four weeks after leaving Golen space, *Spillix* entered the Verjol system; and Carlyle called for a tow to Chaening's World.

Four months, shiptime, had passed from departure to their arrival back at the Jarvis spaceport. On Chaening's World, nearly a standard year had gone by.

* * *

Upon their landing at Jarvis, Cephean pronounced that he and the riffmar greatly needed some time in the forest, and they would leave at once if Carlyle would arrange their transportation. He hated to see them leave; but on the cynthian's assurance that he would return, Carlyle made the arrangements and saw them off on a flyer. All he wanted for himself, for at least the first two days, was to rest.

But instead of doing that, he went directly to see Irwin Kloss.

He waited in the Jarvis offices for several hours before Kloss came in; meanwhile, he considered his journey just past, what he had learned and what he hoped for the future. *Spillix* he had placed in overhaul and indefinite layover—they had sufficient credit from their helter-skelter cargo hauls to maintain their command of her, even in layover—but what he wanted, of course, was to release the ship altogether when he resumed his career aboard *Lady Brillig*. However, there was no word yet from Skan or Janofer, and he held no hope at all for Legroeder's return. Still, he had come so far; he had to persist.

Kloss finally arrived at his office and invited Carlyle in. "You were trying to gather your old crew together again, weren't you, last time we spoke?" he asked genially, showing Carlyle a seat.

Carlyle nodded. "They're on their way. That is, at least Skan and Janofer—that's Skan Sen and Janofer Lief." He sat and looked uncomfortably across the dark-paneled office at the shipowner.

"Good for you," said Kloss. "Have you made plans as to who you want to fly with?"

That threw Carlyle for a moment. Could Kloss have forgotten? No, no—surely he was just being polite. "Well, we hoped that you might have *Lady Brillig* back by now. And that we're not too late. I was gone longer than I'd expected to be, your time."

"I certainly can use you," said Kloss. But his next words

punched Carlyle, leaving a vacuum in his gut. "I can have a ship for you to fly, all right. But I can't say that it's likely to be your old ship." He paused, as though to allow Carlyle to comment; but when Carlyle kept a stunned silence, he continued, "We are going to be adding several ships to our fleet, and we'd be happy to have you with us."

Carlyle couldn't breathe. His head spun and his stomach hurt so badly he nearly doubled over. "You . . . you aren't getting . . . *Lady Brillig?*" he protested hoarsely. But that was what this had all been about! What could he tell Janofer and Skan? It had never even occurred to him that Kloss might not reacquire the ship! "But . . . you said . . ."

Kloss rubbed his forehead thoughtfully. "It's possible I spoke prematurely," he admitted. "I don't recall precisely what I said last time—but in any case, circumstances have changed, and nothing is definite yet."

"When . . . will you know?" Carlyle asked weakly.

"Hard to say," Kloss replied. "The best thing for you to do is to stay in touch with my assistant, Alyaca Perone. Let me call her, and I'll introduce you." He reached for the intercom.

Carlyle's head swam in a void, with no sensation remaining. There was no will in him to fight any longer. Whatever would happen, let it happen. Alyaca. Of all the times . . . of all the people to face now.

While Kloss spoke into the intercom, Carlyle squeezed his arms together across his chest. Trying to hold himself together. Eyes blurring.

The door paled, and Alyaca walked in. She stopped in surprise when she saw Carlyle; but she recovered quickly and produced a businesslike smile, with only the corners of her mouth trembling. Carlyle's chest was so tight he allowed his face no expression at all.

"Alyaca," said Kloss, "this is Rigger Carlyle."

"Yes, we've met before," she said. "How are you, Gev?" She walked over to Kloss' desk but faced Carlyle.

He was stunned to be reminded of how attractive she was, and how unlike a rigger in her poise, her control. "I'm . . . fine," he said, before losing his voice.

Kloss said to Alyaca, "Gev wants to be kept informed if we acquire those ships, and particularly if we reacquire the old *Lady Brillig.* Though I've told him that last is, I regret, unlikely."

"Certainly," said Alyaca. "I remember your being interested in that ship." She maintained a perfectly controlled expression.

"Fine, then. Why don't you show him your office so he'll know where to go to see you," said Kloss. "Gev, thanks for coming in. Let me know if there's anything else we can do for you."

Carlyle numbly followed Alyaca. When they were in the privacy of her office, he stood near the door and said, "Well . . . hi."

She allowed herself a flickering smile, a real one this time, and said, "Hello, Gev."

They looked at each other for a minute, and then he said, "Well—I guess I should be getting back. And I'm sure you have work to do."

"Actually, I don't," she answered. "I was just getting ready to leave the office."

They looked at each other again, for what seemed five minutes to Gev, but was probably closer to five seconds. He couldn't read her expression. There was sort of a smile at her lips, and her eyebrows were raised expectantly. A dozen feelings rushed back to him, feelings he had forgotten in only four months. He wondered if Alyaca had forgotten. "You have a new job, I guess. You didn't used to handle this kind of business," he said, gesturing uncomfortably. She nodded. "I got in touch with my friends," he said, bobbing his head. "They're coming back here, and we'll be together again. All but one of us."

Silence. Then she said, "That's good to hear."

"Well, yes. And Cephean's still with me. The cynthian. He's off in the woods again, with his riffmar. I think I told you about him before."

"Yes, I remember."

"So, well, it seems as though things might be working out at least sort of the way I'd hoped."

Alyaca finally stirred. She picked up a filled pipe from her desk, lit it carefully, and inhaled from it. She held the smoke for a moment, then exhaled. The scent was of brintleaf, a relaxant herb harvested to the south of Jarvis. "Good," she said, blinking.

"Alyaca—"

"If you were going to say," she interrupted, "that we should go out for the evening, I don't think it's a good idea."

Carlyle's chest pounded with conflicting urges, and he blurted, "I think . . . right now it wouldn't be such a good idea. I need to rest . . . and we'll be seeing—"

He stopped. "Oh—" he said. He flushed and began trembling.

"Hey Gev, I didn't mean to make you—"

His words tumbled out over hers. "Alyaca . . . the way I left . . . that time. I'm sorry. I really am. There was just no way I could help it—I tried." His eyes watered.

"I understand," she said softly.

He started. "Do you?" he whispered. His thoughts went forward and back; it was hard to see her, with his eyes so blurry, but he thought her gaze was kindly. Perhaps she did, after all. Perhaps she did.

Three weeks passed with excruciating slowness. There was no word from his friends, and no word from Cephean either. Finally, lonely and worried, he flew out to the forest and went looking. He found the cynthian living in a tree bower with the riffmar. They spoke together and walked, and Carlyle spent the night in a nearby cabin. Cephean was having a good vacation, it seemed, and he wanted to stay for a couple of weeks more.

"But you're coming back, aren't you?" Carlyle asked nervously.

"Ho yiss," said Cephean.

Reassured, Carlyle flew back to the Guild Haven.

Still there was no word from the spaceport, and none from Kloss Shipping. He spoke with Alyaca but did not see her; they remained amicable at a distance, and that seemed best.

Four days later, she called with news that sent his mood plummeting. Kloss was definitely *not* reacquiring *Lady Brillig*. But he was buying a ship of the same model, a somewhat newer ship named *Guinevere*. She would be arriving at the Jarvis spaceport soon, where the registration would be transferred.

"Irwin said he might consider changing her name to *Lady Brillig II*, as a gesture to you and your friends," she said over the phone.

"No!" Carlyle shouted angrily. Trying to make another ship be *Lady Brillig* would be worse than letting the name die.

Alyaca looked startled.

"Sorry," he said, more soberly but still fuming. So what was the meaning of a name, anyway? He could fly this ship. Or he could probably, eventually, track down his old ship to her present owner and perhaps fly for him. But she would no longer be *Lady Brillig;* she'd be something else. So was it the ship that mattered, or the name, or the people?

"Let me know when it's in," he said finally. "My friends still haven't arrived."

Walking through the spaceport the following week, he saw—he was almost certain—*Lady Brillig* sitting on a pad, being readied for flight. The ship's name was *Caravelle III*.

He turned away bitterly, not willing to approach closely enough to actually determine whether she was *Lady Brillig* in fact, or just another ship which looked like her.

Cephean returned a day later, to his intense relief; but when he greeted the cynthian, Cephean's response was muted. "Is anything wrong?" he asked worriedly.

"Ssssssss," muttered the cynthian, his ears twitching. He looked up at Carlyle with unblinking eyes.

The cynthian seemed all right physically. Carlyle looked at the riffmar. One, two, three . . . eight. "Cephean, where's the other riffmar?" he cried. "One of the young ones. What happened?"

Cephean sputtered. "G-hone," he whispered. "H-man-ss t-thake, k-hill!" He hunched mournfully. (*Grief. Anger. Need.*)

"Oh no, Cephean!" cried Carlyle. "How, Cephean, how?"

The cynthian did not answer. He padded into his own quarters, with the riffmar troupe following in disarray; and, sadly, he began to work at a melon. Carlyle felt helpless to do anything except watch and stay with the cynthian until they could speak of other things.

Cephean's grieving mood seemed to pass quickly. But he refused to say more about the lost riffmar, and Carlyle did not press him. He would say only that soon he could begin growing a new group of riff-buds.

Carlyle sat in the Guild restaurant, sipping a roasted coffee and moodily watching the movement of ships, some distance away on the field. A waiter appeared and said that a rigger was at central exchange, trying to locate him.

"What rigger?" he asked, his heart stopping.

"I believe the name was Lief. Janofer Lief," replied the waiter.

Carlyle felt a series of lurches in his breast that lasted for a count of ten. He grunted, tried to clear his throat, and waved his acknowledgement to the waiter when he found that he could not speak at all. He ran to the central desk in the Guild lobby. The area was crowded. First he peered around to see if he could spot her; then he went to the front receptionist.

"It's possible she went to the central exchange desk if she was trying to locate someone," said the receptionist. "Why don't you try there?"

Of course. That was where the waiter had said she was. He went to the central exchange desk and asked the man there if he had spoken with Janofer.

"I just got here," said the man. He pointed to a woman sitting in an alcove behind him. "Talk to her. She'll know."

Carlyle went around to the alcove; he was keeping his emotions from exploding, but he felt the dam beginning to give way. He had to find Janofer while he could still talk.

"You're looking for Janofer Lief?" the woman asked, before he could say a word. "She was looking for you, too. She heard that you were in the Guild restaurant, so she went there."

Carlyle closed his eyes until the blood stopped rushing in his head. Then he ran back toward the restaurant, taking another route.

He met Janofer coming out of the restaurant.

She was dressed in a dark jumper, with a red belt, and with her hair long and silvery. Carlyle stood—unable to move, to speak, to breathe. He thought he might begin to cry, but he couldn't do that, either. The pain in his chest swelled until it engulfed his entire body.

Janofer smiled crookedly, biting her lip. "Hi, Gev."

Carlyle choked—then ran to her. She grabbed him and hugged him tightly. "Oh, Gev, it's so good! It's so good!" She kissed him on the neck and grinned and hugged him again.

He grinned, too, but he couldn't speak for about a minute, until Janofer stepped back and gazed at him.

"You came," he managed to say. "I knew you would."

"Of course!" she cried. "How could I not, after you came all that way? And you have to tell me how you reached us!"

"I wasn't even completely sure that I'd really reached you," he confessed. "It might have been some sort of crazy—"

"It wasn't," she said. "Oh, it was crazy enough—what hasn't been, lately?—but I knew *that* was real. As soon as we go meet Skan, you can tell me all about it."

"He's *here?*" Carlyle exclaimed.

Janofer nodded happily. "We came in together from Theta Aregiae. He's waiting inside, in case you showed up there." She took his arm and marched him back toward the restaurant. "You look great, Gev."

He blushed. "You look exactly the same," he said, though it was not quite the truth. Oh, she was beautiful and graceful, and she was a wonderful sight; but her face seemed fuller and softer, and there were a few lines he didn't remember, and her eyes weren't as quick and ethereal as in the memory-visions he had carried for so long. But should they be? he wondered. Haven't you learned?

Skan rose from a table to greet them. He shook his head. "Gev, you crazy lunecock! You were real, after all. I wondered, I really wondered." He seized Carlyle by the upper arms and embraced him. "So now tell us. I had the feeling that you might have been in some kind of spot when you called us. How did you do that, anyway? And what about Legroeder?"

They all sat, and for hours they drank and ate and caught up on the events which had separated them. When Carlyle asked what had happened originally to make them break up the crew, Janofer said, "I wrote all about that in a letter—" and she stopped and put fist to her forehead, "which I forgot to leave for you, which I discovered a month later when I found it in my bag. Oh damn, Gev, I'm sorry."

Carlyle said dizzily, "That's all right." He swallowed hard

and went back to his original question. "What happened after *Lady Brillig* was sold?"

Janofer looked at Skan, then back at Carlyle. "Well, Gev, it seemed like time to go different ways. Our last flight hadn't gone too well."

"What went wrong?" he asked in bewilderment.

"We had . . . problems . . . as a team. We missed you a lot. But we had some trouble bringing *Lady Brillig* in."

Carlyle looked from one to the other. "But you always worked together beautifully." He started to say that they had worked beautifully with *him*, too, at times when he'd needed them. But they wouldn't have understood that.

Skan said, "Time changes things, Gev. We were having problems. It happens."

"You two?"

"And Legroeder," said Janofer. "So when we lost the ship, we decided it was best to try going our own ways." She poked at her glass and stared wistfully across the table, and for a moment looked at neither of them.

Carlyle hesitated to ask more; but there was so much more to hear. Things which had happened of which he was not a part. Since breaking the team, Janofer and Skan had been to many places, with different crews. They had met once during their travels, at Andros II. Skan had tried to dissuade Janofer from rigging into Golen space; but she had wanted the excitement, had been feeling a little desperate, and had wanted to see if the stories were true. "Bernith is not a place you want to go," she said. "Or Golen space, either."

"Didn't you go to Denison's Outpost?" asked Carlyle.

She shook her head in puzzlement. "Why did you think that?"

Carlyle thought of a Thangol/cyborg he would have dearly loved to kill. He explained the story to Janofer. She nodded, unsurprised, when he mentioned Merck's name. "Pathological liar," she said.

When the stories had all been told, including the unhappy news of Legroeder, they looked at each other sadly and quizzically. Carlyle felt strange. "I guess maybe it was silly, then, bringing you back here," he said uncomfortably. "I had thought—"

"Not silly seeing each other, not by any shot," declared Skan.

"And," said Janofer, "we'd like to give it another try. Times keep changing, and maybe it will work again, even without poor Legroeder. What is there to lose? We can try a flight in the dreampool theater here."

"We have a ship available," Carlyle said slowly. "Not *Lady Brillig*, though. Some ship like her, called *Guinevere*."

"Good, wonderful. But first I think we ought to try a session in the pool, just to be sure. Don't you, Skan?"

"It would be the best thing."

Carlyle realized suddenly how long it had been since he'd used a dreampool. Cephean and he never had used the one on *Spillix*.

"Legroeder," whispered Janofer sadly. "Do you think there's *any* hope he'll come?"

Carlyle shook his head reluctantly. "I just hope he's still alive. We can wait awhile, though—in case." He decided to change the subject. "Anyway, I want you to meet Cephean soon. Maybe he'll join us in the dreampool."

Frowning to himself, he wondered how *that* would work out.

The next morning, though, he got a call from Alyaca Perone. Kloss had a cargo shipment to be carried in *Guinevere*. "He said that if you're ready to fly with a crew of at least three, he'll put in a priority request for you with the Guild. Otherwise, he'll have to let another crew take it. The shipment must go today." Her image smudged slightly on the videphone as she moved her head. They had a poor connection. She steadied and looked back at him. "Have your friends arrived?"

Carlyle missed a breath and said, "Yes. Yes, they arrived yesterday. I'll have to see whether they're ready to go out again on such short notice. What's the destination?"

"Hainur Eight."

That wasn't too bad, distance-wise. It was less than a lightyear away, the nearest star system to Chaening's World. A short distance through real space, however, did not necessarily mean an easy hop through the Flux.

"Round trip?"

"Yes."

"I'll have to check with Janofer and Skan," he said feverishly. "And Cephean." He was nervous as hell. Could they fly so soon? He wished that *anyone* had called him except Alyaca.

"It has to go today. Irwin wants you to have first chance, but if you can't make it he can't guarantee that you'll be able to take *Guinevere* later."

"I'll have to call you back," he said.

Immediately he called Janofer and Skan and outlined the situation to them. "I know we were going to go into the dreampool first, but this may be our only chance to get a ship like *Lady Brillig*, and that's kind of what I was hoping for."

Skan frowned, but he shrugged when Janofer allowed that she guessed it was all right with her. "But only because it's a short haul," Skan cautioned.

Carlyle called Alyaca right back. "It's all set. We'll be ready to go this afternoon." A thought occurred to him, and he added, "And we need a modified rigger-station installed for Cephean. Make it stern-rigger station. You can model it after the one on *Spillix*. Field four, bay fifty-eight." He clucked thoughtfully, blinking at Alyaca.

She nodded, but with what emotion he couldn't tell. "All

right. If you can be aboard and secured by fourteen-oh-oh, we should have no problems."

Carlyle signed off and strode into Cephean's quarters. "Morning," he said.

"Sssssss?" Cephean was breakfasting on milk-melon with the help of the younger riffmar. Idi and Odi were sunning. The cynthian was in a sullen mood.

"Want to fly with us today?" asked Carlyle. "Janofer and Skan and I are taking this ship *Guinevere* on sort of a short trip, to check ourselves out with each other. And if you want to come along—you know—I'd like to have you. You're welcome to come. You can meet them on the ship. If you don't want to do any actual flying, you don't have to. You can just come for the ride if you want."

Why did he suddenly feel so guilty? (He sensed *loneliness. Desolation.*)

"Sssssss. H-no," said Cephean, turning away, turning back to his food.

"Cephean," he said earnestly. "I want you along. This will be my first trip back with them, and you—you've sort of flown with them, in a way. They won't know you, but you'll sort of know them, so you'll have an advantage."

Cephean was mute.

"Please. I *want* you to keep flying with me."

Cephean slurped at the partially crushed melon. His eyes flashed as he licked his jaws; he seemed to be weighing Carlyle's words. "H-all righ-ss," he hissed.

Carlyle, Cephean, and the riffmar met Janofer and Skan in the departure area. Janofer greeted the cynthian with delight; Skan was gracious but stoical. Cephean himself said little, except, twice, "Hyiss-yiss." The riffmar huddled shyly in their cart, and Cephean watched them protectively.

The shuttle tube carried them out to *Guinevere,* and after they settled into their living quarters they gathered on the bridge. Carlyle was surprised at how closely the ship resembled *Lady Brillig*, but how many trivial differences there were, in decoration, in small bits of gear, to make her feel very different. He checked the special rigger-station for Cephean and asked the cynthian to sit for some adjustments. "Is Cephean planning to fly with us?" Skan asked. He sounded dubious.

"Probably he'll stay at the fringes," said Carlyle. "But he wants to work with us."

Janofer beamed. She was buoyant and friendly. But Carlyle thought that some of the original Janofer, some of the mystery, was missing.

As they took their stations, he wondered if he was the only one who felt awkward.

The tow's shadow fell across them as it descended to mate with *Guinevere*. They lifted smoothly, and soon they were in space, watching Chaening's World shrink against the void. The tow accelerated them for an hour, and then they were alone.

Guinevere was speeding out of the Verjol system at a tangent to Chaening's World's orbit when the three riggers, with Cephean whistling softly in the background, extended their net into the misty realm of the Flux and pulled the ship along with them. Carlyle laughed out loud in the acoustical chamber of the net. The others seemed to breathe in time with his laugh, as they dropped into a deep, canyonlike valley.

This is good. But I do wish that Legroeder could be here with us, he remarked.

The valley walls rose on both sides of the speeding rig. It was a mysterious and forested valley, shimmering in full sunlight. He expected someone to reply to his lament about Legroeder, but no one did.

After a time, Skan said, *Let's all stretch a little and see how we're doing*.

Janofer responded at once, extending her reach down from the keel position and forward with glittery silver arms which quivered as they flew. Carlyle reached upward and forward, creating symmetry; and then, out of sheer exuberance, he reached even further than Janofer and pointed the way like a long silver bowsprit. Skan, in the com-station, expanded his presence to form a torus-shaped halo encircling both Janofer and Carlyle. *This feels comfortable*, said Janofer hopefully.

Carlyle voiced agreement, but the truth was that he felt just a bit uncomfortable. He had grown used to the pilot/command position while flying with Cephean, and— *Cephean, are you there?* He heard an indistinct muttering, and the ship swayed slightly as though a tail had been switched. Cephean was there.

Gev, how does it feel to you? asked Janofer.

Fine. But he felt a certain sense of being out of place, out of time. He was being treated as quite an equal, though Skan retained the guiding role (which was fine, since Carlyle was not familiar with the route to Hainur Eight); but equality, he realized, was a new feeling to have in this crew. Before, he had been the apprentice, not quite fully qualified.

Skan? You?

Just fine, love. Gev, I think it would be best if you pulled in a little. Stormy weather ahead.

All right. Carlyle eased back from his long reach and rode pointing cautiously into the wind. He saw no stormy weather ahead, himself, but perhaps Skan could see farther. He bounced lightly up and down in the nose of the rig, wishing that this ship were *Lady Brillig*.

Where is the stormy weather? Janofer queried. *I don't see anything but clear skies, a clear golden path.*

Straight ahead, love. This valley breaks out soon, and things will change. I want us to be ready.

I see that things will change. But I don't see a storm.

It was unusual, Carlyle thought, for Janofer to be so direct with criticism. But then, he had never really seen the two in disagreement. Peering far ahead, all he could see was the valley breaking open near the horizon, and beyond that golden-red clouds like a sunset (although the sun was still high overhead). He assumed that Skan was aware of something they hadn't seen yet.

They continued to fly at high speed toward the end of the valley. Janofer asked Skan what it was that he saw. She was becoming concerned, because she still did not see an agreeing image; and so was Carlyle.

Out there where the earth falls away, and you see a light sky over storm clouds, and a darker area which looks like labyrinths. We have to go through the storm clouds and down into the labyrinths.

There was silence for a few moments, except for the wind.

Skan, I don't see any of that, said Janofer worriedly.

Gev, how about you?

No, Skan. Sorry.

Sorry, my—

What I see is layered golden clouds over a fiery plain, said Janofer, ignoring Skan's outburst. *You, Gev?*

Carlyle focused hard. *Not sure. I see the clouds, but the rest is fuzzy. Feels like I could go either way. Or maybe neither.*

Wonderful, said Skan sarcastically.

Carlyle held his tongue, but he was upset. They could be in for problems ahead, and time was evaporating. They would reach the end of the valley soon; and he had never expected to find Janofer and Skan at odds this way. Had he been naive when he flew *Lady Brillig,* or had they purposely kept it from him? Or was it Legroeder's absence, now, or the new ship? Or. . . .

Get your image set, Gev. We don't have time to play, Skan ordered sharply.

Carlyle was startled by Skan's tone. The com-rigger had never been the gentlest of people, but in the past he had always been careful to keep his anger out of the net. *I'm working, Skan.* Peering ahead, Carlyle suddenly saw Jan-

ofer's golden clouds over an inflamed plain. He started to
speak, to confirm Janofer's image. But through that vision,
as though it were a transparency, he saw something else:
storm clouds, angry clouds, and beneath them smoking canyons, branching.

Both Janofer's and Skan's visions shimmered in front of
him. He hesitated. A decision had to be made. Which
seemed the more real? Which seemed to hold the course to
Hainur Eight, to their destination?

It was so hard to tell. Listening to Cephean mutter and
hum in the stern—and trying to read his thoughts, hidden as
they were behind a private cynthian demeanor—he realized
that in fact *neither* image seemed right to him, or real.

But that could not be. . . .

Gev, speak up, said Skan. *Janofer, we'll have to go with
mine if Gev can't decide.*

Guinevere flew on the wind, drawing closer to uncertainty.

Closer to possible danger.

Carlyle found himself dancing backwards into the net—
exploring, not the terrain ahead, but the terrain within the
thoughts of his crewmates. The images were unclear—
snatches, fragments, pinwheeling bits of mood, of illusion.
He should not be doing this—using the net in flight as he
would use the dreampool to explore the inner worlds of his
friends—but he was doing it now instinctively, and he had to
trust his instincts. It was quite possible that this ship was in
trouble if there was conflict or, worse, if neither of the visions was true to a safe course to Hainur Eight.

Janofer's thoughts were the most accessible, and what he
saw there gave him pause but not immediate worry. She was
constructing images of her internal life, images of her relationships with others. She wanted to fly a glowing path
through the clouds; she wanted desperately to fly it. Shimmering in those golden clouds were love and friendship, and
thoughts of Skan and Gev and dozens of other persons

whose identities were a mystery. She wanted so badly to rig a course on that golden path because beneath it lay a plain of hellstone and the blaze of war. Beneath those clouds lay fear and failure—and the torn and smoking ruins of luckless ships and crews.

No wonder Janofer held the ship's bows high. But Skan was beginning to bear downward, hard, in the net. *Gev, are you helping or dropping out?*

Skan's tone jolted him around to the com-rigger's thoughts. Time slowed for him as he delved through his friends' hearts; he knew there were moments yet in which to reach his decision. But the blackness of Skan's words, the growling impatience opened a window through which he could peer. And he did peer, and what he saw jerked his breath away. Dark, smoldering anger—and beneath it the labyrinthine canyons of Skan's personal depression, bottomless, swallowing light and vision, death-seeking. Skan's depressions, which all of his friends had known on occasion and dealt with, was something he had always avoided loosing in the net. But now it was into the depression that Skan, consciously or not, wanted to carry them.

Skan, are you trying to kill us? he cried out without thinking.

Gev, damn you, what is that supposed to mean?

What do you see, Gev, where shall we steer? called Janofer.

Her urgency was well founded. The ship was leapfrogging ahead. Beneath them glowered flaming land and fearsome labyrinth; overhead floated golden clouds, and flashing storm clouds. How could this have happened? Janofer aiming for impossible dreams, and Skan for a more devious suicide than Cephean had tried, so long ago, on crippled *Sedora*.

Carlyle did not speak; he acted. He projected, instinctively, an image of his own—and his thoughts were so powered by alarm and desperation that they overwhelmed the others completely. He drove forward an image that he knew: luminous amber space, the golden clouds Janofer had wanted broken to a peculiar twisted infinity. It was the luminous amber which he saw when he held a glass of ale to a light and stared through with unfocused eyes. Glazed luminous space with out-of-focus bubbles. At the bottom of the ale were darker regions, where the glowing amber was fuzzy and smoky and obscured by objects: shattered refuse, quarry debris, broken planets, the cluttered reefs of a massively depressed mind. Carlyle steered upward toward the light, toward the infinity; and he found himself being helped by at least one other rigger.

Gev, whispered Janofer, *where are we steering? Do you know the way?*

He did not, but he could not say so. His two friends were steering to disaster, and any other course was better. It hurt him to hear such fear in Janofer's voice, such uncertainty. *Can you help Skan?* he asked desperately. *Do you know why he wants to do this?* Even as he spoke, he flew determinedly upward away from the darkness. The ship moved as though in molasses, or true amber.

After a time he could find no reference points except the vague direction of the light source above, and disaster below.

No, Gev. I should have known, I should have known. Especially without Legroeder. Please—do you know where we are going?

Janofer's fear made him tremble. These were people he had loved, people he had adored. How could this trip have become so catastrophic? Was the ship even moving, now? *Gev?*

No. No, I don't. He was paralyzed by his own fear, now; and the ship hung in amber space, suspended.

Caharleel! Sssssssssss! Caharleel!

Cephean! Yes! he cried.

There was a peculiar moment of transition, as Cephean

slipped forward in the net, curling his claws out into space on both sides, grasping *something*, and as several other things happened. The amber viscosity dissolved around them, and the ship began sinking and rising in response to the net. A curious terrain appeared, slippery gleaming panes and corners sliding through the medium, like fantastically sized cubes of water ice slipping through a vaporous golden liquor. Light flashed and sparkled through the medium, reflected and refracted from a source which might now be anywhere.

Skan's influence in the net subsided almost to nothing, as though suppressed, and Janofer's shrank as though withdrawn. Cephean gathered himself and, with a whisper to Carlyle, leaped.

For a strange minute, the cynthian carried the ship almost singlehandedly. Then Carlyle resumed his efforts, but he allowed the cynthian to thrust the ship and to guide him. *Guinevere* slipped down between two narrowly separated planes and back up through a treacherous channel which angled and twisted past the corners of numerous drifting cubes. By the time they cleared that maze, they were flying again toward the light.

Cephean, do you know where we're going? To Hainur Eight?

Hyiss-yiss, hoff khorss!

How can you know that? Carlyle was astonished, but he felt totally secure with the cynthian's guidance. *How did you learn the way?*

Hyor fren-ss, Caharleell Hi ssaw iss hin ss-their mindss h-when h-we leffft-ss!

(*What? The cat?*) Skan's voice was far away; he was watching from the innermost edge of the net. He sounded calmer, now, and distantly interested.

(*Seem to be doing very well together.*) Janofer was withdrawn, with Skan, but was very interested in watching.

Cephean, I'm amazed, said Carlyle. Bending at the waist

like a diving swimmer, Carlyle steered the speeding ship
under several looming, unfocused bubbles. He wondered if
they were going to surface in the head of a glass of ale. It
felt right to him. It felt perfect, flying with Cephean. *Can
we carry it all the way?*

Hoff khorss, Caharleel!

Carlyle nodded and banked, and the ship sliced upward
through clear space and leveled out in a lighter realm. A
frothy lane stretched out straight to the horizon, and at the
end of it glowed their light source, a setting sun: Hainur.

An hour later, in the subjective time of the Flux, Carlyle
and Cephean brought the ship upward through layers of
foam and cream, and *Guinevere* popped to the surface, into
a universe of stars and eternal night.

Gev. Cephean.

Yiss?

Carlyle was so surprised to hear Cephean respond so easily to Janofer that he forgot to answer himself. Janofer
peered at them, causing them both to hesitate before leaving the rigger net. Her eyes caught both of them at once,
and by a silent appeal she coaxed Cephean to show his full
countenance in the net. Cephean blinked, his eyes coppery
and black. He regarded Janofer with an uncharacteristic degree of courtesy.

To Janofer, Carlyle said, *You and Skan must have been
tired from your journeys.*

*That's not the reason for what happened, and you know
it,* said Janofer. *We would never have made it in if Cephean
and you had not done such a beautiful job of flying.*

Yiss, said Cephean. *Caharleel h-ands hi heff ffly h-many
t-thimes.*

So we have, Carlyle said. He felt warm and nervous. For a
long time he had been resisting the suggestion that Janofer
was making to him right now. But perhaps it was time to
stop resisting. Janofer was right. The real team here wasn't
Gev and Janofer and Skan, and it never had been. His real

teammate had been there all along. *I guess we're not finished, are we, Cephean?*

H-no. Ffly h-more, hissed the cynthian. His ghostly image vanished from the net. Carlyle met Janofer's gaze and allowed her an embarrassed smile. Then, together, they left the net to join Cephean and Skan on the ship's bridge.

EPILOGUE

RIGGER'S WAY

Carlyle rested a hand on the back of the cynthian's furry neck. Cephean craned his eyes back as though to look at Carlyle's hand; but he said nothing and remained crouched, looking with Carlyle across the field of the Jarvis spaceport. *Spillix* stood ready for flight, with an empty pad on one side of her and a fat freighter on the other. She seemed a mere slip of a vessel compared to most of the commercial ships visible on the field.

"A good ship, Cephean. I think we ought to stick with her as long as they let us command her. That could be quite a long while." Carlyle picked his teeth and thought about it, then nodded to affirm his own words.

"Hyiss," said Cephean. He dipped his head and gently nibbled at one of the riffmar. They were arrayed in a cluster before him, with several of the smallest leaning into his forepaws. "Yiss."

They were alone, now. The return to Chaening's World had gone smoothly. Janofer had ridden with them, to watch and keep company; but Skan had said good-bye on Hainur Eight and was now on a ship bound for the southern reaches of human space, with a Thangol and another human as crewmates. Janofer would be leaving soon on a ship out of Chaening's World. She said that she would try to keep in touch; and Carlyle believed her, within reason. Keeping in touch was no easy thing to do.

For just the two of them, then, *Spillix* was the ideal ship after all.

"Good," Carlyle muttered, thinking of all things taken together. He patted Cephean's shoulder and put his hand in his pocket. Before they left, he should call Alyaca again, to say good-bye. "Do you think you'll want to look for your home world one of these days, Cephean?" he asked.

The cynthian did not reply immediately, but his breath escaped with a tiny whistling sound. "Fferhaffs," he said finally. "Fferhaffs, Caharleel." (*Longing* and *confusion* and *wistfulness* welled out of the quiet of his mind.)

"Maybe we will, then," said Carlyle. He raised his eyes from the silver ships on the field to the evening stars, sprinkled against the darkening sky. There was the source of dreams, and he could look at them forever. But he lowered his eyes again and watched the ships. They were the source of dreams, too—and reality.

"Maybe we will at that, Cephean. Maybe we will."